navigating the darwin straits

edith forbes

seal press

Cover design by Clare Conrad
Text design by Anne Mathews
Cover photograph by James Randkley/Tony Stone

Library of Congress Cataloging-in-Publication Data

Forbes, Edith, 1954–
    Navigating the Darwin Straits / Edith Forbes.
        p.cm.
    ISBN 1-58005-049-2 (pbk.)
        1. Young men—Fiction. 2. Children of gay parents—Fiction. 3. Internet industry—Fiction. 4. Seattle (Wash.)—Fiction. I. Title.

PS3556.O662 N38 2001
813'.54—dc21   00-066146

Printed in Canada
First printing, March 2001

10   9   8   7   6   5   4   3   2   1

Distributed to the trade by Publishers Group West
In Canada: Publishers Group West Canada, Toronto, Ontario
In Australia: Banyan Tree Book Distributors, Kent Town, South Australia

To Helen and Herbert Wunderlich,
whose wisdom and warmth were offered
when most needed.

navigating the darwin straits

prologue

If scientific truth is to be believed, the human race is both a fact and an improbability. Like rolling snake eyes a dozen times in a row. The likelihood of our coming into being is vanishingly small, but then, here we are. After countless happenstance sproutings and prunings of natural selection, one of the twigs still carrying sap is *Homo sapiens*.

It all could have happened differently. If a different shoot had been nipped off by drought or predation back in the Cretaceous, we might never have evolved. No satellites would bounce intelligible speech from here to Tokyo and back. No guitarists would play for small change in the subway.

Looking back at my own life, a million moments leading to one particular moment waiting for a bus, I can easily believe that our existence is an improbability, miraculous or catastrophic depending on who is choosing adjectives. Change one moment, and I might not have been standing where I was. If the bus had come sooner. If it had been raining. If I had never been approached by a stranger with no concern for probabilities. If I had never fallen for a woman who did not fall for me.

I can follow the thread back and back, to my birth, or even before my birth, to the night when my mother lapsed from prudence into drunken, what-the-hell defiance at a college fraternity party. Of all the narrow escapes in my career, that moment may have been the narrowest. But perhaps it was also a sign that I was destined to survive, if my DNA could manage to splice itself together even as my mother was heaving up sour beer into a frat house sink and my father, whom she'd met that night and never saw again, was passed out on his roommate's bed.

chapter one

A few months after she bought the first car she had ever owned, my mother decided to pack up whatever would fit inside it and move us back to the place where she grew up. I don't know that it was really a decision. More like a convulsion, an all-systems red alert of claustrophobic panic.

At the time this happened, I was on a soccer team, not playing in games, just practicing and wearing a uniform and waiting on the bench in case a dozen other bigger, stronger, faster guys all blew out their knees simultaneously. After one of my team's games, Mom and I were walking home and suddenly, for no visible reason, she stopped dead in the middle of the sidewalk and stood there staring at the shrubbery in our neighbor's front yard.

"I've had it with green," she said. "I feel buried by all these trees."

I looked up and down the street, which did have a lot of trees. I had thought trees were good.

"There's nothing but trees here," she said. "Except where there's a building, and that's worse. Everywhere you look, there's a tree or a building, blocking the view. I can't stand it, Jordy. I've got to get out of here before I take a chainsaw and do something I'll regret later."

I thought she must be seeing something I wasn't. She sounded frantic, and my mother never sounded frantic. She was too practical for that. It was as if all the trees had turned into giant Venus flytraps and she was the fly, but I couldn't see it. All I could see was a street with houses and trees, the same as every other day, and I liked the trees.

It scared me a little, the way she was acting. In the eleven years of my life, I'd never seen her come close to falling apart, and if she ever had, I'm sure I would have known about it. Until very recently, we had been living in the cheapest possible studio apartments, and if she had wanted a place to go catatonic without me knowing, the only place available would have been the bathroom.

For years, the rule that had governed our lives was short and definite: "We can live without it." In five words, my mother dispensed with every buyable object in existence, unless it was immediately required for physical survival. It didn't matter what other people had, she said. She was not going to buy something with money she didn't have.

With me, she tried to make self-denial into a game, like it was a daily adventure to eat off a card table and sleep on a mattress on the floor. The two of us were explorers, or Trappist monks, or island castaways, people for whom it was a test of wits or willpower to live on nothing. We were hobo pals, scoffing at luxury, reveling in a cigar stub found on the sidewalk, or in our case, the perfectly usable toys and cookware that other people called trash.

Once when I was about six, before she'd gone back to college, she found a coil of electric cable that someone had thrown in a dumpster. Crazy, she thought. That stuff costs money. She borrowed a pair of electrician's pliers, and we spent an afternoon turning the wire into soldiers. First she cut the cable into short pieces and stripped off the outer insulation at each end; then we bent the black and white inner wires to make arms and legs. At the top, she looped the copper ground wire into a circle, to make a head. At the bottom, she nipped off the ground wire and shaped the cut piece into a rifle or a sword.

When we were done, I had a squadron of guerrillas, one arm and leg black, one arm and leg white, a torso in a white tunic of insulation and a tip of copper poking out under the bottom of the tunic, like it was a company joke for them to leave their flies open. Their limbs could be bent and rebent to make them crouch, run, kneel and fire, crawl on their bellies, or climb the leg of a chair to shoot sniper bullets. In my battles, they always beat the yard-sale plastic soldiers, who had much fancier weapons but were all stupidly stuck in one position.

Mom called them clown commandos, and said they were our own personal army. Different from other people, maybe, but tough and resourceful, and just like us, they would triumph in the end. For the time being, we were down and out, completely broke, or even beyond broke, deep in debt. But it wasn't forever; it was only until the game was over. Better days lay ahead, if we could just hang on.

Sometimes I wondered if the same could be said about elementary school. That better days would come, if I could just hang on. In elementary school, that was the sum total of my aspirations—to hang on, to get through, and with all my limbs intact.

I had always been small, and as I got older, I only got smaller. According to medical charts, I had started my life in the twelfth percentile for size. I then lost ground, slowly but steadily, until I settled around the seventh percentile. Translated into practical terms, this meant that almost all the boys my age were bigger than I was.

I could guarantee that at least one of the almost all, usually one who was somewhere up around the eightieth or ninetieth percentile, would discover that he could get credit for brilliant wit by pointing out that my mother was a queer. Or, if he stretched his imagination, a lesbo. Or, if he made the truly awesome leap to two words, a diesel dyke. And then I, being a sucker, would fly at him like a rooster flying at a fox in defense of his flock. The results were predictable.

Once, a lot later, I saw a sign in a cafe, shiny varnished wood with a carved motto: "It isn't the size of the man in the fight, it's the size of the fight in the man." I thought, if that's really true, then why are there all those weight classes for boxing and wrestling?

Luckily, there's a reason the human skull has been evolving toward the outermost limits of the birth canal. After a few years of poundings, the brain inside my human skull finally devised a defensive strategy. Not that I became Bruce Lee and started flattening villains twice my size. I simply became a different material, one with no blood to make bruises and no nerves to register the sensation of a fist hitting soft tissue.

I figured I had three choices. I could be Teflon and slide through situations with nothing sticking to me. I could be Kevlar and let everything bounce off without making a scratch. Or I could be bungee rubber and let myself stretch and stretch and then, *boing*, bounce back into my own shape. I liked the sound of bungee rubber best, so that's what I became.

When I found my head tilted back, looking up at a mouth spewing insults, I didn't fly out with my fists and ask to be pounded to a pulp. Instead I metamorphosed. I became stretchy, springy, easy to bend, impossible to break. "A shrimp? You exaggerate. I'm not nearly that big. An ant at the very most. More likely a flea, or an ear mite. My mother's a queer? Why, thank you. She'll be so pleased you noticed."

When the fists landed, all they hit was a rubber band. *Boing,*

8

boing, boing, coil, stretch and recoil, over and over. After fifth grade, I never started another fight. I was Gandhi, with a big mouth and rubber bones.

Unfortunately, just about the time I figured out how to get along where we were, we left. Mom had calmed down a little from that first moment of blind panic, but not so much that she ever sat down and made a rational list of pros and cons, go or stay. She just needed to get out of Oregon, period. She didn't seem to care that our lives were finally on track, that she'd finished college and had a good job, that we were living on a nice street with houses and lawns, that it had been almost a year since she'd gotten a call from the guidance counselor, suggesting I needed to find more constructive outlets for my anger. None of that mattered. All that mattered was that there were trees on every side of her and she couldn't breathe.

The trees were just an excuse, I knew that, but the reality behind the excuse wasn't a whole lot more rational. Her name was Rachel, and she had recently decided that Mom and I did not fit into the life she wanted for herself. As far as I was concerned, it was good riddance.

It wasn't that I had anything against girlfriends. I'd been happy, a few years before, living with Cindy. She knew most of the card games ever invented, and she liked both me and basketball enough to call me Dr. J, after her favorite player, Julius Erving. The only bad part about her was that she didn't stay around long enough. Her job had run out at the end of our second summer, and the next university that hired her was two thousand miles east, in Indiana.

With Rachel, the leaving was the good part. It was like having a bug zapper in the living room, the whole time she was around. She was so tense and irritable, it seemed like every little move I made set off a spark, *bzzzt,* another bug getting fried. Even her name sounded like a bug zapper. Hazlett. Rachel Hazlett. She worked in a bank, and if she'd had her way, the whole world would have been as clean and tidy as bills from a cash machine and everyone under the age of eighteen would have been kept in storage somewhere. I couldn't figure out why Mom ever fell for her. I suppose some people would have said Rachel was pretty, but I couldn't see that she had anything else going for her.

After Rachel left, I expected Mom would be upset for a while, but that after some time had passed, she would settle back into we-can-live-without-it mode and our lives would get back to normal. Instead she loaded us into the car and headed off into the void.

chapter two

Mom didn't often talk about the place where she grew up, but when she did, she always said it was beautiful. Probably there's been an astronaut who said the same thing about the face of the moon.

When I first saw the place, that's what I thought it looked like, a moonscape with breathable air. I wouldn't have called it ugly any more than I would have called it beautiful. There just wasn't anything there.

On the map, Kilgore was a town, and it did have buildings, but to me it didn't look much different from the expanse of nothing that surrounded it. Main Street was a mile wide, four full lanes plus diagonal parking. I thought at first the town must have had delusions of grandeur sometime in the past and really thought it was going to need those four lanes. But the truth was, the people who lived there were so used to nothing, they wanted plenty of it around them, even when they were driving down Main Street.

The street was paved, but the wind still kicked up clouds of dust, collected from a hundred miles in all directions. The twin rows of buildings looked like they were the only thing stopping the dust from blowing all the way to the Dakotas, and most of the buildings looked like stopping that dust was the only reason for their existence. Exactly three cars were parked on the street, two in front of a grocery store with gas pumps and one in front of a cafe. A lot of the other storefronts were boarded up, and their signs were faded and peeling. Out by the interstate ramps, the Pizza Hut and truck stop had been busy, but the downtown felt like a movie where some sinister force has killed off all but a handful of the inhabitants.

My grandparents' ranch looked a little more alive than the town. The buildings were still in use, most of them, and I saw more vehicles than I'd seen on Main Street. In fact I saw so many vehicles, it was hard to believe they all belonged to my mom's family. We hadn't even owned a car until she finished college, but here I counted five pickups, three cars, a minivan, three ATVs, two snowmobiles, three tractors and two big trucks. Some of them looked ancient, a couple were up on blocks, but there were more of them than there were people to drive them, even counting the two little kids.

For that matter, there were more vehicles than there were trees, so I guess Mom was happy. One thing was certain about this place: a person would never feel smothered by the vegetation.

Before we came, Mom had tried to explain to me about the family and why I'd never met them, when most other people's grandparents would have been waiting outside the delivery room door all ready to coo over the squalling prune that was their genetic link to eternity. It seemed that my grandparents had a different idea about eternity. In their view, my mother was on her way to a very hot and unpleasant one, and as long as I was associated with her, I was in danger of the same fate.

When my mother told them why she couldn't marry my father, my grandparents had made the here-and-now too hot for her to stay, so she'd headed for the West Coast and anonymity. She did send them a birth announcement, but when they sent no reply, she didn't say another word to them for eleven years. She was stubborn. She'd put up with the previous owner's smell on all her clothes before she'd go back to Kilgore and beg her parents for help. I think we only went back now because she finally had a degree and a good job and didn't have to beg them for anything. And because, for some reason, she wanted me to know them.

From the way Mom talked about Grandma, I expected her to be iron-jawed, looming and scary. Instead I found out where my seventh-percentile size chromosome came from. The others in the family, Granddad and my aunt and uncle, were more or less average, like Mom, but Grandma was tiny. She was nice, too, as long as we were talking about animals or cooking or her garden.

It was only when human beings came into the conversation that she'd get a red glare in her pupils, as if her vision of eternity was right there burning inside her eyeballs. Sometimes when I looked around at the red dust hills and the pathetic wisps of grass struggling to stay alive, I thought that Grandma had made this place the way it was, that the furnace glare from her eyes had swept full circle, horizon to horizon, and scorched the land clean.

It made sense that she lived where she did, twenty-five miles from a boarded-up dust trap of a town. When she looked at the human race, she saw evil and corruption so foul that an eternity at a thousand degrees Celsius couldn't purify it. Out here she didn't have to look at the human race very often. Out here, she could smile and hum to herself as she set lettuce transplants into the ground and even smile at me, a human being, if I was helping her.

I could understand Grandma being here, but I still couldn't see why Mom wanted to. Her new job paid a lot less than she'd been making in Portland, and she had to drive forty-five miles to get to it. Also, for the first year we didn't even have our own house. We were living with my grandparents, and every night at dinner, Mom had to look across the table and see Grandma with that glare in her eyes, like she was calculating how many BTUs Mom would put out when she started to burn.

Grandma could see that Mom was dug in and unafraid, so she didn't waste much breath trying to argue with her. Instead she worked on me. Whenever she could catch me alone, she would start describing all the indescribable torments that awaited my mother. She said my mother was a depraved person, an iron spike through the living flesh of Christ, and unless she changed her life, an eternity of torment would be no more than she deserved. Then, when she thought she had me softened up, she would switch tactics and start talking about the possibility of mercy, if only my mother would acknowledge how vile her whole past life had been and repent.

Somehow, Grandma could make it all sound completely abstract, even when she was talking about torment and suffering and iron spikes passing through flesh. As if she were reading from an accountant's balance sheet of rightness and wrongness and who deserved what. As if a particular diameter of iron spike deserved a particular number of millennia in hell. It never felt like she was talking about a real person, whether it was my mother or the one with the nails driven between the bones of his hands.

The worst of it was, I couldn't even argue with her. Mom had told me I had to be polite in these conversations and that I couldn't talk back, no matter what Grandma said and no matter how much I disagreed with her.

Mom hadn't told me not to ask questions, however, so that was what I did. Especially I tried to pin Grandma down on what she meant by the word "vile," as applied to my mother. Was it wearing clothing that other people had given away? Was it getting pregnant and dropping out of college for six years? Was it not having a husband?

I knew well enough what Grandma thought was vile, since I'd been hearing about it in the schoolyard for most of my life. I just wanted to make her say it out loud. She was in a Catch-22 because she couldn't explain it to me without talking about something she didn't think people should even know about until they were married. So she would scowl and mutter something about "those women your mother knew."

I demanded more details. What was it about Rachel that Grandma thought was vile? I said I agreed Rachel was annoying, but I wouldn't have gone so far as to call her vile. Was it because she was so picky? Because a door slammed gave her a headache for the rest of the day? Because she could fuss for hours over her hair, which was silver blond and fluffed out into a gigantic swoopy hairdo that made her skull look too small for a full-size brain?

For sure, the last thing Grandma wanted was to hear any details about "those women." If I kept on giving her enough of them, she usually gave up and changed the subject, and I counted that as at least a draw for Mom's and my side.

Sometimes, instead of trying to fend Grandma off, I actually tried to talk to her about Oregon, and especially about Cindy. I couldn't muster much enthusiasm for defending Rachel; she was just a tool for prodding. But Cindy was different. She was someone it made no sense to dislike, and occasionally, on my braver days, I tried to convince my grandmother of that. I talked about how Cindy used to write nonsense rhymes for me and read them out loud, and how we had watched basketball together, Cindy rooting for the 76ers, because she had grown up in Philadelphia, while I cheered for the Blazers. I talked about how she loved gardening, just like Grandma, and how we ate dinners on a picnic table in the backyard, with tomatoes and cucumbers she had grown.

For some reason, it bothered Grandma even more to hear that

Cindy was nice than it did to hear that Rachel was annoying. And it bothered her most of all to hear about the masses of pink roses that climbed the front of Cindy's house and sprawled over her backyard fence, roses that grew with abandon in the mild, rainy Oregon weather, while in Kilgore, Grandma had to labor ceaselessly with her hoe and the water sprinkler, battling thin, rocky soil and the harsh desert climate to keep her little patch of green alive.

Before long, the moment I even mentioned Cindy's name, Grandma would start to scowl, and if I went on talking, the scowl would get deeper and deeper, until finally she would cut me off by saying something like, "The devil can put on a smiling face, but he's still the devil." Neither one of us was very happy about these conversations, but if she wasn't going to lay off about my mother and hellfire, then I wasn't going to lay off about Cindy's roses.

I think it took us about six months to work our way to a compromise. Bit by bit, in an unspoken truce, we began to limit our conversation to the purely physical world and the present place and time. I stopped mentioning human beings, my own previous life and the state of Oregon; she stopped mentioning human beings, the afterlife and God. It didn't leave either of us with much to talk about, but at least we could spend afternoons together, hoeing weeds or cutting up vegetables to freeze, in moderately comfortable silence.

When I first started school in Kilgore, nobody knew much about Mom, except that she had a computer job with a mining company over in Seco Springs, the county seat. So I didn't get ragged about her. Instead I got ragged about all the other ways I was weird, which covered a lot of ground, from my haircut and clothes to the music I liked to the way I talked. After a while, it zeroed in on the basics: that I was short, that I came from the city and that I didn't know squat about livestock, dogs, guns, pickups or fishing.

I did know about sports, though, and about computers, and these probably saved me from being euthanized as a runt by the offensive line of the school football team. My bungee-rubber being metamorphosed into a new persona, a digital-brained database of sports statistics. Whenever one of the eightieth-percentile mesomorphs started looking hungry for someone to humiliate, I would toss out tidbits of trivia, the first player to score a quadruple double in the NBA, Babe Ruth's slugging percentage, Julius Erving's career point total, the record for blocked shots in the NCAA tournament, like someone scattering chunks of hamburger to divert a Doberman pinscher.

Sometimes it worked, sometimes it didn't, but one result was that all the guys assumed, without thinking about it, that I had been named Jordan after Michael Jordan. I thought it might be hazardous to correct their arithmetic, so I never pointed out that Michael Jordan hadn't yet started high school when I was given my name.

As quickly as I could, I tried to acquire some of the knowledge that counted in Kilgore. Mom taught me how to ride, on a steady, slow-witted retiree named Sawdust. I didn't exactly fall in love with horses, but in the end I could ride well enough not to break my neck, and I could avoid sounding stupid on the subject, as long as I didn't try to sound smart.

I asked Granddad to tell me about cattle, but that was hard going for both of us. Granddad's knowledge was so instinctive, he had trouble putting it into words, and my eyes simply didn't see what his eyes saw.

How did he know a cow was about to calve? Just by looking, he said. She looks different. She acts different. Different from what? Different from the way she usually looks and acts. How did he know when she was sick? She acts different. Like she does when she's calving? No, different from that, too.

He could walk through a pen of fifty identical cows and tell me something about each one: this one's had only bull calves, that one weaned a seven-hundred-pounder, the one over there you want to keep an eye on when she has a new calf because she'll knock you down. I'd ask, "Which one over there?" and he'd say, "That long-bodied one with the almond-shaped eyes," and I'd look and see fifty long bodies and fifty pairs of brown eyes, all of which looked somewhat almond-shaped but really closer to round.

I gave up on ever having anything to say about livestock and instead concentrated on guns, which were simpler. From the moment we arrived, Uncle Fred had been saying he would teach me how to shoot. He kidded Mom about her having turned into a pacifist off in the city, since she'd never taught me to shoot or even given me a toy gun.

"There's nothing to hunt in the city, except other people," she said.

There were lots of things to hunt around Kilgore, but Uncle Fred said prairie dogs were the only wild animal that did enough damage to bother about.

"You have to thin 'em out a little," he said. "Otherwise they'll keep on multiplying and gobbling up more and more good pasture. Kind of like those California people, over on the western side of the state, gobbling up all the land along the mountains. I guess we're lucky we're not scenic. I'll take prairie dogs any day. At least we can shoot a few of 'em, keep the numbers reasonable."

We started off with targets, and when I had practiced until all my shots landed somewhere on the target, he took me out to a prairie dog town, one he said covered about two hundred acres. I had thought the whole county was about as bare as land could get, but that prairie dog town took bareness to another level. Every last wisp of grass was eaten down to a stub. All that remained were some scattered clumps of sagebrush and yucca, an expanse of rock and dirt, and hundreds of low round humps, marking the prairie dog holes.

Uncle Fred and I settled down to wait, and before long a head popped up out of one of the holes. The body followed, and the prairie dog perched upright on his mound, chirping.

"He's yours," said my uncle.

I aimed the .22, but my heart was pounding so hard the sight was wobbling all over.

"Take it easy," he said. "It's not a twelve-point elk."

When my aim was steadier, I squeezed the trigger. The .22 made its little firecracker snap, and the prairie dog spasmed into the air. I felt a terrific rush of excitement and leapt into the air myself, shouting, "I got it."

But the prairie dog didn't keel over and lie still, the way dead people do in the movies. It kept twitching and thrashing until finally Uncle Fred raised his gun and shot it again. Then it did lie still.

"Bad luck, not to get it clean with one shot," he said. "But good work, hitting it on your first try."

We shot a few more, until they got smart and stopped popping out of their holes, but I never got the same rush as the first time. I was too afraid I wouldn't hit one clean and would have to watch that thrashing struggle again. Every time I squeezed the trigger, I held my breath until I was sure the prairie dog was still.

After a while, some crows and magpies appeared out of nowhere and flapped down to pick at the carcasses.

"Undertakers," said Uncle Fred. "They hear a .22 and think dinner. Same thing with farm machinery. You'll see 'em right behind a combine or a swather, looking for the mice and snakes that got cut down with the crop. It's almost scary what some birds can figure out."

Shooting wasn't the only skill I learned from Uncle Fred. A couple of miles from the main ranch buildings, there was an abandoned shed that Mom was having made over into a little house for us, and my uncle was doing a lot of the construction. He said I could help anytime, and when I came, he showed me how to measure accurately and cut with a power saw and hammer nails straight.

He was a good teacher, but it didn't take long for me to know I wouldn't want to do this kind of a job all my life. For Uncle Fred, the work was automatic and he never seemed bored. His mind didn't wander into daydreams, or if it did, his body didn't wander with it. Every move he made was strong and economical. He'd make one little tap to settle a nail point, then two big whacks and the nail was in. It was like watching an athlete, to watch him work.

I couldn't work the way he did. My mind did wander, so my movements were never economical. Again and again, I would return to the present and realize my hands weren't moving because I was thinking about something else, and after a few hours, I grew bored.

While guns and power saws weren't likely to be the tools of my future career, they were very useful to me in the present moment, at school. They added a whole new dimension to my sports-encyclopedia persona. Thanks to my uncle, I could casually let drop that I had spent my Saturday framing in a wall or knocking off prairie dogs, and I could almost see guys deciding that I wasn't as totally weird as they had thought.

About the time I started inching upward on the approval scale, my mother started skidding downward.

I suppose people were bound to find out the rest of her story sooner or later. Mom knew how to keep her mouth shut strategically, but she refused to lie outright or change how she acted. She wouldn't flirt with men or string them along just to keep her cover.

For a while, I was her cover. There were plenty of whispers about my bastard status, but my existence certified that she had acted as a heterosexual, at least for thirty seconds. The first innuendoes hinted that she must have been "wild," meaning that it had been more than thirty seconds and with lots of men besides my father. That theory withered quickly as she went to work, came home, helped Grandma cook supper and wash up, and spent her evenings quietly in her parents' living room. She was never seen in bars.

With men she was friendly but matter-of-fact. Now and then I did see a man try to flirt with her. She was a single woman, and in Kilgore single women were outnumbered about four to one by single men. Her response was not negative. She would just look a little blank, as if the man had started speaking Chinese. I don't think she emitted the slightest whiff of pheromones, and for sure she didn't notice the ones the men were giving off.

She could have continued this way for quite a while, with people a little puzzled but nothing worse, and with Grandma biting her tongue because all "those women" were safely in the past. Instead she fell in love.

Even then, if she had picked someone different, she might have had a discreet little fling with none of the eightieth-percentiles in the schoolyard any the wiser. But she had to pick a person who was, in Kilgore's dried-up puddle, almost a celebrity.

Pat Lloyd wasn't someone you'd expect to be a celebrity. I saw her almost every time I went into the Kilgore Mercantile to buy a Coke, and in all those times I never figured out she was the person who had the whole town in an uproar. At the store, she hardly said a word, except "That will be $12.40" after she rang up an order of groceries. If Kilgore was as close as you could get to nowhere, then Pat seemed as close as you could get to nobody.

She had lived her whole life in the same poky little town and worked at the same job in the same poky little store, her own father's store, no less, and I think she must have decided there was no need for her to talk because there was never a moment when her father wasn't talking. He was always there at the counter, yakking away like a talk-show host, using his customers as an excuse to tell stories and make jokes, and she was always a little off to the side, silently ringing up the order and making change and packing the food in bags, as perfectly camouflaged as the toads I would almost step on in Cindy's garden.

And then one day, completely out of the blue, she hires a guy to dynamite the hilltop behind her house so that she can carve a giant sculpture into the rock. I'd seen that sculpture every day on the way into Kilgore on the school bus, and sometimes heard people arguing about whether or not it was indecent, but until I met Pat outdoors, away from her father's store, I never realized that she was the person causing all the controversy.

To me, the statue looked crude, not very realistic, but it was as big as a barn, so you couldn't help noticing it. A lot of people in town were upset because the subject was a naked woman, sleeping, and they didn't want kids like me seeing her. I couldn't figure out what they didn't want us to see. The woman was huge all right, and maybe startling, but she wasn't in any way sexy. The half of her that was finished looked like rock and not at all like someone warm and breathing you could put in a daydream.

More than anything else, I thought the carving was a little spooky: a gigantic, vaguely human shape growing out of a rock cliff. The rock was rough, webbed with cracks and striped with shades of tan and rust, and often, when the light hit it in a certain way, I couldn't see the carved shape at all, just the textures and colors. At those times, the woman in the sculpture looked camouflaged, like Pat.

If it hadn't been for me, Mom and Pat might never have come to know each other. Mom's job was forty-five miles in the other direction, and she almost never came into Kilgore unless there was an event at the school. It wasn't by design that I introduced them. It was pure happenstance, one of those collisions that seem like not such a big thing at the time, and it's only a lot later that you realize they've changed your life.

chapter three

When Mom had started making decent money, the second thing she bought, after a car, was a bike for me. A new one, too, not prehistoric like the car. I had ridden it all over the place in Portland, and I did in Kilgore, too, but in Kilgore that became another proof of my weirdness. In Kilgore, the kids used their bikes to turn wheelies in the school parking lot or to ride the three blocks to the Mercantile to buy a snack, or if they were up for a major expedition, they might go as far as the Pizza Hut out by the interstate ramps. That was it. Choosing to pedal a bike twenty or thirty miles, because I liked it, when I could have bugged Mom for a ride, that pretty well cemented my status as an alien species.

People in Kilgore had a highly adjustable definition of distance. If they were in their cars, they acted like twenty-five miles was practically next door, and forty-five miles was just a little down the street. But the moment they were under their own muscle power, everything changed. If they had to walk more than half a block from their parking place to a store, it was cause to write a letter of complaint to the governor. Out on the ranch, I'd never seen Uncle Fred walk more than a hundred yards. Farther than that, he took a pickup, or if the terrain was too rugged, an ATV or a horse. It was fine to sweat, if you were working and there was no way around it, but to sweat and call it fun, that was weird.

In spite of my weirdness, I did have a couple of friends in town, keyboard junkies like me, and one weekend one of them invited me to stay over. I struck a deal with Mom. She'd bring me and my bike into town on Saturday, and on Sunday I'd ride it back out to the ranch, the whole twenty-five miles, because I thought it was fun.

It was about noon on Sunday when I headed home, and warm for October, easily warm enough to be happy riding a bike in shorts and a T-shirt. The road was paved for the first few miles, then it turned to gravel. Right after the change, you came around a corner and there was the infamous rock sculpture, up on a hilltop, looming over a little house down in the creek bottom.

That whole first stretch of gravel road was a teeth-rattling gauntlet of washboard, probably from all the people putting on their brakes to look at the sculpture. When I hit the washboard, I slowed down myself to keep from bouncing right off the bike. I glanced at the sculpture once, just long enough to see that someone was working on it. After that, I kept my eyes straight ahead, picking a path through the bumps, creeping along barely faster than a walk.

I passed a mailbox, and a moment later, seemingly out of nowhere, something black and white came shooting out into the road and knocked my bicycle over, sending me sprawling in the gravel. I felt teeth tearing into my leg, and I started yelling. I tried to get up to get away, but my feet had gotten tangled up in the bike. The creature was a fury, snarling and biting, and the gravel was scraping my arms and legs almost as bad as the teeth. I had one arm up, to keep the teeth away from my face, and I kept trying to stand up, but one of my feet was hung up between the wheel spokes and I couldn't pull it free.

Suddenly, I heard a woman screaming commands and the biting stopped. The black and white fury turned into a dog, crouched and cowering and surprisingly small, just a little collie half my size.

The woman grabbed the dog's collar, and I finally managed to free my foot and stand up. That's when I realized this was the woman I had seen, or not seen, at the Kilgore Mercantile. She was shaking, she was so upset, and I was bleeding all over the place, but for that first minute all I could do was look from her to the statue and back again and think, that was you? The one screaming? The one who carved this rock? The one people are mad at?

Because out here, with just the hills and grass—no father, no shelves of canned goods—with her hand gripping her dog's collar, her face white as a sheet, her voice stammering questions, she wasn't camouflaged anymore.

I must have been in shock, because I hardly felt the cuts and scrapes. I was too amazed at this metamorphosis. I was fascinated, too, and in a flash I understood what was really going on. It wasn't the statue that made people mad. It was the person carving it and what it meant. Now it all made sense. Out here, away from her camouflage, it was obvious. She was a lesbian, and the statue was somebody she had loved. That was the real issue, not what the statue was or wasn't wearing. I almost laughed, because the whole town was lined up like two armies, everyone with a position for or against, but no one was saying out loud what the fight was really about. I couldn't wait to tell Mom.

All of a sudden the shock wore off and I realized my leg hurt like the blazes. The scraped skin burned, and a deep cold ache cut toward the bone. I began to feel dizzy. Pat locked up her dog and helped me to her house, where she sat me down and brought me gauze pads to press on the cuts. She called the doctor and my mother, and then helped me out to her pickup to drive to town.

On the drive, she seemed to feel like she had to explain.

"It was my fault, not the dog's," she said. "She's not naturally vicious. She's high-strung. Border collies need work, and I've been too busy to give it to her. Something in her must have changed, from being left alone too much."

"What will happen to her now?" I asked.

"I'll have to have her killed."

I guess you can't always predict what's going to hurt the most. My leg was sore, for sure, but it wasn't a big deal. The cuts would heal and anyway, I was bungee rubber and could recoil out of range. Teeth couldn't get at me, inside, any more than fists could. But when she told me the dog would be killed, that did get at me, way down deep.

Pat seemed pretty calm about it, but I kept seeing the dog, crouched close to Pat's legs, trembling with fear, shrunk with chagrin, knowing she had done wrong and would be punished. She looked way too small to be a serious threat to anyone. It made positively no sense that she had to be killed.

All the way to town, I argued with Pat, trying to convince her that it made no sense. For one thing, I wasn't dead, so it was way more than an eye for an eye. And for another thing, the dog might have had a good reason to go after me. I wasn't a sheep, or something you would kill only if you were hungry. I was a human, and humans were the species that went around murdering and raping and torturing each other and inventing stuff like gas chambers and crucifixion and computer-guided missiles to do it all more efficiently. So it wasn't completely unreasonable that a creature with nothing but teeth to defend itself might want to launch a preemptive strike.

Couldn't she just keep the dog tied up, instead of killing it? Couldn't she pay more attention to it? She said herself the attack was her own fault, that she had been too busy, working at the store, carving her sculpture, and had left the dog alone too much.

Pat listened to me the whole way and never argued back.

26

"I'm the one who should be killed, if there were any justice," she said.

"But why does anyone have to be killed?" I said. "There's no reason."

She flinched a little, but she didn't answer.

"You said she isn't vicious," I said. "You said she's changed, and that must mean she can change back. Can't she?"

"I don't know."

"But we have to try. It's only fair."

Pat didn't tell me right then that it wasn't only a question of what she and I wanted. She just said we could try, but she didn't sound hopeful.

The next weekend, I called Pat and asked if I could come visit, to see the dog again. She sounded surprised that I wanted to, but said sure. When Mom and I got there, we found that Pat had already gone and bought a few sheep, to give the dog some work, to see if work might help. She said in the past she'd always kept a few sheep, for training her dogs, but then she had gotten too busy with her sculpture and didn't have time.

The dog's name was Lucy. Now that I had a chance to look at her closely, I thought she was beautiful: silky black and white, lithe and quick, with eyes that tracked every move Pat made. On the outside, she was alert and graceful, but on the inside, it seemed, she was all nerves, wound up tight, and if a couple of them got crossed, they jangled the whole system.

The moment Lucy saw me, she shrank away, crouching close against Pat's legs. Pat told me to talk to her, quietly, and I did, babbling anything that came into my head, trying to persuade her that I could be trusted, trying to explain that I was a seventy-pound tech brain who wouldn't even frighten Miss Muffet. According to Pat, Lucy had attacked out of fear, not aggressiveness. I thought if I could teach her to trust me, then she might trust other people, too, and if she lost the fear, then she might lose the viciousness and not have to die.

After a while, Lucy did allow me to touch her, to stroke her head, but the whole time my hand was on her, she looked braced and miserable, enduring torture because she knew it was what Pat wanted. Pat worked her with the sheep every day, and I visited several times, trying to get her used to me, but no matter what I said or did, she never stopped looking miserable. In the end, Pat said it was no use. Lucy would never be trustworthy.

What she didn't add, but what I knew from Mom, was that all of Pat's neighbors expected the dog to be put down. It was a code in this part of the country, not legally spelled out, but accepted by everyone, including Pat. A dog who turned vicious must be killed. And I could see for myself that we were making no progress. With Pat there, talking to her, reassuring her, the dog could almost keep herself from flying apart. But Pat could not talk to her twenty-four hours a day.

Only once did I see Lucy look whole and happy, when Pat took her out to work sheep one last time. I'd never seen anything like it. It was like the two of them shared a brain wave or something. Pat stood almost still, making tiny movements with her hand and quick low whistles, and the dog went racing out and back and around, gathering the sheep, shifting them here and there. The commands were so subtle and the reactions so fast, you would have sworn the dog was mind-reading.

Lucy seemed to fly, skimming the ground, heedless of rocks and holes, circling, darting. Then suddenly she'd stop, belly to the ground, gaze fixed on the sheep, holding them paralyzed. And then she'd be off again, racing, like the sandpipers whose steps are so quick they seem not to have legs, only a cushion of air between their bodies and the ground. In the end, when the sheep had been herded into a pen, Pat gave the dog some words of praise, and Lucy flopped down in the grass, panting, with what looked to me like a smile of triumph.

And then the look passed. She became aware of Mom and me and tried to shrink herself into invisibility. The help had come too late. She couldn't learn to trust, and it was only when she was lying dead on a sterile metal table that I could stroke her fur and lay my cheek against her head and not feel her tremble.

I couldn't understand how Pat could be so calm about it all. When Lucy was out working, the two of them had seemed like part of one another, like the dog was a piece of Pat that could detach itself and go tearing around a field. But then, at the vet's office, she just stood there with a hand on Lucy's head, stroking her, saying "I'm awfully sorry, Lucy, old girl," and watched the needle go in. When the dog sagged down onto the table and stopped breathing, Pat sucked in her own breath and got very still, but she didn't make a sound. She just stood a little to the side and watched as I threw my arms around the warm, limp body and cried.

Afterward, I kept thinking, didn't she love her dog? I'd known Lucy only a little while and I loved her, so how could it be that Pat didn't?

I was stupid to think that, but I didn't know Pat then.

In the following months, my mother would have the same trouble. It was impossible to tell what Pat was feeling, unless you happened to catch her by surprise, the way I had when Lucy first ripped up my leg. Her temperament was like a mountaineer, everything necessary for survival packed up into the smallest possible space and carried on her own back. At least that was how she seemed.

Pat also didn't seem to mind much what people thought of her. She wasn't defiant about it; she didn't resist conformity any more than she conformed. She just did what she did, and if it happened to be what other people expected, that was pure coincidence. She had an amazing capacity for not noticing certain things. My mother was in love with her for almost a year and she didn't notice. Mom used to go out when it was ten degrees above zero and sit up on that rock while Pat was chipping away with her hammer and chisels. They would stay up there for hours, and Pat would keep warm because she was working, and I would keep warm because I was running around with Pat's new puppy, Skipper, but Mom would be sitting still and slowly congealing while they talked. And the whole time, Pat thought Mom was just being nice, keeping her company while she worked.

Poor Mom. We came home after one of those visits, and she said, "Do you think she likes me at all?"

I said, "I'm sure she likes you, but I don't know if she *likes* you."

I'd seen Pat's face light up when we came to visit, but it wasn't any big, blazing flash. More of a cautious creep, like she didn't want to risk too much too fast. And besides, if she was in love, why wouldn't she say so? It was clear as daylight how Mom felt about her.

Later, I figured out that Pat didn't see what other people saw, particularly about herself. Like her sculpture, for instance. Turns out she had started carving it with the idea that it might somehow bring back the woman who had ditched her. The woman's name was Alma Rose, and she was a truck driver who had come through Kilgore now and then. And then one day she stopped coming through.

Pat didn't know where she was, and even if she had, she didn't think Alma Rose would want her to come chasing after her, so instead she stayed put and started making the sculpture. As if Alma Rose might see it from the interstate and come back. Pat hadn't thought it through at all. She just felt the need to make the thing, so she called up a guy with dynamite. She didn't even consider what people in town might think, not until the two armies lined up and she was in the middle.

With Mom, Pat was the same way. She wasn't politely ignoring Mom's interest. She truly wasn't aware of it. When she and Mom finally did sort themselves out, we found out she thought Mom had been coming to visit so that I could play with her dogs.

Her dogs, for Pete's sake. That was the opinion she had of herself.

Not that I didn't love her dogs. I did, especially Skipper. After Pat had Lucy put down, she got Skipper to keep her old dog Lulu company. He was a prince, sharp as a tack, and he didn't care a whit how big I was or where I came from. Still, it was more than a little strange for Pat to think Mom would sit there for hours just so that I could play with him. We could have got a dog for ourselves if that was all she wanted.

It was typical, though, of how Pat could see some things and not others. On the one hand, she could see that I loved her puppy, could guess that I might be taking some ragging at school, could understand how the dog might feel like a refuge. On the other hand, she couldn't see the way Mom looked at her. I figured her first lover, Alma Rose, probably had to put on a sandwich board that said, "I love you, Pat," and the back probably said, "Yes, I mean you." That's almost what Mom had to do.

It took Mom about nine months to get up the courage, and there were a lot of times in those months when I was afraid she might give up hope.

"What if Alma Rose is the one great love of her life?" she said once, in a moment of complete discouragement. "A person doesn't spend years carving a gigantic image of someone unless that someone is pretty darned important."

Dealing with college, job, house, Mom never doubted herself, never deviated from practicality. She had an unshakable conviction that if you worked at it, you could get somewhere. But as soon as she fell in love, confidence and common sense both went out the window and she second-guessed herself at every step.

With Pat, Mom's dithering was worse than it had ever been, because she felt like she was competing with a ghost. Sometimes she asked Pat to tell us about Alma Rose, and we always came away with the impression of someone utterly dazzling. Alma Rose was charming. She was lively. She was beautiful. She was funny. Okay, yes, she was also changeable, unreliable, moody, but somehow everything negative came out sounding like cayenne pepper, the spice that adds interest.

It didn't help that these conversations mostly took place in the shadow of a ten-times-life-size replica of all that perfection. You could take almost anybody—Margaret Thatcher, Mrs. Dumpling or the lady at the post office—and if you blew them up to sixty feet tall and carved them into a hilltop, they'd start looking like a goddess, too. I thought a little demystification couldn't hurt, so I told Pat once she should carve a stomach and intestines into the inside of the sculpture and let kids crawl around inside. She laughed, and that made me think Mom had a chance. If Pat had been irretrievably devoted to some lost love, she wouldn't have thought the idea was funny.

I was almost as eager as Mom was for her and Pat to get things worked out. For one thing, I liked Pat. She was the antithesis of a bug zapper, and she also wasn't likely to pull up stakes and move to Indiana. But more than that, she was making Mom crazy, to the point of being unbearable. Mom was forever fretting and stewing, analyzing every little hint in Pat's behavior, venting all of her uncertainty to me because she had no one else she could talk to about this particular subject.

"Just tell her, why don't you," I said, after the nth repetition of her hopelessness.

"But I must look as dull as oatmeal, compared to . . . you know. How am I supposed to compete with her?"

"You're here, and she's not," I pointed out. "And maybe you could stop apologizing for being a stable person."

Mom laughed at that, which was a relief.

A few weeks later, she finally did work up the nerve to make her move. She had to make three or four tries before Pat really believed her, and then a little more time had to pass before it wasn't too much too fast, but in the end, thankfully for both of us, Pat said yes.

They didn't move in together. They both agreed, no way, not as long as I was in school in Kilgore. But Mom and I had moved into our new house by then, so at least Pat could come stay with us without getting scorched by Grandma's disapproval.

From then on, Mom was a lot happier, and at home I was happier, too. Pat was easy to be around, even easier than Cindy. She wasn't bothered by noise, because she didn't notice it, and since she didn't have the faintest idea how to talk to a kid, she just talked to me as if I were an adult. Not that she talked much. But if she did, it could be about anything and you couldn't usually guess ahead of time.

She had all these thoughts that had spent months, maybe years, in the dark inside her head, and when they came out into the daylight, they could look a little strange. But strange was good, I thought. We got talking once about religion and Grandma's god, and I asked her if she believed in an afterlife. She said, "Not if you mean an eternity on a cloud playing a harp."

Then she smiled and said she thought some of the laws of physics might apply to a person's spiritual life, too. She said, "Look at how nature is so stingy with materials. It won't throw away a hydrogen atom without making an explosion. So why would it throw away a mind?"

"Then what do you think happens to us, if we don't go to heaven or hell, but we don't disappear either?"

"Maybe we get broken down and recombined," she said. "Like carbon and hydrogen. Maybe around the time that I die, some dog breeder somewhere will find he has a puppy that goes and hides under a chair, and some mother somewhere will be worrying about her five-year-old who can read and write but hasn't learned to talk."

She was smiling the whole time she was saying all this, so I couldn't tell if she really meant it.

Another time I asked her why she hadn't ever gone in search of Alma Rose to try to persuade her to come back, the way most people would have, why instead she had stayed in Kilgore and carved a rock.

She just shrugged and said she didn't figure you could force people into things.

chapter four

It's a mystery to me, how people know so much about other people's private business. For months, Mom had been suffering through her hopeless yearning after Pat and I didn't hear a whisper, but I could swear that within twenty-four hours of their first kiss, the whole town was buzzing.

The first take on the story was that Pat was a conniving predator who had corrupted my innocent mother. That version didn't last long, probably because Pat had lived in Kilgore forever and her neighbors knew her too well: not even the wildest imagination could turn her into a conniving predator. The second take was that my mother must be the predator and Pat the innocent victim of urban wiles. That theory didn't hold up either, because a barn-size rock carving of a lesbian lover wasn't an innocent-victim kind of production.

In the end the story got fragmented. Sometimes both of them were the villains, and the victim at risk was the world around them. Sometimes both of them were victims, and the villain was a corrupt society. And then there was a contingent who thought that people's personal lives were their own concern, but this group didn't speak up much because it believed in minding its own business.

The parents in town might quibble about fine points of morality, such as whether my mother was evil or merely weak, but the kids at school didn't care about fine points. Their view was simple: I was earthworm castings and the lowest of the low could look at me with scorn. Possibly a few kids didn't share this view, but they kept their mouths shut.

If there was a time in my life when I stretched bungee rubber to its outer limit, it was my last year and a half in school in Kilgore. It was no longer enough to shoot prairie dogs and spout sports trivia. I was surrounded by boys whose voices, like mine, still made embarrassing skids up into the treble and who lived in mortal fear that someone might think they were queer. They vented this fear by snapping wet towels at each other in the locker room and by snapping me with wet towels, verbally, anytime and anywhere. The girls weren't any refuge either. They didn't taunt me, but they kept well clear, for fear that I might transmit the lesbo label from my mother to them.

Pat survived in Kilgore because people had known her for thirty years before they learned she was queer and they couldn't totally change their minds about her, and besides, there was nowhere else to buy groceries. Mom probably got cut a little slack, too, because she'd grown up here and everyone knew her family. She hardly ever came into Kilgore anyway.

As for me, I was an alien. I had no history in town and nothing to sell that anyone needed, and there was no reason why I should not be the receptacle for any trash anyone felt like dumping.

It was a measure of my desperation in my ninth-grade autumn that I took my two feeble years of sitting on the bench with a soccer team in Oregon and went to the junior high football coach to see if I could try out as a place-kicker. Mr. Ross also taught science and supervised the two PCs in the corner of the library that the school rather grandly referred to as its computer center. Those PCs were my most frequent refuge from real life, so Mr. Ross knew who I was and knew I was a hacker. I guess he hoped my grasp of computer logic would somehow translate into perfectly calibrated trajectories on my kicks, because he allowed me to try out.

He corraled the quarterback Scott Alderman to be my holder and took me out onto the field to show what I could do. I half-expected Scott to pull the ball away at the last second so that I would fall on my butt, like Charlie Brown in the comic strip, but Mr. Ross was standing ten feet away, so Scott held the ball properly. I tried half a dozen extra points, and by some miracle four of them went through the uprights and so did one of my three longer field-goal tries. That was better than anyone else they had, so I became a football player.

At least it gave a microscopically more respectable identity to my weirdness. All place-kickers were weird, right? They were little and had foreign accents, and they spent games off by themselves on the sidelines, loosening their leg and muttering superstitious incantations under their breath. For two hours once a week I had a niche, and I was safe.

Safe, that is, provided I never had to try an actual kick in an important situation. I was torn between daydreams and nightmares, the daydream that I would kick a miraculous forty-yard field goal and win a game and everyone would forget about the rest of my life, the nightmare that I would miss a critical extra point and lose a game and suffer quadruple ignominy. As it turned out, our team was usually so far behind that a field goal was never even considered, and when we did score a rare touchdown, Mr. Ross would opt for a two-point conversion instead of a kick. For the first six games of our season, I was asked to kick only twice, extra points, and one was good, so I was passable.

In the last game, my dream/nightmare realized itself. We actually had a chance to win. We were two points behind with twenty seconds left in the game. It was fourth and four on the twelve-yard line. A field goal would win the game, so Mr. Ross sent me onto the field.

In the NFL, a field goal from the twelve-yard line is a chip shot, an automatic three points in the bag before the kicker swings his leg. But as I walked onto the field, I thought the goal posts had disappeared down the wrong end of a telescope. This was a joke, wasn't it? Someone had poked a couple of toothpicks into the ground an inch apart, and I was supposed to send a football through the gap.

The rest of my life in Kilgore depended on this moment. The roaring in my ears easily drowned out any noise from the little six-row grandstand. I was probably hyperventilating, but somehow I kept myself from fainting and measured out my steps behind the holder. My other nine teammates bent forward into their set, and eleven defenders tried to hex me with their eyes, and I realized I was praying fervently to Grandma's ruthless god that he might make an exception and help out a nonbeliever just this once.

The snap count was three. I heard the holder bark once, then a second time. I'll never know for sure if what came next was a reply to my prayer, or whether one of the linebackers on the other team had seen the desperation on my face and out of some inexplicable rush of pity had leapt forward to rescue me. All I know is that before the third bark from the holder, a body came hurtling across the line of scrimmage, knocking two of our linemen aside, and whistles were blowing, and our opponent was called for offsides, a five-yard penalty, and instead of fourth down and four at the twelve-yard line it was first down and goal at the seven, and I was safely back on the sideline watching our quarterback throw an interception on the very next play. The game was over, another defeat added to our season's perfect record of failure, and I had done nothing either to retrieve my reputation or to sink deeper into ignominy. If what happened was a reply from Grandma's god, then it must have been in tongues, because

I couldn't decipher the message.

Then winter came, and there was no possible way to talk myself onto the basketball team, so I was back where I started. Except that I now had a closer acquaintance with a boy named Duane Selby.

Living perpetually on the outside of situations, I sometimes got a better view of them. Even in my uniform, I was on the outside of the football team, so I could sit back and observe the curious situation of Duane Selby. Before I played football, all I knew was that he was big and tough and that he taunted me about my size and parentage with what seemed a particular and personal venom. Then I got to watch him play football every day, up close, and I saw someone who played as if his life depended on it. He was reckless, fearless, single-minded. It was not a game with him, and he did not look like he was having fun. He just had to play and play well, as if he would cease to exist if he didn't.

He was definitely the best athlete on the team. In Kilgore, that didn't mean he was world-class or even that he'd be good enough to get a scholarship somewhere. It only meant he was half-decent, but still, that was better than the rest of us, and I couldn't see why he didn't play quarterback. I sometimes saw him throwing the ball in practice, and he could throw twice as far and a lot more accurately than Scott Alderman. He had quick reflexes, too, and he was taller than Scott, tall enough to see over the linemen. In spite of all that, the coach had Duane play running back, which made no sense.

I also wondered why Duane hated me so much. It went way beyond the other kids, who had a pack mentality and just wanted to look cool in front of their friends. With Duane it felt like rage, like he was a cauldron inside and something about me made him spill over and pour fire. The other kids made sure they had an audience when they had thought of some new and clever way to call me a runt and my mother a queer, but Duane usually picked a time when no one else could hear.

His insults weren't clever—he wasn't very articulate—but they were spoken with what sounded like heartfelt fury. He would pin me up against a wall and hiss in my ear that I had computer circuits in place of guts and if my dick was as small as the rest of me I must have to do it with rabbits. He didn't seem to take a shower as often as other people, so the whole time I was pinned there I was breathing in stale sweat and barn chores and coal smoke, and I had a close-up view of the grime that had worked itself into the pores of his neck. I tried to stay away from him, but he sought me out. He never hit me. He just grabbed me so that I had to stay and listen, and then leaned down so that his VDT-green eyes were looking right into mine and told me all the ways I was a worm.

When I'd been on the team a while, I found out more about him. I had already asked Pat and she had told me he had four sisters, no brothers, and that his family had a very small ranch south of town. I didn't know just what she meant by small, or any other details about his family, until the day I left my windbreaker behind in the locker room.

Duane and I had one habit in common. We both dressed and left as fast as we could after practice. I had plenty of reasons not to hang around for the locker-room horseplay, but I couldn't see why Duane didn't, when he was a star player. I found out why when I went back to get the windbreaker.

As I approached the door, I heard guffaws, so I stopped. I stood there quietly, curious to hear what the guys laughed at when they didn't have me around.

" . . . sleeps in the barn," I heard a voice say.

"Makes it handy, doesn't it? He can have a sheep one night, maybe a cow the next . . . " More guffaws.

"His mom's a retard, off in the bin somewhere . . . "

"She's not a retard. She's a psycho."

"What's the difference?"

So which did people think was worse, a psycho or a queer?

"I bet his dad doesn't mind, having her gone. He can have a different sister every night . . . "

"They all sleep in one bed anyway. He can just roll from one to the next . . . "

"Gotta keep everybody happy."

"Wonder if his dad ever lets Duane have a turn?"

"Naw, Duane just gets the milk cow . . . "

For one crazed moment, I wanted to burst into the room and tell them they were all pea-brained creeps, but then I decided I wanted to live to see my next birthday. My mouth stayed shut and I slunk away, leaving my windbreaker where it was. I felt queasy, but I half wanted to laugh, too. So Duane was the king of the worms, and I was his subject, a serf worm to be whipped at will.

The next time Mr. Ross came and peered over my shoulder at the computer screen, I turned around and asked, "How come Duane doesn't play quarterback when he has the best arm?"

Mr. Ross looked startled and then said awkwardly, "We need him at running back." It was lame and he knew it.

"He could still run the ball if he played quarterback," I said.

"It takes more than an arm to be quarterback. The quarterback has to be smart. He has to make decisions fast . . . "

No, the quarterback gets to tell other people what to do. Can't have a worm as the boss, even if he's the king of the worms. Keep him at running back, where he does what he's told.

From then on I watched Duane hurling himself at linebackers like a man with a death wish, and I thought, I'm luckier than he is because he minds so much more than I do. It occurred to me to tell him about bungee rubber, but then I thought, he would probably obliterate me if he thought his serf worm was feeling sorry for him.

If I had been queer myself, I probably would have fallen in love with Duane right then. As it was, he became a minor obsession. For some reason I decided I had to win him over. I felt almost the way I had about Lucy, after she ripped up my leg. I couldn't stand watching her shrink away from me. I couldn't stand knowing she had to die because a human had failed. Probably it was stupid, wanting to make friends with someone who hated me, but there it was.

With the dog, the attempt had been too late, and I had no reason to think I would have any better luck with Duane. He wasn't afraid of me. He despised me. It wouldn't do any good to show him I wasn't a threat. He already knew I wasn't a threat. Trying to conciliate him would only make him despise me more.

Instead, the next time he shoved me up against a wall and told me I was a piss-ant, I coiled myself into bungee rubber and sucked in enough breath to say, "I'm not a piss-ant. I'm a shit-beetle. It's a completely different species."

It made him pause. Probably the next insult he had planned now sounded like a non sequitur.

With a little less conviction, he said that my balls must be made out of Jell-O.

I said, no, it wasn't Jell-O, it was butterscotch pudding.

This time he seemed to lose his train of thought entirely. He stared at me and his eyes narrowed, trying to see if my self-mockery was also mocking him.

"Shit-beetle, huh. Is that what I should call you from now on?"

I tried to shrug, but my shoulders were still pinned against the wall. "I answer to Geek-Brain, too. But I like Shit-Beetle better. More colorful."

"You really are weird, aren't you?"

"Everyone tells me I am."

All of a sudden his grip loosened. He kept his hands where they were, to remind me that it was he who would say when I was free to go, but at least I could breathe more easily.

"Okay, Shit-Beetle, how is it you know so much about computers?"

This was progress, but it might be instant regress if I said it was because my school in Oregon had a lot more than two computers and its science classes weren't taught by a football coach who also policed the lunchroom.

"My mom works as a computer programmer, over in Seco," I said.

"Really? She must be rolling in it then."

"Oh, sure, rolling. She figures that by the year 2010, she'll have paid off her student loans and her car loan and her construction loan and her credit cards and we might be able to buy a CD player."

"Now you're shitting me. Computer types get paid a ton of money."

"Not in Seco Springs, they don't."

Regardless of my mother's salary, I could see that I had climbed a notch in social status. The question was, would the change require some new humiliation to restore equilibrium?

"So, Shit-Beetle, it must be a real thrill, living in the same house with a lez."

Evidently the answer was yes.

"A thrill?" I said. "Sure, every minute. She does laundry. She reads the newspaper. She cooks dinner. The excitement never ends. What could be more exotic than watching a lez wash dishes? It must be so dull, being stuck with a straight mom, watching her wash—"

Too late, I remembered that his mother was "off in the bin" and not home washing dishes. I shut my mouth and hoped I was not about to get obliterated in earnest.

His grip clamped down again, but he didn't say anything. He seemed to be calculating what fate I deserved.

A little desperately, I said, "Listen, could we please leave our mothers out of this?"

He thought some more and slowly his grip relaxed. "Good idea," he said.

That was the strange beginning of what was, in a peculiar way, almost a friendship. It had one unspoken but absolute limit. No one else in school could know that he didn't utterly despise me. So we observed our peculiar rituals. Around the other kids, he called me Geek-Brain but otherwise ignored me. I never said a word to him. When no one else could hear, he called me Shit-Beetle, and we talked, sort of. If we were in a place where anyone might see us, the whole conversation took place with my shirt front gripped in his fist or my shoulders pinned against a wall.

I was curious to see where he lived, but I knew it would never happen by invitation. At Christmas, I finally found a way. Duane's dad had posted a notice in the Mercantile advertising homegrown turkeys, and I pestered Grandma until she agreed to put her name down for one. Then I demanded to go along when it was picked up. It was Granddad who made the trip. He said he had some business to talk about with Earl Selby, something about running some cattle on shares. Since the Selbys didn't have a phone, he thought this would be a good opportunity.

When I saw Duane's house for myself, I found out several things. One was that Duane only slept in the barn when the weather was warm enough, maybe April to November. The rest of the family didn't all sleep in one bed, either. His dad slept outside on the porch for the same months that Duane was in the hayloft, and the four sisters shared the two little bedrooms inside the house. In the winter, Duane and his dad both slept in the living room, one on the couch and one on a camp cot.

When I saw Earl Selby, I didn't think he looked like someone who would be ravishing a different girl every night. He just looked very tired, worn down and discouraged. He reminded me of one of Granddad's old pickups, the kind that has springs poking up through the seat and holes in the floorboards and a tailgate that won't stay shut and you can't figure out how the thing keeps running, unless it's out of habit.

Duane didn't tell me about sleeping in the hayloft right off the bat. When we first arrived, I thought he was going to call me Geek-Brain and not talk to me at all. He hung off by himself, sitting on the camp cot. Then his dad told him to take me outdoors and find something to do, because he and Granddad wanted to talk about business for a while.

There wasn't anywhere indoors for us to go. The sisters had disappeared into the bedrooms and shut the doors. The rest of the house was all one room, a kitchen at one end, then a table, then the couch and some armchairs and the camp cot. The heat came from a coal-fired heater in one corner, which explained why Duane always smelled like coal smoke. At this moment, the kitchen end of the room was a mess, with buckets of turkey innards on the floor and bits of fat and membrane and pinfeathers stuck to the counters and sink. The turkeys themselves were out on the porch, keeping cold.

Even though the air was freezing, it was a relief to go outdoors. The house smelled of coal and old food, and every object in the room was frayed or dented or dusty. The walls were coated in soot and grease, from too much heat and human moisture confined in too small a volume of air.

Outdoors was another world. Not that it looked any less poor. The sheds were patched up out of a miscellany of plywood, asbestos shingles and tin roofing, and the farm yard was littered with piles of scrap lumber, rolls of barbed wire and old rusty farm equipment, all half buried in weeds. Not a single object looked either new or well kept.

Still, the air was icy clean, and there were animals everywhere, and the animals did look well kept. Two dogs hung at Duane's heels wherever he went. In the henyard a flock of chickens scratched happily in the dirt. A horse and a milk cow dozed in the sun beside the barn. A half dozen pigs of various sizes wandered wherever they pleased. I thought Earl Selby must carry all the worries for everyone, because none of the animals looked the least bit worried or discouraged.

Outdoors, Duane became different, too. He started to look happy, and it made me realize I'd never seen him look that way before, not even on the football field when he'd broken free and run for twenty yards and everyone was cheering. At those moments, he just looked like someone who has been saved from execution for the time being. Out here, he looked happy, like he really was a king and there was nobody telling him that he and his subjects were worms.

For a while we wandered around randomly, watching the pigs nose around in a manure pile and throwing rocks at a tin can. Then he took me into the barn and showed me the corner of the hayloft that was his sleeping space in the summer. He said if he had a warmer sleeping bag, he'd stay there in the winter, too, and I could see why. The barn smelled of hay, not coal smoke, and I could hear the ripple of the creek that ran behind the buildings. From where we sat, slouched against hay bales, the door of the loft framed nothing human and nothing ramshackle, just the blue of the sky, the clean, wind-carved profile of the hills and a dusting of snow among the gray-green sage, rusty brown rocks and dry golden feathers of grass.

My mother had said from the beginning that this country was beautiful, but it wasn't until I saw it from Duane's hayloft that I thought so myself.

It's hard to believe he and I kept up our masquerade for the whole of that winter. A person would think we were having a love affair, as covert as we were. In public, I was Geek-Brain. In semi-public, any place where someone might come along and see us, I was Shit-Beetle, pinned against a wall, miming being picked on, when in fact we were talking about this and that and nothing much at all. On the rare occasion when we were on our own together, when Granddad went to discuss business with Earl Selby, or a couple of times when I found a way to have Duane over to the ranch, we became ordinary friends, fooling around on Uncle Fred's snow machines or target shooting or wrestling, one arm against two to make it a contest.

I didn't think the sky would fall in if we talked in a normal way at school, too, but Duane seemed to think it would. He had lived in Kilgore a lot longer than I had, so I figured he must know more about it than I did. He never said anything out loud about our masquerade, but he made it clear without words that I could never act like his friend at school.

I had thought I was the one with the obsession, but sometime in midwinter it dawned on me that he was the one who started most of our conversations. Once he had sought me out to pour venom on my head. Now he sought me out even more, just to talk, and it really was about nothing. "Hey, what's happening?" "Not much, how about you?" "Did one of the pigs yesterday." "Math test was a bear." So on and so on. He needed me, for some reason, but it wasn't to talk about the meaning of life. Maybe it was because I had as big a family skeleton as he did, so he thought I couldn't be sneering at him.

By mutual agreement, neither one of us ever said anything about the other one's mother.

At the end of April, the sky did fall in, which is bound to happen when it is being held up by fakery.

What happened was simple: bad timing. I said something funny, and he smiled, for a fraction of a second, and that fraction was when four members of the football team came around the corner of the building, planning to have a quick smoke. What they saw was Duane with his hands resting on my shoulders, smiling at me. Unfortunately, he didn't have the acting skill to keep his hands where they were and let his smile curl itself into a sneer and spit some taunt at me and shove me away. Instead, he leapt away from me as if I had turned into a hot stove and then looked guilty.

"Well, look at these two faggot love-birds. Like mother, like son . . . "

"Makes a change from the milk cow, huh Duane?"

For about ten seconds, nobody moved, and those ten seconds lasted into next year. I figured Duane had two choices. He could try to salvage his own life by pounding me into oblivion. Or he could jump off a cliff here and now.

I was a goner either way. But I also knew pretty definitely that I wasn't going to be in Kilgore my whole life, if I could just stay alive. Duane didn't know that. He knew exactly the opposite, that his dad couldn't buy him a warm sleeping bag, much less a ticket out of town.

I could already feel the blows, not the ones from his fists, but the ones inside, the ones that would hurt, if he turned on me. I wouldn't have blamed him if he did—not too much anyhow—but he didn't. I had heard of soldiers throwing themselves onto the barrels of enemy rifles, and now I had the chance to see it for myself, without going to war. Duane led off with a couple of curses and followed with his fists, and I saw him get in a few good punches before three of the guys pounded him to a pulp. The fourth one took care of me, all by himself, and I can't say the punches I got in were very good ones.

I have a hazy memory of hearing kids shouting "Fight! Fight!" and seeing more and more faces crowding into the circle around us and feeling a couple of kicks hit me in the ribs and then I blacked out. When I woke up, I was in bed with my ribs taped and bruises all over.

As soon as I felt like talking, Mom asked me if I wanted to move back to Portland. I said heck no, or those gorillas would never stop beating their chests and yodeling.

The next thing she said wasn't a question. "You're going to the high school in Seco next year. They have more than two computers, and maybe you won't have to show the science teacher how to use them."

I knew my going to school in Seco had nothing to do with the number of computers, but it made a cover story.

Then I asked about Duane.

"No permanent damage, but he's pretty beat up," she said. "They broke his nose. The good news is, he bled all over them, so when a teacher arrived to break up the fight, they couldn't duck into the crowd and leave you guys having to say who did it."

That wasn't all I wanted to know, but I couldn't ask the rest, about what would happen to him next year, since he couldn't flee to a bigger school in Seco Springs the way I could.

"So what happened, Jord?" she asked. "Why were they after you two?"

I shrugged. "They saw Duane talking to me, and I guess that made the two of us queer."

"What do you mean, saw him talking to you? They already know you guys hang out together sometimes. Don't they?"

There was no way I could explain to Mom the style of Duane's and my conversations at school. I shrugged again and said, "You want me to try to make sense out of what goes on in those guys' heads?"

The fight did have one other result, which was that a lot of the people who up until now had believed in minding their own business decided that Duane's broken nose and my cracked ribs were their business. At first it looked like the principal, Mr. Treadwell, was going to suspend the four gorillas for a few days and leave it at that. But he couldn't get away with it. According to Pat, who heard almost everything there was to hear in Kilgore, some people who never got mad were mad about this and they weren't about to let Mr. Treadwell mutter "Boys will be boys" and let things slide. In the end, the four were suspended for the rest of the year and also, the part that counted, barred from playing either football or basketball the following year.

I don't think any of the parents, except possibly Mom and Pat, had any inkling what the fight had really been about. The parents thought we were being picked on because of our mothers and because

Duane was poor, which was part of it. They didn't know about the rest, and for sure none of the kids were going to tell them. So they thought, okay, the culprits have been punished and it's over. They had no idea what school was going to be like for Duane from now on.

I sometimes thought back on how Duane always had his hands on me, one way or another, and I wondered if he had wanted it that way. But he'd never made the slightest move toward either affection or sex, and I was more inclined to think it was just a habit, from the strange way our sort-of friendship had begun. In any case, it didn't matter what he had actually felt. All that mattered was what the other kids thought, and if they thought he was queer, then he was going to be made as miserable as if he were in fact.

There was nothing I could do to make his life any easier, except to stay away from him. It worried me that he would misinterpret my staying clear, so I tried to write him a letter, but I didn't know what to say. What could I say? "They're creeps and it doesn't matter what they think, and if life were fair you would be the quarterback . . . "

I finally muddled out some sort of scrawl about how Mom was arranging for me to go to school in Seco next year and I was going to miss watching him run the football. I don't think I succeeded in writing a single word of what I was really thinking. I asked Mom to do the envelope on her computer at work, addressed to Mr. Duane Selby, neat type, no return address and metered postage. I hoped it would look like a mass mailing. I didn't think he'd want even his sisters to know I had written to him.

I never heard anything back, and I never got another chance to talk to him. Sometime in October, after I had started school in Seco Springs, Pat told me that one day, instead of going to class, Duane had walked out to the interstate ramp, stuck out his thumb and was gone.

chapter five

Seco Springs was a much bigger puddle than Kilgore. The high school had almost twelve hundred kids, so news became old news quicker and there were plenty of other geeks, nerds, retards, faggots, runts and spazzes to keep me company. People had heard about the fight, but the twin distortions of distance and news reporting had transformed the story into one that made my life a lot easier. As it was reported in the Seco paper, four players on Kilgore's junior-high football team had beaten up two other players on the same team. The injuries were serious enough that the four attackers had been barred from team sports for the following year.

So I started off in the Seco Springs high school as "the football player who got beaten up," which was a better rep than I had expected. Also, Mom had decided she needed four-wheel-drive for the back roads in winter, so she had traded in her twelve-year-old Toyota wagon on a seven-year-old black and silver Ford 150 pickup whose first owner had decked it out with chrome and running lights on every available surface. Hopping out of that rig every morning didn't hurt my rep either.

I found my niche fairly quickly, with the nerd group, and amazingly, no one ragged me about Mom. Some people knew she had a brain job with the only big company in town, and they seemed to make the same assumption Duane had, that she made a ton of money. I kept my mouth shut and let them think that, because it seemed to divert their attention from her personal life.

In Seco, I had a new problem.

When I first met Reba, I didn't know she was going to be a problem. All I knew was I couldn't take my eyes off her. I saw her first in my English class. Every day she sat in the back corner staring out the window, never volunteering a word. If Mr. Gallen tried to spring a question on her, she would answer in a voice that sounded half-asleep but most of the time said something pertinent enough to keep her out of trouble.

Outside of class, Reba hung out with the nerds, but she wasn't a nerd herself. She couldn't be classified that easily. Her clothes were random. One day she looked like she belonged on stage with a rock band; the next day she'd be wearing an old green rag pullover, like she'd been raking the yard before she came to school. Some days she wore black from head to foot. Some days she decided to step out, wearing scarves and jewelry and lots of color. As far as I was concerned, it didn't matter what she wore. She was beautiful. She was definitely too beautiful to be a nerd, no matter who her friends were.

But she wasn't cool, either, not by the usual standard. She didn't hang with the right crowd, and she was too eccentric. The only classes she didn't sleepwalk through were art and drama. She maintained a tidy C average in everything else, just enough to avoid getting hauled in for chats with the guidance counselor. She was going to be a set designer, she said, and she didn't want to clutter up her brain with information she would never need, such as algebra. She said that Alzheimer's disease was caused by information overload, that it was the brain crying "Enough already!" and shutting down its circuits one by one. In her view, it was never too early to start a prevention program.

Reba liked me right away, mostly because I had lived on the West Coast. If the airlines had planned their schedules three years ahead, she would already have bought a one-way ticket for California, for the day after graduation. Portland wasn't quite as good as San Francisco or L.A., but she still wanted to hear anything I had to tell.

I more-than-liked her right away. She was bold. She looked boys straight in the eye when she talked to them, and she never giggled. She had dark, dark hair and eyes, and on the days when she decided to step out, with a deep red scarf around her throat and gold earrings and some sort of loose dark jacket and skirt, I couldn't look back at her for very long or I would have passed out.

Even if I had had the courage, I couldn't have asked her out on a date. I lived forty-five miles outside of town and didn't have a driver's license yet. As it was, I hung out with her whenever I could, at lunch, after English class, and sometimes after school, if she didn't have a play rehearsal, but it wasn't nearly enough. It was only an hour here and there, and we were never alone. She traveled in a pack—five guys like me, who dreamed in computer assembly language and loved any field of study that used Greek letters, plus Reba, who loathed computers and mathematics equally.

As the weeks passed, I grew progressively more desperate to break free of the pack, somehow. I tried volunteering for the stage crew, but that only meant that I saw her in a different pack, a compound of oddball artsy types and cool kids, plus Reba. Plus me. The rest of the drama crowd were surprised that a nerd would venture so far from the computer room, but hands were needed and the theater world was supposed to be bohemian and broad-minded, so they tolerated me hammering nails and scurrying around with props as long as I didn't expect to sit with them in the lunchroom. The trouble was, I still didn't see Reba alone.

Then, in winter term, one of my wishbones or shooting stars must have panned out. Reba decided not to act in the play, only to design the sets, and that meant more of her afternoons would be free. Now all I needed was a way to shed my fellow nerds after school. Unfortunately, I suspected that the rest of the pack had been picking out shooting stars, too, and they weren't all going to retire graciously and leave the field to me.

But my star turned out to be the right one, or so it seemed. One afternoon in late January, a big storm started to blow in and as the six of us were standing in the entrance hall, looking out at the snow whipping past on the wind, Reba said to me, "I told Mom about you having to wait for your ride home. She said you could come to our house to wait if you want."

When the rest of the pack started making noises about coming along, too, she said, "Mom's being charitable, because Jordy can't go straight home. She doesn't want the whole gang."

So Reba and I said good-bye to four very sullen-looking guys and stepped outdoors into the gale. As we walked down the street together, leaning a little against the wind, ice crystals blew against my cheeks and into my eyes, stinging, and I thought nothing had ever felt so good.

At her house, she told me she'd been lying. Her mother didn't know anything about my coming there.

"I just got tired of being a party of six all the time," she said.

I stared at her, and inside me all the shooting stars reversed direction and started bursting upward like rockets. She had picked me.

Then panic struck. What did I do next? We were alone in her house. Her brother was off at college. Her parents wouldn't be home until five. This was my chance.

I must have been gaping, because Reba started laughing. "Stop looking like a trout on a hook. My dad doesn't keep a shotgun, you know. He's a dentist. You just have to be out of here before five, and you would be anyway, to meet your mom. You don't mind having to walk back downtown, do you?"

I closed my mouth and shook my head, no, I didn't mind. How could she be so calm?

She flopped down in an armchair with one leg over the side. "Grab a seat somewhere. I'd offer you a Coke, but my mom keeps count. She thinks they're bad for me, so she'll only buy me three per week. Those are gone by Tuesday. If I want any more, I have to buy them myself, and I'd rather buy CDs."

I sat down on one end of the couch, or perched, really, since I didn't quite feel ready to settle in. Reba saw my tea-with-the-queen-of-England posture and said, "Are you still worrying about my parents? The only thing they would mind is my not telling them you were here. But I don't want to tell them, because then Mom will start grilling me about you. Does your mother grill you about girls?"

"No. Not that I've ever put her to the test. I've never had . . . anybody."

"Would she grill you if there were somebody?"

"Probably not. She's, well . . . " I stopped. Did Reba know about my mother? "She would probably wait for me to tell her. She's, like, super-scrupulous about ever assuming anything about anyone until they tell her."

"What else is she like?"

"My mom?" That was like trying to describe Pat's sculpture from six inches away. "She's a computer programmer."

"*Duh*. The whole world knows that. What else?"

I told Reba the obvious stuff, that Mom had grown up on a ranch outside Kilgore, that she worked hard, was practical, not romantic, and stubborn as a mule if she thought something was important but reasonably easy to get along with most of the time. I thought it was strange that Reba was so interested in my mother, but it seemed like I couldn't tell her enough. Every time I paused, she'd say, "And what else?"

I was becoming a little annoyed, actually. Was she just waiting for me to come out and tell her the good stuff in plain words, that my mom was queer? And if that was all she wanted to hear, why didn't she ask? I was feeling punctured, too. No more shooting stars. She just wanted the inside gossip and had to get me alone to get it.

After she said "What else?" for about the fifteenth time, I said, "Why don't you ask me whatever it is you want to know, instead of angling? Usually you're pretty good at saying what you mean."

Would she ask, in plain words?

But she was already several jumps ahead of me.

"I'm not angling. I want to know everything. And I want to know about your—what would you call her? your stepmother?—too. All I hear is the gossip. About the sculpture and so forth. I want to know what's true, that's all. There's so much b.s. passed around."

Now I felt like a dope. Obviously she didn't need me to tell her, in plain words, about my mother's marital status. Kilgore wasn't that far away, not to anyone who was curious.

So I told her about Pat, too, and that was easier than describing Mom, because I had gotten to know Pat from the outside in instead of from the inside out.

"She fools people," I said. "It's like they find out too late that the chair they've been sitting on has opinions about them. They don't notice she's there, and then she says something and they discover she's been watching and thinking the whole time. People were stunned when she started that sculpture, but now that I know her, I can see that she is exactly the kind of person who would do something like that. Most people yak away about themselves all the time, so the things they think and feel get scattered around in public and mixed in with

56

what other people think and feel. But Pat keeps it all inside, so it's like this boa constrictor that you've raised inside a box for ten years, just tossing in mice every once in a while, until one day you lift the lid off the box and find out the thing is huge."

"She sounds a little strange."

"She isn't, really. She trains dogs, and she has art prints on her wall. You'd like her. She's really smart."

"Why didn't she ever leave Kilgore?"

"She was going to. But then her mom died, and her dad wanted her to stay and help at the store. So she stayed. It's been over twenty years, so I guess she must like it. More or less."

Reba shook her head. "Now that is truly strange."

Almost before I knew it, quarter to five had rolled around and my time was up. A whole hour, and we hadn't talked about anything I was hoping to talk about, and now I had to leave. I thought this was probably the first and last time Reba would invite me to her house alone. She had gotten her inside scoop on my mother and Pat. Now we could go back to being the party of six everywhere we went.

When I left the house to walk downtown, the wind had risen to a howl and that was fine with me. I could howl a little myself and no one would hear. How had I fallen into the delusion that someone as fine as Reba would bother with a seventh-percentile circuit board?

I tried to act normal when Mom picked me up, but she has radar.

"What's biting you?" she asked.

"Nothing."

"Are people giving you grief again?"

"Nah, the kids here are fine."

"Something else, then?"

"Mom, it's nothing, okay?"

She knew it wasn't, but she is determined not to be like Grandma, so she didn't push me. If she had, I would have lied. For sure I wasn't going to tell her I had had an hour alone with the most beautiful girl in the school and had stupidly let the conversation get stuck on my mother.

The blizzard was for real. The next morning all the roads were closed. I was glad—it was only putting off the inevitable for a day, but a day is a day. All too soon, I would go back to our gang-of-six routine, with nothing gained except that four of the six would be mad at me. I half wished the roads would stay closed for a week.

Instead, the county sent out its battalion of mega-plows, the kind that look like they were designed to rescue the Donner Party from its fate in the high Sierras. In less than a day, all the roads had nice neat viaducts cut through the head-high drifts, and I was back at school.

I was right that the other guys were mad at me, but I had miscalculated Reba. So I found a new way to look like a dope. After school the pack gathered, the way it always did, but I hung back near the edge, waiting to see what plan would develop, the library, something to eat, browsing CDs, or maybe nothing. It seemed like a bad moment to be pushing myself forward, so I didn't say much. Then all of a sudden, Reba was standing in front of me, scowling. She grabbed my sleeve and said, "Are you coming, or what?" Turned out she was expecting me to come to her house again, and now she was annoyed that I had forced her to make an issue of it, instead of acting like it was automatic.

I tried to hide my surprise under a bunch of baloney about being occupied with a math problem, but it wasn't any good. The guys were bugged at having my privileged status shoved in their faces again, and Reba was bugged that I was so obtuse. I felt bad for about two minutes. Then Reba and I were alone together and she had shown that she wanted it that way, as a matter of course, and I didn't care if all my other friends had gone home to stick pins into an effigy of me. I was flying.

I returned to earth again in her living room. We might be alone, but we weren't together, not yet. She seemed permanently planted in her favorite armchair, with her leg over the side, and that armchair might just as well have been a fort. I couldn't find a way to approach her when she was in it. There was a stereo cabinet on one side of it and a huge potted plant on the other side, so there was absolutely no way I could inch myself a little closer and a little closer, talking the whole time, until finally I was close enough to let a hand brush some little part of her, a sleeve maybe, just casually, to see what happened. If I wanted to touch her, I would have to fling myself across twelve feet of open carpet, brazenly, all bridges burned. I didn't have that much courage.

Instead, we talked. On Mondays she split her ration of Coke with me, but otherwise all the days were about the same. She dumped her books on the floor and flopped into her armchair. Sometimes she stuck some CDs into the player. Then she asked me about Portland, or about Mom, or she talked about movies and all the ways she would have done a set design differently for one scene or another. She was fun to talk to, and I wouldn't have minded continuing the conversation forever, if I hadn't felt like my insides were a bag of rags soaked in paint thinner, about two degrees away from spontaneous combustion.

Sometimes I tried to steer the conversation in a more fruitful direction, with the idea that if I couldn't sidle closer to her physically, I might be able to verbally. I tried to get her talking about who was dating whom at school, or did she like to dance, or what kind of boys did girls generally go for, or which movie stars did she like. I thought if I could start the conversation down the right track, I might eventually inch my way to the information I really wanted. Did she like me at all?

I found out plenty of her opinions. She liked Mel Gibson and Brad Pitt, didn't like Tom Cruise. She liked Demi Moore and Jodie Foster, didn't like Michelle Pfeiffer. She said most of the dating couples at school were the perfect mating of an airhead with a neanderthal. She did like to dance, but she said it was always the wrong person who asked her.

That was my opening and I leapt, cautiously. "Who would be the right person?" I asked.

For a minute, she looked like she was holding her breath and might actually answer. I know I was holding mine. Then she screwed up her face into joke mode and said, "Brad Pitt, of course. Who did you think?"

Was this going to be the routine for the rest of my life, best buddies separated by twelve feet of carpet?

Then one day, out of the blue, Reba said, "Does your mother ever stay in town for the evening?"

"Not very often, why?"

"I was thinking we could go to a movie or something."

"You and me?"

"Yeah. And your mom, I guess. You couldn't exactly ask her to wait in the car. Anyway, I'd like to meet her."

"You want to meet my mother?"

"Sure. You are my best friend, aren't you?"

"Yeah, I guess. I mean, definitely."

I wasn't sure whether I was happy or not. First she wanted to be introduced to my family, as if we were engaged or something, and then she pronounced us best friends. But in most people's vocabulary, "best friends" meant definitely not engaged, or even dating. "Best friends" meant there was almost an incest taboo against dating. So what did Reba mean by it?

When the big evening came, she turned very squirrelly. We had agreed to get a pizza and go to a movie, all with Mom along, but she didn't want her parents to know that Mom was with us. She said her parents would see my mother as a radioactive substance that might contaminate their daughter.

I was perplexed. First, she wanted to be introduced to my mother, as if we had reverted to the nineteenth century and had to ask permission to begin a courtship. Then, she wanted her own parents to think we were on a date by ourselves. But no matter how closely I looked, and I was looking closely, I couldn't see that there was anything definite between us. I had always thought people fell in love first and then told their parents, but she seemed to want to tell all the parents before she told me. And apart from the scenes that played inside my own head, I wasn't at all sure there was anything to tell.

Our "date" didn't clarify the situation. For the first few moments, all three of us were awkward, but when we got to the pizza place, Reba and Mom discovered their first female bond, negotiating all the details of the pizza topping. From then on the conversation was amicable, but not exactly profound. I hardly remember any of it. I think it was mostly about careers and what it was like to be a programmer and what Reba's parents did.

The movie was *Ghost*. Reba and Mom loved it, but I'll never know what I thought of it, because there was a scene right at the beginning that left me too paralyzed with self-consciousness to make any objective judgments. I was just grateful that movie theaters are dark. Here I was with Reba in the next chair, almost touching me, and up on the screen Demi Moore starts molding some wet clay on a potter's wheel. She's wearing a thin sleeveless cotton shirt and nothing else, and she has her hands wrapped around this soft slippery mound of clay, and she's caressing it and squeezing it up through her fingers, and all the while Patrick Swayze is right behind her with his hands all over her body. The scene seemed to go on forever, with that soft rounded pillar of clay squeezing up through her fingers, and some romantic song throbbing accompaniment, and me wishing I could sink down through my chair and out of sight, because Reba looked more than a little like Demi Moore and that scene was way too close to home for my comfort.

The movie was Friday night, so I had to wait the whole weekend before I could see her again and perhaps get a clue where we were going next. On Saturday, she called me, but it was only to talk about the movie. She seemed fixated on that scene with the clay. I kept trying to head the conversation off toward Whoopi Goldberg and how funny she was, and Reba kept coming back around to Demi Moore in just a shirt with her hands on that clay, and I started to wonder if she had been reading my mind and was teasing me.

When I went to her house on Monday, something had definitely changed. For one thing, she forgot to offer me my half Coke, and then she didn't toss herself into her armchair like an old banana peel. She kept jumping up and walking around, and finally she said, "Come upstairs to my room. I feel like the living room has eyes and ears."

As I followed her up the stairs, my heart was racing. I'd never kissed a girl. What if I did it wrong? What if she decided I was gross?

She closed the door, then sat down on the edge of her bed and pointed to a spot next to her, not right next to her, but close enough. This was territory made for inching.

My face felt hot, so I knew I was flushed, but she was, too, so it was okay. I slid my first half-inch closer.

She turned and looked at me, straight in the face. Her eyes were very bright, glowing, I thought. She looked scared, too, and that made me braver, so I ventured a whole inch this time. I calculated it would take five or six more moves, less if she helped a little.

I saw her take a deep breath and that made me hold mine. Was she going to say something that would close the whole gap at once?

"Jordy, you're the best guy I've ever known," she said. "No contest."

I thought the blood was going to pop my eardrums. I was trying to think of something more poetic to say than "I feel the same about you," but all I got out was "You . . . " before she stopped me.

"Don't say anything," she said. "I've got to say this all at once, or I won't be able to."

Her eyes looked on fire. She was ten times more beautiful than Demi Moore.

"I've never told anyone this before," she said. "You're the first person I've ever wanted to tell."

I leaned closer. Did I dare try a kiss?

"I trust you not to freak out, the way other people might," she said.

Huh?

I felt a first little prick of ice, melting and spreading. I think my face must have locked itself into a death stare, because she suddenly looked confused.

"This is harder than I thought. I can trust you, can't I?"

I felt like I should be a cartoon character, grabbing my head with my hands and giving it a twist, to free my face from paralysis.

"Yes, you can trust me," I said, instead of howling.

"It's that . . . well . . . I mean, I wanted to meet your mom . . . that is, I already knew, but even so it was good to just, like, talk . . . I mean, she doesn't like green pepper and I don't either . . . "

If I hadn't been about to cry, I would have laughed. As if everyone who hated green pepper must be queer.

She got the actual word out, eventually, and I said no, I wasn't freaked out. Not in the way she was worried about. Annihilated, maybe. Obliterated, maybe. My heart was solidified in liquid nitrogen, my gut was weighted down with lead, but no, I was not freaked out. I just thought she was the only woman I would ever love, and that was doom enough.

For her, pronouncing the word yanked the stopper out of the bottle and the whole story came gushing out. She told me about a girl in the junior class who was to die for. She told me about her father's wisecracks about gay soldiers wanting to take their pantyhose and blow dryers with them into combat. She told me she didn't like hanging out with other girls because they thought she was weird when she didn't giggle with them about boys. On and on. She also told me several times what a good friend I was, and with every repetition, my heart twisted into a tighter knot.

Neither of us had a thought to spare for the time. We forgot about it entirely, until her mother's voice chimed down the hallway, "Reba, dear, are you home?" There were two quick knocks on the door, and then it opened. Reba and I both jumped to our feet, looking as guilty as if we had been caught naked and steaming with passion.

And that was how the two of us officially became an item.

Reba got grounded, of course, for sneaking a boy into her room, but it was token, just a week. Her mother was too relieved to find she had a boyfriend to be seriously angry. As soon as the week was up, I was warmly welcomed again, downstairs. The ration of Cokes was doubled, and whenever Reba's parents saw us together, we were bathed in benevolent smiles. Why shouldn't they smile? We were a model teenaged couple, unswervingly faithful and pristinely chaste. We didn't even hold hands, except occasionally in public where people seemed to expect it.

Our status as an item became common knowledge at school, too. Since neither of us was inclined to join the wider dating circle, changing partners every time the music stopped, we were thought to be really and truly in love, Romeo and Juliet almost. The other guys in our pack envied me furiously, and I got a ton of status points in the school at large. Reba didn't gain any points at all, snagging me for a boyfriend, but she did gain a great cover story. It was the perfect arrangement for both of us, except for one small detail. I was still in love with her.

If people could turn off fruitless love like a faucet, we wouldn't have bathtubs overflowing with poetry, and as far as I was concerned, it would have been a good trade. I'd have thrown out every line ever written, and tossed in music, too, if that was the price of ending the pain. Instead, I tortured myself, for two and a half years. When we graduated, Reba and I were the longest-lasting couple in the school, by far, and everyone assumed we would get married.

Between ourselves, we were the best of friends, sharing everything.

I had tried my hand at acting. Reba had deigned to touch a computer keyboard. Neither of us was very successful, but we gave ourselves points for having broadened our character. We could talk about anything, except that one small detail.

Reba told me about every passing fancy for this girl or that one, all of them unavailable. She was counting the days until she could move to a place where she might meet someone who was available. She talked longingly about L.A. For my part, I daydreamed out loud about hooking up with a high-tech R&D company, some place small with a few really smart people who manipulated computer logic the way Uncle Fred handled his tools, some place where the work was new and radical and made you think. I also told her things I hadn't told anyone, about the Kilgore school and my time on the football team, and a little about Duane.

When we got our driver's licenses, Reba could come out to the ranch more easily, so she got to know Mom and Pat better. She also got to meet Skipper. Technically, Skipper was Pat's dog, but by now Pat was staying at our house more nights than she was home, and whenever she was there, Skipper slept in my room and shadowed every move I made. Pat would watch him picking up sticks for me to throw and hovering beside my feet when I was reading, and she would smile, a little ruefully. She said that Skipper might still be her dog, but I was Skipper's person. Reba got along famously with him, which only added to my torment by adding another way that she was perfect. I didn't think I could love someone who didn't like dogs.

Sometimes Reba asked me if I had my eye on anyone, and I always turned the answer into a joke. I would bow with mock courtliness and say, "Am I not sworn to you, milady? Until I meet a maid whose beauty outshines yours, I am your consort and slave."

Reba was of three minds about my true emotional state. Sometimes she thought I must be too in love with technology to have any interest in sex. Sometimes she thought I might be attracted to other boys, but deep in denial. Sometimes she approached the truth, that I was afflicted with a poetically hopeless secret passion, but lacked the talent and courage to transform my hopelessness into art. In fact this was only half the truth. I also had inherited a share of my mother's pragmatism. I could see clearly that there was no one else at Seco Springs High School who was likely to become as good a friend as Reba, and I didn't want to mess things up by making an awkward and useless declaration of love. Poetry I would willingly pour down the drain, but not friendship, not in that desert.

Reba and I fooled her parents and the whole high school, but there was one person we couldn't fool. I had been blind about Reba for several months, but my mother had her figured out in one evening and me figured out soon after. She asked me what was going on with us, in a way that made clear that she knew, at least partly. So I told her, partly.

I said that, publicly, Reba and I were dating, but in fact we were just good friends, because Reba had no interest in boys. I said I thought it was a good joke, going to a party, dancing every dance together, letting people think we were totally devoted, and all the while Reba is pining away for Lorraine Kimball. I didn't mention what it was like for me, the slow dances, smelling her hair, feeling her body brushing against mine, just lightly, here and there, feeling currents race across my skin, and knowing all the while that she was just smiling at the joke, that her nerves were as calm as if she were dancing with a broom.

Mom guessed anyway. "You like her, don't you?"

If I said no, she would know I was lying and she would start worrying that I was brooding. She never used to be a worrier, but something must happen to people in their thirties, because for the last year or two she had been worrying about me all the time. If she thought I was brooding, she would probably extrapolate it all the way to my being suicidal. I decided she would worry least if I said yes, I did like Reba, but it was no big deal.

"She's pretty," I said. "We have a lot of laughs. It would be nice if she were straight, but she isn't. It's not the end of the world."

Mom was going to worry no matter what I said, but my being casual kept her worries down near the baseline. She just said, "Don't be too hard on yourself about it. Don't take it personally that she doesn't think you're pretty, too."

If she could make a joke about it, then she was only averagely worried. Luckily, she wasn't a mother hen, even in her thirties.

Only once did I come close to telling someone what I really felt, and for some reason, that person was Pat. Maybe she happened to catch me at the right moment. Or maybe it was because she's so quiet. She might not say anything, but at least she doesn't say the wrong thing. She used to climb up to a hilltop and sit on a rock and stay still for an hour, watching her dogs nosing the rocks and bushes, mapping the recent history of the hill. I didn't know anyone else who seemed so content to stay in one place and absorb all the little details close at hand. She reminded me of a pool in a hollow, collecting the runoff from the slopes around it. She stayed there, quiet and still, and before I knew it I was talking to her, my thoughts flowing down the slope into the pool.

It was a Sunday morning, the morning after the junior prom. Reba had thought it would be a lark to dress up and go, so I had rented a monkey suit, bought her a corsage, the works. She had looked stunning, the way she always did when she decided to step out, and the two of us had spent four hours touching but not touching, until the inside of my suit was soaked in sweat. As the dance was winding down, there was a general move to go somewhere and park. People were ragging us about how we would never go along, how we always had to be so private, and all of a sudden Reba said to me, "Let's go along. Why not?"

In the truck, she said, "Don't you think we should do it once, just to see what it's like? We're seventeen already, and I'm curious. Aren't you?"

Curious wasn't the right word, but I said yes. The truth was, I felt a little sick at the idea of "seeing what it was like" with my best friend who was also the ghost of my fantasy life. My fantasies did not picture scientific experiments on the seat of a pickup.

Still, I wasn't about to say no, so we followed some other cars out to one of the regular spots on a dead-end gravel road north of town. All the way there, Reba kept talking about how her period was due in two days so we would be safe, and how she thought she had to try it once with a boy, just to be sure she wasn't making a mistake. Probably she was talking so much because she was nervous, but I really wished she would shut up about all the logistical considerations.

Once we parked, she did shut up. We kissed for a few minutes, and then somehow we got enough clothes off for me to get inside her. When I came it was more hollow than it had ever been with just her ghost. She was very sweet, stroking my hair and kissing me some more, but it was clear without any words that the experience had satisfied her curiosity and I hadn't miraculously persuaded her to fall in love with me.

I didn't tell Pat all the details. I'm not sure I told her much at all, in words.

I had slept late, and when I got up, Pat was at our house with her dogs. Mom had gone off somewhere, for a ride I think. It was warm, mid-May, and the hills were as green as they ever got, which was not very. Pat was sitting out on the front porch with a book, and the dogs were lounging in the sun. When I sat down on the step, Skipper came over wanting his ears scratched, so I sat there rubbing his ears between my fingers and thinking that this particular morning of my life should have been different, shouldn't have felt so rotten.

We all sat like that for quite a while, silent. Skipper would stay to be scratched indefinitely and I didn't think I had anything I wanted to say and Pat was just being the way she was.

Then, out of nowhere, she said, "I used to wish sometimes that I could be a dog."

I tried to laugh. "How come? So that people would scratch your ears?"

She shrugged. "Just simpler."

I looked at her other dog, Lucky, who was only half-grown. She was dozing in the grass, her ear flicking now and then at a circling fly. Pat's old dog had died a year before, so she had only the two young ones.

"You wouldn't live as long," I said.

"No."

"But no one would expect you to talk."

She smiled then. "No."

"Maybe I should try being a dog for a while," I said. "It couldn't make things any worse."

"Depends who your owner is."

I laughed then, a little crazily. "So I'm doomed either way. Dog or human, I get to be miserable. But if I'm a dog, I don't have to be miserable for as long a time. So maybe it would be an improvement. And it's not like it would be any big change. I'm already a loyal dope who wags his tail whenever she gives me a scrap. Which is all I'm ever going to get from her. A scrap. Am I stupider than other people or what?"

I picked up a stick and threw it. Skipper ran and picked it up, but at least he had the dignity not to bring it back.

"I put a guy through that," Pat said slowly. "In high school."

"Why did you do it?" I asked. "Was it an ego trip or something?"

She winced, and I thought that was going to be the end of the conversation. But after a minute, she said, "It wasn't intentional. I was all disconnected inside. Nothing to do with him. I didn't realize

69

how hard it was for him, being my best pal. I needed the friendship, that's all."

"Did you—?"

She waited.

"Nothing." I picked up another stick and threw it. Once again Skipper picked it up and kept it for himself. Smart dog, I thought.

"Where is he now, your best pal?"

"He lives about sixty miles from here. He's got a wife and kids."

"So he got over it."

She smiled. "I'm not someone you don't get over."

I looked at her. She wasn't ugly, but she wasn't pretty either. She looked like a person you would want with you on an expedition to explore the Arctic. Solid.

"How long do you think it took? Him getting over you."

"Until he fell for someone else."

Great. It had been almost two years, and I hadn't met anybody close to as fine as Reba.

"That makes me feel a lot better," I said. "I've found somebody perfect. Now I just have to find somebody who's better than perfect. And of course she'll be waiting to fall all over me, since I'm so wonderful. Shit."

I could see Reba's face, last night, with the moonlight on it. I could see her expression, apologetic, grateful and colossally indifferent. You've answered my question, thank you, now let's be friends again.

"I hope you didn't—"

Once again, Pat waited for me to finish the thought.

"I mean, am I crazy or is what she did more than usually cold? Or is it something anyone might do?" I stopped. My eyes were starting to burn, and I didn't want to cry, not in front of someone. Then the damned dog came over and started licking my hand, and I couldn't stop myself. Pat still didn't say anything. She sat there quiet while my tears ran down into the dog's fur, into the silence.

"Let's just see what it's like, she says. What was I supposed to say? No, I don't want to. I've thought about it every day for two years but, no, I don't want to. Wasn't I curious, she asks. Who, me? Oh, sure. I'm curious what it would be like to stick my hand into the blender, too. Let's do that next. As if it wasn't bad enough before."

I was gripping Skipper's ruff and I must have gripped too hard, because he let out a yelp. I let go, and right away he nosed my hand, forgiving. I didn't feel forgiving, not yet.

"Does she know?" Pat asked.

"Know what?"

"How you feel about her."

"Are you kidding? I'm not that big an idiot. No, she thinks it's all a big joke that we're putting over on everyone else. Some joke. Jordy, the straight man. And last night was purely scientific. Testing, testing, one, two, three . . . "

Pat was quiet again for a long time, and then she said, "I don't think she would have . . . if she'd known. That would be cold. Reba isn't cold."

"You don't think so?"

She shook her head. "She just didn't think. About what it might be like for you. The same way I didn't."

"Did you . . . ?"

This time she finished my question. "No, not with him. We kissed once, that's all."

I hadn't thought that anything could make me feel better, but hearing that Reba wasn't cold helped a little. That was before I found out she was going to be the pattern of my life.

chapter six

Two weeks after my high school graduation, I moved to the Bay Area. It was one of the times when I actually heard a *kerchunk* as I was knocked onto a track different from what I had planned.

In my mind, I had been in L.A. ever since Reba first told me she was going to be a set designer for the movies. She and I had made a pact that the moment we had our high school diplomas in our hands, we were gone. I had no clear picture in my mind of what I would do in L.A., just that I would be there, because Reba would be there.

My mother did have a picture in her mind, and it wasn't of me waiting on tables and hanging out with Reba while she tried to grease her way into the Hollywood system. Mom was pragmatic, relentlessly pragmatic. In her picture, I was going to college. Since she was still paying off her own student loans, I had two choices. I could go to our state's university immediately. Or I could pick a state I liked better and get a job there until I had established residency.

She said, "You're going to be an indentured servant no matter what, but at least if you pay in-state tuition, it won't be for half your life."

I wasn't sure I wanted to be an indentured servant at all, especially since it wasn't clear that the servant's master would keep to its half of the bargain. As far as I could see, college graduates were being downsized along with everyone else.

I did know, however, that I wasn't spending four more years in a state where high culture was a satellite dish. I told Mom I was taking option two and going to California.

She said that was fine, and then added, "Let's hope it still has a university system by the time you're a resident."

I didn't tell her I might not ever need its university system. I just muttered something about what a great place Berkeley was and started packing. Reba's parents had bought her a car, and she and I had it all planned out—we would drive to L.A. together, find an apartment to share and then find jobs.

"What kind of job?" Mom wanted to know.

"Maybe I'll wait tables in some fancy place where I can watch the movie stars."

"You're under age. You can't serve alcohol. I doubt you'll see many movie stars at Taco Bell."

"Then we'll start a business cleaning rich people's houses."

"You're not qualified to clean anyone's house. Even if you were, a couple of million immigrants are in line ahead of you."

"Then I'll pump gas."

"In that case, you've already been replaced by a computer."

"Mom, you're bumming me out."

"I'm trying to."

Turned out Mom had her own idea, and it didn't include either L.A. or Reba, unless Reba was willing to change plans and move to the Bay Area. One of Mom's friends from college was part of a tiny start-up company in Sunnyvale. The company had just reached the point where they needed one more body, very cheap, to do routine grunt work like software testing and shipping and miscellaneous errands. The body had to know about computers and be willing to work for almost nothing. For that, I was qualified.

"But I don't know anybody in the Bay Area," I said.

"You don't know anybody in L.A. either."

"I'll know Reba."

"Innocents abroad. It's your choice, but this job is your chance to play with computers all day long. If you go to L.A., the only computer you are going to see is the one with keys for large and small orders of fries."

I knew she was right, but still, sometimes it's aggravating to have a mother who is unfailingly reasonable. Why couldn't she be wrong once in a while? Why couldn't she urge me to become an accountant or insist that I join the Marines? Couldn't she be tyrannical and misguided, just for one minute, so that I could vow to follow my own star, no matter what, and exit the room in stormy defiance? Instead, here she was, encouraging me to strike out on my own, opening the way for me to do exactly the thing I'd always wanted to do.

"Who is this friend of yours?" I asked. "Do I know him?"

"I don't know. Do you remember a guy named Greg Milloy?"

I did remember him, a little. He was a nut with dreadlocks who talked a mile a minute about philosophers with German names and always acted like his computer science classes were a scheduling mistake that he hadn't bothered to correct because he could knock off the assignments during the ad breaks on *Star Trek* and collect another easy A.

Mom said, "If I were prudent, I probably wouldn't let you anywhere near him. He's more than a little crazy and he has no detectable standard of ethics, only a standard of technological elegance. Still, he knows most of what there is to know about computers, so you might learn something. He says his company's goal is to design the next product to be swallowed up by one of the amoebas in Seattle or Silicon Valley." She grinned at me. "Who knows? If you're lucky, you might catch the burp after the gulp and become a millionaire."

The light in California was different from other places. Blinding. In Kilgore, it was sunny most of the time, but the blue of the sky looked infinitely deep, so that any light that bounced off the earth would just keep going, on and on, back into space. In California, the blue was washed out, as if the sky had a surface that had faded from all the sunshine and the faded surface kept reflecting the light back toward the earth, so that it never got away. Instead, the light kept bouncing back and forth and multiplying, until you had to squint or buy sunglasses.

I found a place to live, three guys looking for a fourth in a dumpy three-bedroom ranch halfway between El Camino and the Bay. The three bedrooms were occupied, so I got the cubbyhole that was supposed to be the den, for a rent that would have paid for most of a house in Kilgore.

The living room looked like a stereo warehouse. There was almost no furniture, just a couch, one chair and a dining room table that was shoved against a wall and piled with videotapes and CDs. The rest of the room was filled by four mammoth speakers and two towers of electronic gear. One tower had an amp, a tuner, a CD player, two tape decks and an antique turntable; the other, a thirty-six-inch TV, a little nineteen-incher, and two VCRs. A jungle of wires hooked the system together, so that inputs and outputs could be routed through every possible combination of components. The two central mountains of gear were surrounded by foothills, stacks and stacks of CDs, videotapes, cassettes and even some old LPs. The whole setup belonged to Mike, who worked in a mega-electronics store. My other two roommates were students, too broke and too busy to own much of anything except their textbooks and computers, which they kept in their own rooms.

In the kitchen I found one saucepan and one frying pan and some plates and eating utensils. The house had a broom but no vacuum cleaner, and no one seemed concerned about the lack, even though half the floors were covered in gold shag carpet. It didn't take long before I wasn't concerned either. The dirt worked its way down into the pile, and you really didn't notice it much.

Ethnically, the house was like a random census sample. If we counted all ten parents and step-parents belonging to the four of us, we could trace ancestries back to Africa, Asia, Europe and Latin America, and even leaving aside Mike, who never discussed his religious background, we could claim either current or historic affiliations with Catholicism, Judaism, several varieties of Protestantism, New Age spiritualism and scientific rationalism.

The one blank was my biological father, who was more or less an anonymous sperm donor, Caucasian. My mother hadn't told me much about him because she didn't know much herself, except that he was a business major with a loud laugh and he wrote about sports for the campus newspaper. Their one-time encounter at a beer brawl had not included any conversation about religion or family history.

The other guys thought I was a little backwoods and naive, coming from Kilgore, but on the other hand, I had a job with a high-tech start-up and that was highly cool. When they found out my mother was a lesbian, it wasn't cool or not cool, just unexpected, because of where I came from. They ragged me a little about shooting prairie dogs, but it was friendly ragging, and for almost the first time in my life, I felt like it might be safe to let bungee rubber turn back into muscle and blood. I didn't care if I had to live in a cubbyhole and eat from the microwave. I was really happy to be away from Kilgore.

My job was two miles away, a fifteen-minute test of reflexes on my bicycle. California seemed to have as many motorized vehicles per capita as my mother's family did, but here the houses weren't several miles apart. At rush hour the traffic reminded me of a marching band, the larger part of the formation trying to go north or south, the smaller part trying to go east or west, a hundred-square-mile grid of cars negotiating an elaborate crisscross, with me on a bike in the middle, trying not to get killed.

At the far end of the ride was Ultimall, Inc., my employer, which despite its grand title was just one small suite of offices in one corner of one building of a gigantic business park. My first day there I wandered for twenty minutes among a complex of parking lots and five-story stucco-faced cinder-block buildings until I finally found a door numbered 23375 and a tiny sign with the name of the company. When I walked in the door, the size of the company increased by fifteen percent, from seven to eight.

My boss said they didn't have any more offices, so my workspace was a desk and a terminal in one corner of a room otherwise fully occupied by computers. I liked it, actually. With all the cooling fans going, and the disk drives, each on its own frequency, it was like floating in a bath of white noise. The only drawback was that the air conditioning couldn't keep up with all that energy output, so the temperature was generally in the eighties. On my first day, I thought I was going to get heat stroke. Then one of the programmers clued me in that I was already hired and didn't have to dress for a job interview any more. After that I wore jogging shorts and a T-shirt and eighty-five degrees suited me fine.

My mom was right about my boss—he was a little crazy. He had shed the dreadlocks in favor of a head shaved bald, but otherwise seemed a lot the way I remembered him. No one at the company called him Greg. He was known as Mips, only in his case the acronym stood for "millions of ideas per second," not "millions of instructions." I thought he must be a mutation or an alien hybrid, because it didn't seem possible a human brain could work that fast.

Mips talked in fast-forward, but even that wasn't fast enough to keep him from sputtering in frustration at the slowness of his motor neurons. He said having to talk was like having to run all his data through a modem, the weak link in the system. Even with the fastest modem available, the processor had to spend most of its time idle, waiting for the modem to catch up, and that was how his brain felt, like a processor idling while his tongue and jaw laboriously transmitted information. Everyone else at the company learned to talk fast, too, because if you talked slowly, his fingers would start picking up pencils and snapping them in two, involuntarily.

Besides Mips, who was the chief tech-brain, there were five other programmers, two of whom were also graphic designers. The business brain of the outfit was a guy named Guthrie Stone. He had been born on a commune in upstate New York, and he loved to explain in elaborate detail how you could run an enlightened company, like Ben and Jerry's or Patagonia, and still make millions. I didn't think the explanation required all of his circuitous elegance. At three dollars per pint and two hundred dollars per windbreaker, it seemed to me there was plenty of room for enlightenment and millions both. He was more idealistic about those companies than I was, maybe because he had more personal experience with their products. Before he reached kindergarten, his parents had abandoned the commune in favor of a very lucrative import business.

I didn't like Guthrie much. His beard was too neat. I mean, it was always exactly the same length. He must have trimmed it every other day. Every third day at the outside. Like he had found a length that projected exactly the right degree of "natural manness" and made sure to keep his beard that length all the time. Also, he was one of the army of Californians who bombed around the suburbs in four-wheel-drive sport utility vehicles, as if the climate might suddenly change and bury Sunnyvale in eight-foot snowdrifts.

Luckily, I had almost nothing to do with Guthrie at work. He was always complaining that the company was overloaded on the technical and design side, but then Mips would point out that they didn't yet have a product to sell, so the technical and design side was where most of the work was. Guthrie seemed to think the product was optional, that all we needed was a package and a good sales pitch. He said the techies were wasting too much time worrying about a few bugs.

Mips, on the other hand, was fanatical about the product. It was going to be something real, something revolutionary, something utterly cool and brilliantly designed. It was also going to make a ton of money. If Guthrie could find an enlightened way to structure the profits, that was fine, that was his show, but Mips didn't want to hear the details. Coding, he paid attention to an inefficiency that might add a nanosecond to response time, but when it came to money, he said, "I want all the figures rounded to the nearest million."

That line was a standing joke, since Ultimall hadn't yet shown a dollar in profits, much less a million. Officially the company was part employee-owned, but that was another standing joke. What it meant was that in addition to our salary, we were all earning a little piece of the company every month. When Guthrie first explained it to me, he tried to make it sound like it was a matter of deep principle, until Mips chimed in and said, "No, it's just a way for us to pay you a lot less money without looking bad. A share of this company is worth zip right now, as you know. So think of it as a lottery ticket, with about the same odds."

Mips didn't really believe what he said about the lottery ticket. He believed, absolutely, that the company's product was going to make a killing.

"How could it miss?" he said. "It's the coming version of the national pastime. It has all the right elements. It's fun. It's mindless. It's mesmerizing. It spends money. And when you're done, you've bought a big pile of new stuff."

For marketing purposes, the product had the same name as the company, Ultimall, but in-house, everybody called it Shopnotize. My job was to run it over and over and over, trying out every possible idiot thing a user might try to do, and making notes whenever the program failed. I found out fast that Mips had described the product to a T. Essentially, it turned a group of websites into a virtual shopping mall and then applied the psychological principles of video games, the carefully calculated alternation of reward and frustration, the gradually escalating level of challenge, to suck the user into a more and more compulsive pursuit of the next purchase. Unlike a video game, though, this program spent real money.

Mips had conceived and designed the whole program, and he loved to talk about it, in any odd moment by the coffee machine or pausing in a stairwell. As he talked, his hands traced shapes in the air, as if he could see a program flowchart right in front of him and was pointing out details. Sometimes he forgot that he was holding a mug in his hand and his coffee sloshed out onto the floor, but he didn't notice it, because all he saw was the flowchart.

"Really, it's two programs," he said. "One for now, one for the future. Right now, we can't put in the whole light show. Too many people get onto the net through a modem. You can't run full-scale graphics through a modem. Not even a Buddhist monk has that much patience. So we handle most of the graphics on the customer's machine. The online catalog just sends a little skeleton of information about the product, which the user's machine extrapolates to make a whole image.

"Someday, everybody will be wired into the Web directly. Then we can really do a show. But for now we're stuck with modems. We're writing both programs simultaneously, and we can sell the concept to catalog companies as present and future in a single package, no bump of transition. Already every little pizza parlor is scrambling to set up a web page. We're going to make it so that's not enough. We're going to make it so that every catalog company has to have a storefront in Ultimall, or they're nowhere."

Only the clothing wing was far enough along to be tested.

"Clothing is the flagship," Mips said. "It's the nicotine of shopping. Most serious shoppers start out with clothing. Also, it's the place we can really have fun with tricks."

Some of his tricks were amazing. In the Fitting Room, I could scan in a full-length photograph of myself and try on clothing from the stores in the "mall." I entered my height and weight, and the program analyzed the photograph and told me what size would fit. If I wanted, it could suggest which colors would go well with my hair and skin. Then I entered an item number, and there I was, onscreen, dressed in that item.

The real trick, though, was that when the program displayed my image dressed in a catalog item, it slightly altered my body proportions. In my case, it made me a little taller. If I had been fat, it would have made me a little thinner. If I had already been tall and slender, it would have increased my chest size or tapered my waist, or adjusted the ratio of legs to torso. Then, when I made an actual purchase, the adjusted proportions became the baseline. If I tried on more clothes, my proportions would be altered a little more. With each new purchase, my image moved another notch closer to perfection, until some outer limit of credibility was reached. At that point, the program would go to work on hair and face, darkening any grayness in the hair, brightening mouse color with a tint of chestnut, touching up a nose or a chin or an eyebrow, shading skin tones to harmonize with the current outfit. The changes were subtle and clever, like a flattering portrait painter. I still looked like myself, but that self began to look more and more like a movie star.

The program had a dozen different ways to find the outfits in the first place, from the scrabbling frenzy of the bargain basement all the way up to a kind of GPS-guided wilderness trek through the ultra-upscale boutiques. In every shopping mode there were strategic decisions, obstacles to overcome or circumvent, moments of frustration and moments of exultation. The game was irresistible. I didn't even care about clothes, and I still would get hooked. Before I knew it, I would have ten or twelve outfits charged to a credit card and my image would be looking like an eighteen-year-old Brad Pitt. Maybe not quite, but as close as I'd ever get.

Luckily for me, I wasn't spending real money. My mall was fictional, a collection of imaginary online catalogs I had created to test the program—L.L. Pea, Land's Beginning, J.C. Nickel. Instead of colors like teal, burgundy and forest, my catalogs had pigeon, grape juice and bog, and I had scanned in outfits from sci-fi movie stills and *People* magazine.

"The whole point is to have fun," Mips said. "Let someone else do the dull stuff. Someone else can code boring database searches so that boring practical people can find every single navy-blue blazer in the world and have them sorted by price. We're not aiming at those people. They're all tightwads anyway. We're after the dedicated recreational shoppers. That's where the money is.

"Our mall has to be more fun than a real one. Otherwise, who'll come? But it can be, I'm sure, and someday a million catatonically bored store clerks will thank us. If we're even halfway clever, we should be able to send those clerks the way of the village blacksmith. Transform them from real-life drudges into fondly remembered relics."

If the clothing department flew, Mips had sketched out ideas for all sorts of other products—sporting goods, electronics, tools, cookware, books and CDs, seeds and nursery plants. In the sports department, the user could play around filling a backpack with different combinations of gear—stoves, tents, lightweight clothing, freeze-dried food—and, with each arrangement, see how much the pack weighed and how much space was left. In the electronics department, he could assemble a fantasy home theater. In the seed and nursery department, he could scan in a photograph of his house and yard and add theoretical plantings of shrubs and flowers from the catalog, and the program would show what the plantings would look like in two years, five years, ten years, all assuming, of course, that the weather was ideal and the care meticulous.

Right now, all the other parts of the program were as theoretical as the plantings in the nursery department. The clothing department was the vanguard, and the company would live or die on its success.

The worry was not that the product itself would fail. The worry was that another company would get a similar product on the market before we did. Guthrie, especially, fretted about this possibility.

"It doesn't matter if we're the best," he said repeatedly. "Look at Betamax. Look at Apple. We either have to be the biggest, or we have to be the first. There's no way we can be the biggest, so we had better be first."

Mips agreed with him, but he was convinced we could be first and best both. He didn't quite grasp the reality that the other programmers couldn't crank out code at anything close to his speed. He was forever setting deadlines that he could have met easily and then fuming when the project failed to meet them. His reaction was to assign more and more of the work to himself, and even then he was the only one who met the deadlines. The others were hardly slackers. It went without saying that the work week was sixty or eighty hours, for everyone. But somehow, at the end of those hours, Mips would have written two or three times as much code as anyone else.

He also was the one who figured out all the big design problems. I would see Artie, staring at his screen and muttering to himself about how it couldn't be done, and then I would see Mips peering over his shoulder for a few minutes, saying, "Maybe you could try x . . . ", and then I would see Artie, typing again and muttering that he should have figured it out himself, it was so obvious.

Mips simply saw the solution. He didn't have to work it out. He looked at a logic problem and saw the solution and couldn't tell you himself how he had found it. Artie and the others practically thought he walked on water. They couldn't stay mad at themselves for not seeing what he saw, because they didn't believe he was entirely human.

Their view was shared, only half-jokingly, by Mips himself. He told us that when his wife divorced him, they both had the same complaint, that the marriage made them feel like videotapes running at the wrong speed. He also said he doubted he would find any woman he wouldn't drive crazy, because even his cat got jittery and started climbing the curtains when he was at home.

To the degree that Mips could be responsible for any living creature, he had decided he was responsible for me. It didn't mean all that much. He had his cat on a self-feeder because he couldn't remember to put out food every day. In my case, his feeling responsible meant that he sometimes paused from thinking about Ultimall to ask me how I was getting along. Since he knew my mother, he thought he should try to act as a parental figure in her absence, but it didn't come naturally. He was only a couple of years closer to her age than he was to mine, and it wasn't his style to be prudent, moderate or wise.

I was fascinated by him. I could have sat for any number of hours and listened to him talk about programming. It was like watching Ken Griffey Jr. play center field. Effortless. Like the computer was an extension of his own mind. Within a few months, I had decided there was no way I would ever quit this job to go to the university. I could learn everything I needed to know right here and get paid for doing it.

On one of the days when Mips attempted an avuncular chat, we talked a little about careers. I think he knew that, as a wise uncle, he should be advising caution and a college degree, but he couldn't do it. He did say that college could be a blast, if you didn't take it too seriously, but then he added that he would never advise anyone to get a degree in computer science.

"Why waste college on stuff you can learn at work?" he said. His own degree was in philosophy. He had taken electrical engineering and computer science on the side, just enough to give him a framework and a vocabulary.

"Anyway, I don't like hiring people with CS degrees. Some of them are okay—true geek fanatics. But too many of them are cautious grinds who just want to be sure they will have a job when they graduate. They don't even like computers that much. They just want a nice, safe job. And they'll grind out code all right, but that's not good enough. I want people who are a little over the edge. I want people who will take a risk, even if they might go down in flames. I want people who would be hackers even if there were no jobs and they had to wait tables to support their habit."

"But what about my mom?" I blurted out. "She's like caution packaged for retail sale. Why were you friends with her?"

Mips actually had to think for a millisecond before he answered.

"Extenuating circumstances," he said. "She's not a grind by nature. But a person can't risk going down in flames if she'll be taking a kid with her. Not that people don't. But they shouldn't. Anyway, you don't think it was risky enough, telling her parents about herself and getting kicked out of the house? And I never said everyone in CS is there for a job. Some people are there because it's the only thing that interests them. Still, I'd rather hire people who did something else, too. Maybe I'm an egomaniac. I'd rather start with a blank slate and teach the person myself."

"I'm a blank slate," I said.

"I know, but we can't afford another programmer right now. Not until we have a product to sell. We need you to get the thing tested." He grinned. "Too bad we aren't a meg-amoeba. Then we could put it out there and let the customers do the final testing. But we're just a speck, so we have to rely on Jordy, the super-consumer, the Clark Kent of online power shopping, the man who can hit the credit limit on his gold card in less than ten minutes and never leave his armchair. We're going to make millions."

"Doesn't it ever bother you, trying to turn people into compulsive shoppers, encouraging them to go into debt?"

"Not if it makes me rich," he said. "I didn't make this culture. I'm not forcing anyone. If people are suckers and I can make a profit off them, then hurray for me. It's not my problem if people don't have brains to go with their greed. Would you rather have a system where there's no reward for being smarter than other people? Russia tried that, and look where it got them."

My own piece of the enterprise was mindless but not boring. It was a lot like playing video games all day, and I hardly noticed the time passing. I would look up and find that it was seven or eight o'clock and people were starting to go home for the day and I would have to drag my mind back to a three-dimensional world.

The key feature I was supposed to test was the manipulation of the scanned-in image. The rest of the program was fairly straight-forward, but the analysis and alteration of a photographic image could be tricky stuff, especially when all the decisions had to be made by the computer and not by the user. I tried everything I could think of to make the program choke. I scanned in physiological extremes—sumo types and jockeys, Manute Bol from the NBA, and Dr. Ruth. I scanned in people dressed in space suits and hoop skirts and bustles. I scanned in gorillas. I entered height and weight numbers that could not possibly match the photo image. I scanned in fashion models who already matched the program's definition of perfection and watched it try to make the image look even better in a catalog outfit. None of this was real brain work, but it was a lot better than keying in orders for French fries. I might be a cabin boy, but at least the ship was going somewhere.

Some months, the company couldn't meet its payroll, and Guthrie went out trolling for new investors while Mips made the pitch to the rest of us to stick with them, even though half our pay that month was going to be a bigger share in nothing.

His pitch wasn't the typical sales pitch. "You'll all be fools to stay here," he said. "You'd be hired in a minute by a meg-amoeba. Probably for a lot more money. Speaking practically, I have to advise you to leave. We're down to about one engine right now. I think we're mostly flying on faith. The only good news is we're saving on fuel. Before long we may be a glider, and then we'll really be saving on fuel. The point is, don't feel bad if you decide you need to get paid in money. We want you to stay, but it's no hard feelings if you go."

I didn't even hesitate. I was plenty used to nothing. As long as I earned enough to pay the rent and feed the microwave, I would survive. I liked all the peculiar messages on the T-shirts I bought at the thrift store. Anyway, if Mips had said he wanted people to go with him to the Andes to search for an alien spaceship landing site, I would have volunteered. I thought that anything he decided to do would be a lot more interesting than what most people got to do in their jobs.

I was fairly confident our precarious situation was temporary and would come right in the end. Mips was simply too smart to be a failure. One way or another, he would find a way to make his millions. Evidently the others felt the same way, because no one quit, even at the low point when more than half our pay was in the form of employee ownership. I would have earned more cash keying in French fries, but what did I care? I was cabin boy and minority owner of a vessel bound for the Spice Islands.

chapter seven

M y first two or three months at Ultimall, I hardly
noticed June. I was too busy learning my job, too caught
up in the prevailing atmosphere of barely controlled frenzy, too
intent on catching every tidbit of computer wisdom that Mips
let drop. Also, I was still in love with Reba.

But it was June who had told me in my first week that I didn't
have to wear slacks and a sport coat to work, and it was June who
started finding a few minutes here and there for quick tutorials in
programming, and it was June who would finally cure me of Reba,
by infecting me herself.

In a world's-nicest-person contest, June would have been a
finalist. She always knew who needed a ride because their car was
in the shop, whose sister had had a baby, who was planning a
weekend up the coast. She found out people's birthdays and gave
them cards. She found time and energy after her seventy-hour
work week to volunteer at a senior center two Saturday mornings
a month and sometimes even managed to fit in baking a cake,
which she would bring into the office to stoke everyone up on

chocolate. In the middle of cutting it, she would always pause to point out, apologetically, that it was a box cake, as if she didn't want to be given more credit than she deserved. It made me wonder if she had a grandmother like mine, who looked on cake mixes as a temptation to the deadly sin of sloth.

Although her office looked exactly like all the others, windowless and cube-shaped, it seemed to hold some charm that drew people, like a kitchen with a welcoming cook. More often than not, June would find herself at lunch hour pinned to her desk, snatching bites of her sandwich as she listened to Teresa's boyfriend woes or Artie's homesickness for the mountains of Idaho or Guthrie's complaints about how hard it was to find a cleaning lady who didn't smoke. I'd spent an occasional lunch hour in her office myself, not airing any sorrows or complaints, because my life was right on track, instead just chatting about baseball, which she liked, or trading my stories about Kilgore for hers about her equally tiny hometown in Minnesota.

Her whole family—parents, grandparents, brothers—were dairy farmers, and when she described their various farming operations, it sounded like the rural version of mergers and acquisitions, like her relatives had bought up, taken out a lease on or married themselves onto almost every piece of land in their area. They made good money, she said, but worked like fiends to do it.

"Seventy hours a week is nothing," she said. "Downright restful."

Then she laughed, a big, generous laugh.

"That's why I came out here. To take it easy. Maybe have a Sunday off now and then. Back home, you never stop. You don't go all that fast, but you go and go and go. You must know what that's like, since your people have livestock. Do they work all the time?"

"For a good part of the year, they do," I said. "And I guess it became a habit with my mom. Even when we lived in the city, she worked every minute of the day. Job and school both. She was going to pay her own way, get ahead, even if it killed her."

"The biggest sin in the book is laziness, right?"

"You got it."

We both laughed.

"And the worst of it is, I can't get rid of the idea," she said. "I look at people who are laid-back, mellow, all those pleasant things, and there's a little voice inside me saying, 'Shiftless.' It's terrible."

"You're not shiftless, that's for sure."

"I'm trying to learn."

"Yeah, right," I said.

During one of our lunch-hour conversations, June asked me if I ever missed Kilgore.

"Not a bit," I said.

"Not anything?"

I paused. At first her question had called up the condensed image, a sort of mental screen icon of some derelict object—a broken windmill, a torn screen door, a rusty satellite dish, creaking and banging as the wind blew dust around it. But her repeated question was like a mouse-click, and the image expanded. I thought about Skipper chasing sticks, and Pat, dropping some offhand remark about the town busybody needing vice the way a vacuum cleaner needs dirt, and my mother, reassuring me that Sawdust lacked the ambition to buck me off, and Uncle Fred, showing me the anatomy of a tractor, and most of all, Reba, looking breathtaking, even in the week before graduation when she shaved her hair down to a half-inch spike cut and sent her parents into a frenzy of willfully self-deceiving worries about her being on drugs.

"I do miss people," I said. "Not the place, just people."

"Same here. I don't miss the mosquitoes or the barn chores, but I miss my family. Especially my brothers. Even if they did have some traits in common with the mosquitoes."

"The whining or the biting?"

June laughed. "The hovering. I'm the oldest, and whatever I did they wanted to be in on it." She waved her hand past her face. "I used to wish I could shoo them away."

"Not swat them?"

"That, too. Well, no, I don't really mean that. Mostly we had fun. But what about you? Who do you miss most?"

That one I couldn't answer right off. I didn't feel like talking about Reba, and I couldn't really sort out who came next, probably Pat, but it seemed a little weird to say her ahead of my mother. But then if I said I missed my mother, it would sound sappy, so finally I turned it into a joke and said I missed the dog.

June didn't deflect that easily. "Oh, come on," she said. "Seriously."

"My friends, I guess," I said.

I had liked June for a long time before it occurred to me to think beyond that. We'd gone through most of the summer, having our casual conversations, and every so often she would stop by my desk and grab a scrap of paper from the recycling box and outline some little piece of programming logic, and in all that time, my attention stayed on the conversation or the scrap of paper. I never really opened my eyes and looked at her, because the part of me that would have wanted to look was still filled by the image of Reba, as clear in my mind as my last sight of her, behind the stupid bullet-proof plate glass at the little one-gate airport in Seco Springs.

But when June and I had that conversation about who I missed, some switch must have flipped in my head. The image of Reba started to waver and fade in and out, like it was getting interference from the next frequency, and before very long, it had been overlaid by a whole new image, from the here and now.

One day, on her way to the coffee pot, June stopped by with some tidbit about sorting algorithms, and as she was leaning over my desk writing, I found my eye leaving the scrap of paper and traveling to the circle of finger and thumb around her pen, and from there moving on to the back of her hand, the bend of her wrist, her forearm, each shape flowing into the next in a soft, curved line, no knobs of bone or strings of tendon, and as I was watching the tiny movements of muscle under the skin of her forearm, I noticed that she smelled really good, a little like orange spice tea, and I started thinking about other shapes of muscle and skin, not immediately visible, and before I knew it my mind was miles away from any information that could be communicated to a machine.

When she stopped writing and asked, "Does that all make sense?" I came abruptly back to reality. I looked at the paper and was forced to confess it didn't make sense, because I hadn't heard a word she had said.

"Is that your perfume that smells so good?" I asked.

Now she was the one distracted. She became very flustered and said she wasn't wearing perfume, it must be her shampoo, and when she tried to go back over her explanation, she couldn't remember what it was she had been explaining.

If she hadn't been so flustered, I never would have dared ask her out. June was half a head taller than me, and two years out of college, and she made at least twice as much money as I did, so why would she want to go on a date with me? But if I could wreck her train of thought with one compliment, there had to be some hope.

I had already asked her out for dinner and a movie, and she had already said yes before it occurred to me that I had no transportation to offer. It wasn't exactly suave, having to postscript the invitation with a request that we use her car, but she didn't seem to mind. If anything, she seemed eager to volunteer the car. It was like it put her back on familiar ground, to be helping somebody out. If the date part turned out to be excruciating, then we could both think of it as her giving me a ride to the movie.

Typically, June was agreeable to anything I wanted to suggest as a plan for the evening. She said she ate every kind of food, and when I asked if there was a movie she particularly wanted to see, she said she would be happy to see anything I wanted. The only thing I wanted was the solid certainty that no one in the movie would be squeezing and caressing any mounds of clay. So we ate Mexican food and then went to see *Alien 3,* which had plenty of slippery, slimy creatures in it, but nobody was caressing any of them.

After the movie, I suggested we get some ice cream. Up to this point, I'd kept a little of myself in reserve, a kind of safety rope, but at the ice cream shop, I went into free fall. She ordered chocolate, two scoops, without a trace of hesitation. No giggling and simpering about watching her weight. No pleas of a lost appetite from all the dripping slime in the movie. Just chocolate, two scoops, with her cheerful laugh and then pure relish, as her tongue swept circles around the ice cream.

We sat on opposite sides of the little round table, and I had to keep reminding myself to glance away now and then, because all I wanted to do was look at her. Even as I was eating my ice cream, I couldn't have told anyone what flavor it was. Every sense was fixed on her, my whole body swimming in a warm bath of joy and hopelessness and arousal. At some point we were going to have to get up from the table, and I was really wishing I had brought along a sweatshirt or windbreaker, to be carried with strategic casualness.

Instead, each time her lips and tongue made another slow luxuriant sweep around the dark, creamy chocolate, I would start muttering to myself, silently: Cold. Ice-cold. Freezing cold. Numbing, bone-chilling, Arctic cold. A couple of times I bit right into my ice cream with my teeth to reinforce the message.

I tried to derail my thoughts with conversation.

"Do you always ask for chocolate?" I asked.

"Usually. Sometimes vanilla."

"Those poor slobs at the ice cream lab. Forty-three flavors and she still wants chocolate."

She laughed. "I'm from Minnesota. We don't like 'things' in our ice cream."

"No Chunky Monkey?"

"Oh, I'll eat Chunky Monkey, if that's what's there. Not my folks, though. It's not how ice cream was meant to be. My dad thinks nuts are a conspiracy to lower milk prices. More nuts, less cream."

She laughed again. "Me, I just don't like interruptions. With chunks, it's like you're getting a massage, and suddenly somebody pokes you in the ribs. I want perfectly smooth chocolate melting across my tongue."

She closed her eyes and made another long sweep around the ice cream. So much for derailing my thoughts.

Somebody else, talking about massages and chocolate melting in her mouth, could have been laying on some extra meanings, but I was fairly sure June was only talking about ice cream. I'd never seen someone so rapturously absorbed in the present. She was completely unselfconscious and completely unaware of me.

I, on the other hand, was aware of every minute detail of her. Like the scar above her eye, a tiny white slash across the reddish blond line of her eyebrow. In some previous conversation, before every inch of her body became an inch I wanted to touch, she had told me she got the scar playing tag with her brothers, misjudging the turn around some sharp metal corner on a piece of farm machinery. Then it had been a story. Now it was an inch of her skin that I wanted to reach across and get to know. My hand could imagine each small sensation, the slender white line through her eyebrow, the smooth skin curving around the bone of her forehead, the curling edge of her hair.

Fighting the pull, my hands clenched and I felt the crunch of sugar cone between my fingers and then the cold ooze of ice cream.

"Damn!"

Even with one hand occupied, June leapt to be helpful. With her free hand, she poured the remains of one water glass into the other and used the empty glass to scoop up the glob of ice cream, laughing all the while.

"What happened?"

"I don't know. It must have been my Schwarzenegger grip."

"Remind me not to arm wrestle with you."

We wiped up most of the mess with napkins, and then I retreated to the bathroom to wash my hands. By the time I came back, my nerve circuits were in better order.

"You want another one?" she asked as I sat down.

"No, one was plenty."

She had finished her own ice cream, so for the moment my nerves seemed safe from renewed derangement. We sat and talked for a while, and it was almost the way it had been before I started noticing her bones. Easy and fun. Except that her conversation was starting to energize a different set of circuits, the ones that were wired into the space behind the breastbone. June's voice was like the rest of her, firm and warm, nothing wispy about it. She laughed a lot when she talked, and there was nothing wispy in her laugh either. She made me want to kid her or make jokes, just to hear her laugh, or to play the straight man, setting her up to be funny.

We got talking about movies, and it turned out she'd seen the two previous *Alien* movies and loved them, especially the second one.

"How can you not love a movie where a woman uses duct tape to strap together a flame thrower and a rocket launcher and then goes blasting in to rescue her kid?" she said. "I especially liked the duct tape. It took me right back to the farm."

"I liked the android," I said. "Probably a bad sign that I identified with him."

"You're nothing like a droid."

"You don't think so?"

"Not at all."

"Not nearly that smart, right?"

She laughed. "That isn't what I meant."

"Okay, so maybe I couldn't survive being cut in two at the arm-pits. But apart from that, we could be brothers."

"Sure, and your little sister is a Powerbook."

"How did you know about her? I've never told you . . . "

We yakked on, for over an hour, and somewhere in the middle of that hour, I started to realize that talking to her, kidding her, listening to her laugh was a lot more dangerous than watching her eat ice cream. Pure physical derangement you could somewhat take care of, first thing in the morning, but once a woman got into that hollow spot behind the breastbone, there was no taking care of it. She became another self, living inside you, that you could see, hear and feel, in imagined scenes, anytime and anywhere.

Walking to her car, I was conscious of her actual self beside me, that faint scent of orange and the fainter-still radiance of body warmth, and her voice, telling me a story about high school, and then there was her other self, the one inside me, rolling out a whole script of imagined conversations in which stories of childhood, leaving home, future daydreams, wove themselves around the curves of her breasts and thighs.

When we pulled up in front of my house, reality intruded. Since she was driving, I couldn't walk her to the door and hope for develop-ments. Whatever I did, it had to be here and now.

"Um . . . Well, thanks for driving," I said. Very suave. "I hope you had a nice time."

"I did have a nice time. Even if the movie wasn't as good as the first two."

"No. Not even close. Sorry."

"I didn't mean it that way. I enjoyed it. Really. It just wasn't . . . "

"One of the all-time greats?"

"Maybe not."

She laughed, and then her laugh backed off to a smile, but she was still looking at me with enough friendliness that I thought, Damn the torpedoes! and leaned across to give her a kiss. Her response would politely be called hesitant. She didn't pull away, but she also didn't linger. To me it felt like a minimum bet, just enough to keep us in the game.

After she drove away, I wondered if it might have felt a little too much like kissing one of her little brothers. But I couldn't make myself any taller, or any older, so I had to hope we'd get beyond that.

A few days later, I invited June out a second time, and she accepted a second time, and after some mediocre food, a fairly decent movie, and some very good conversation, the good-night kiss was exactly the same. She wasn't trying to get rid of me, but she wasn't rushing forward, either.

For our third date, I suggested going across the bay to watch a game between the Oakland A's and my team, the Seattle Mariners. I thought a ball game might feel less freighted with expectations, and maybe we could relax and laugh and I could spend the evening worrying about the shakiness of the Seattle bullpen instead of worrying that she was going out with me only because she was too terminally nice to say no to anyone. A little part of me hoped if we could spend some time laughing and having fun together, she might be caught unawares and fall in love, the same way I had.

Sometimes being half right is worse than being totally wrong. We did have fun together, and she did get caught unawares, and she did fall in love, but not with me. For three hours we sat in the mild evening air, gazing out across flood-lit grass that glowed like an emerald in the darkness, watching the Oakland A's batters try not to flinch as Randy Johnson launched cruise missiles toward the catcher's mitt. June was enthralled. By the end of the game, a dormant passion had been re-kindled, and within a week, she had started playing herself, not base-ball, but softball, in a women's league with one of the other volun-teers from the senior center. Soon after that, she invited me to come watch her play, and then, after the second or third game, she asked if I would be willing to umpire, because her team had a hard time find-ing umpires.

I think sex hormones must interfere with the neurotransmitters in the brain, because at that moment, if I had looked around and ap-plied even the most rudimentary powers of deduction, I would have known that I was out of luck. Most of the other teams in her league had no difficulty finding umpires. They simply recruited one from the mob of husbands and boyfriends who came to drink beer and roar encouragement and instructions from the sidelines. On June's team, I was the only boyfriend available to be recruited.

After I umpired my first game, she and I went to get something to eat, and when she dropped me off at my house, my mental stopwatch clocked the good-night kiss at a measurable beat longer than the oth-ers, and I thought it might finally be the moment to move forward, now, while she was feeling so warm with gratitude. We had moved forward as far as my room and about the second hook on her bra, when she suddenly backed off and shook her head and said she was sorry, it didn't feel right and we had better just stay friends. She was horribly apologetic and regretful and awkward, as she put her blouse back on and straightened her hair, and all I could think was that I must be pretty spectacularly incompetent if one piece of clothing was enough to tell her I was not what she wanted.

Two weeks later, June confessed to me with enormous gratitude that I had helped to break the logjam in her heart and open a way for her true feelings to express themselves. Or, in fewer words, she had realized she was a lesbian.

The day after she had told me I didn't feel right to her, the third baseman on her softball team had made a pass at her. The difference in how she felt was so starkly clear that she could no longer delude herself. She said I was the best friend she could imagine finding and she was very glad we hadn't taken things any further than we did. She hoped I wasn't too terribly hurt.

Hurt? Who, me? Well, I'd had no chance to begin with. So this was just a different way of having no chance, right? Shit.

Unlike Reba, June knew I was in love with her, which made her all solicitous about my well-being. I almost couldn't bear it, how extra-nice she was to me. Maybe it would have been easier if she'd been a bitch, so I could just out-and-out hate her. But she was bent on staying friends, and on top of that, her team still needed an umpire, so she refused to let me slink away and sulk. And I didn't actually want to. Yes, I loved her, but I really liked her, too. And, hey, I'd done this scene before, I could handle it.

Except that with Reba, I hadn't had to watch her go home at night with someone else.

> dear pat, help. is it true that only 2% of women are lesbians? if so then why can't i hook up with one of the other 98%? the odds have to be in my favor. or am i a prisoner of freudian psychology, condemned to eternal frustration?
>
> it was bad enough, with reba, but june is even worse. it's odd in a way. they're not at all alike. you know how reba is, kind of cynical and funny and takes no shit from anyone, but june is completely different, friendly and full of life and kind, not a speck of cynicism anywhere. just my luck that the only thing they do have in common is a demographic. (and if it did have to be a demographic, why couldn't it have been brown eyes or lutheranism or something?) jordy

✿

For some reason it was easier to say things to a keyboard. Like I hadn't really committed myself to anything because one mouse-click could blow the whole message away. Writing something with a pen felt like I was setting it down for posterity, so I had better think carefully about what I said.

My leaving Kilgore had prodded Pat into buying a computer and modem, which was a radical step for her, not because computers were high-tech, but because she so rarely bought anything. Mom was getting my emails at work, and Pat figured out pretty quickly that she wasn't going to hear from me very often unless she went online herself.

With me safely away from Kilgore, Pat had moved out to live with Mom and no longer had to watch the tourists taking pictures of themselves in front of her sculpture. She said the tourists had done her a favor, actually, by carrying away with them every last ounce of emotional baggage. The sculpture had begun as a memorial to lost love—blasted and hacked out of the earth, looming over her life. With each new snapshot, the tourists had carried a little piece of it away, and Pat said now it felt as light as one of those life-size cardboard celebrities people pose with as a joke.

Pat took to email like a monk discovering potato chips. When I was in the same room with her, she could out-laconic Clint Eastwood, but with me a thousand miles away and her alone with a computer, she became almost chatty. Right away, she grasped the basic concept that you didn't leave messages lying around in a pile the way you did with regular mail. She'd reply within a day, at most, with whatever thoughts came to mind, and she revealed a lot more of herself in type than she ever had in conversation.

For Mom, computers were work, and her notes to me were mostly functional: Did I have enough money? Did I need any cookware or some new socks? Would I like to fly home for Christmas? I couldn't talk about things with Mom anymore, because everything I did made her worry. For sure I couldn't tell her I was in love with another lesbian. She would take it to mean that she personally had ruined my life. As if she should have turned herself into Betty Crocker so that I would be oedipally programmed to fall in love with a perfect homemaker.

I could tell Pat about it, though. Pat had never had to stop me from grabbing a hot frying pan, so she didn't have such a well-developed worry reflex.

Dear Jordy, I don't know about the 2% statistic. It might be 5% or 10% or 1% or 1/2%, depending on who paid for the survey. Anyway, Freud's conclusions were faulty because he didn't do adequate follow-up studies. If he had, he would have found that people outgrow Oedipus and Electra. First they have to get mother, or father, out of their system, then they can move on. Some people are unlucky enough to get married before they have moved on. About 50%, judging by the divorce rate. At least you should escape that fate. So things could be worse. Pat

hi, pat, did you have to get a parent out of your system first time around, and if so, which one? have you grown up since, or is mom still an electral (?) electric (?) connection? :) j

J, I never thought of it that way. It's so much easier to analyze other people. It must have been Pops I was getting out of my system. A.R. was quite a bit like him in some ways, talkative and lively, a people person. As far as your mother, Donna is sui generis. That's probably overstating it, but she is a different genus from either of my parents. I'm not sure I would go as far as saying that means I am now mature. Pat

It took a good part of the winter, but when the worst of the bruise had been reabsorbed, June and I did indeed become what she had hoped we would, the best of friends. I knew the drill, after all. I'd had years of practice.

Then spring rolled around, and with it a new softball season, and I was back in my spot behind home plate, umpiring her games. It was there, gazing out over the catcher's head at a whole field of attractive women, that I first started wondering if I ever would "move on."

What I felt for June didn't ever go away, it just changed direction, and the basic pattern began to look less like a phase and more like a permanent fate. Reba was the template, June the first copy. After that, by turns, I fell in love with the first baseman, the shortstop and the short fielder. None of them fell in love with me, needless to say. The shortstop had recently celebrated a formal, though not legal, union with the left fielder, and the short fielder was deeply but hopelessly in love with the catcher, who was dating the first baseman.

For a few brief, self-deluded weeks, June had thought she was one of only two straight women on the team. Now that she knew better, there was just the pitcher, who was forty-something and should have been a college coach, and who had a husband at home who disliked sports and would not watch, much less umpire, any of her games.

That left me, old faithful, sublimating my longings into mimicry of the more flamboyant major league umpires, the prolonged bugle call "Steeerrrriiike!" with a sword thrust to the right, the bull bellow "Y'rout!" with a thumb lancing skyward, and the pantomime for safe, the voiceless chambermaid vigorously smoothing the sheets of a hotel bed. Except for the pitcher, the whole team loved me, like a brother. The pitcher loved me like a son.

hi pat, do you think once you've been in love, you can't ever not be? that's how it feels, like a force that has to go somewhere. maybe i don't fall quite as hard as i did at first, but i just keep falling, over and over, and always the same story.

research question for my software testing—if you could change your proportions, would you rather be the same height but thinner or the same weight but taller? jordy

Jordy, I've only been in love with two people, so it's hard to say there's a trend. But it's true, I didn't completely get over being in love with one until I met the other. Probably a psychologist would chide me and tell me I ought to have established a happy, self-fulfilled identity on my own before I let myself fall in love again.

You asked if I would rather have my body be pinched or stretched. Neither, thank you. I suppose that question was connected to the coming miracle of electronic shopping. I'm not the right guinea pig for you to ask about shopping, since I would choose an appointment at the dentist ahead of an hour at Wal-Mart. Clothing stores hate to see me walk in the door. They worry their other customers will think I buy my clothes there.

Let me know when you have the seed catalog up and running. We will challenge it with a photo of the sheep shed and Zone 3 with 12 inches of annual rainfall.

Did Donna mention that Skipper always sleeps beside your bed? Pat

Did she have to tell me that? I hadn't been completely joking, when I told June I missed the dog. You could stay connected to a person electronically, by talking or writing, but with a dog, you had to be there.

chapter eight

❦

" The good news is, Guthrie has found us a new Sugar Daddy. So we are still in business and we can hire four more people. The other good news is that we have scheduled our first release. Officially."

The applause was as thunderous as seven people could make it.

"The final good news is that production will be contracted out. So you won't all be working late packing diskettes and CDs into pretty wrappers."

The applause was even more thunderous.

"Now what's the bad news?" Artie asked.

Mips grinned at him. "The bad news is that the four new people will be sharing your office. No, seriously, there isn't any bad news. We've found some offices on the fourth floor. Guthrie and the new marketing and documentation people will move up there. The rest of us tech-nerds will stay down here, in a buzzing hive of creative brain power."

While everyone else was cracking open bottles of beer, Mips pulled me aside. "You've done your time on the chain gang, Jordy.

What's it been, a year and a half of QA and errand boy? Enough's enough. June tells me you've been programming in your spare time. I think we can squander a few of the Sugar Daddy's bucks and have you program on company time."

"Do you mean that?"

"No, you're a clam and I'm a gull who's about to drop you on the rocks. Obviously I mean it."

"*Yee-hah!* Upward mobility lives." I was grinning. "But who's going to do the QA?"

"The customers, who else? No, not true. Not if I can help it. You'll still do some. The new hire will do some. We'll work it out. There is one other wrinkle, though. Do you have any neurotic bourgeois hang-ups about status? You know, getting a bigger office, working your way up to a window, rank and seniority and all that baloney?"

"In other words, will I agree to stay in the computer room so the new hire can have an office, because you want to hire the best possible person and the best possible person will expect an office?" I grinned again. "What do I get in trade?"

"The man has sharp wits *and* a killer instinct. His talents have been seriously wasted for a year and a half. In trade we will give you a huge, indestructible potted plant. And a new wall calendar. These will create a virtual office out of the air around your desk. The calendar can have any theme you like, as long as it includes enough clothing to avoid embarrassing anyone. Oh, and in the minor detail department, your salary will be a bit higher."

A bit. I was rich. I couldn't believe the number on my next paycheck. Going to college wasn't even on the screen anymore.

To celebrate, I bought a Honda Civic, six years old, but in the California climate cars still looked new when their engines gave out. Mine could have come right out of the showroom. I also bought some new Reeboks and a whole pile of CDs and a better bike, and I overnighted Mom a CD player for her truck because I knew she'd never buy one for herself, not as long as the radio was still working.

I wanted to send Pat something, too, but I couldn't think of many things she would want. You can't buy objects to put inside your head, and that was where Pat spent most of her time.

She did sometimes buy books and art prints, though, so I tried to find an art book that she might like. On her walls she had dreamy impressionist landscapes and a way-too-realistic starving cow by C.M. Russell and some flaming Georgia O'Keeffe flowers, a fairly miscellaneous selection. I tried to calculate what would happen if those three styles got together in one painting, and I ended up sending her a book of technicolor daydream landscapes by a guy I'd never heard of, David Hockney.

When the packages arrived, Mom immediately called up to ask what was the deal, and I told her about my new job.

"I'm launched!" I said. "And right on schedule, as good as the space shuttle. Mips is a genius, you know. There's not a thing he doesn't know. And the work is fun. I don't know why they pay us so much, when it's like playing games all day. But it's a trip to have so much money!"

"It is a trip. But I hope you're not spending every last cent of it the moment it's in your pocket."

"Aw, Mom. Can't you stop worrying for once? Whatever happened to 'Congratulations! I'm so proud of you' and 'What a wonderful surprise'?"

"I'm not worrying, just thinking ahead. And I am proud of you. But it's not a surprise. They'd have been crazy not to start you programming."

Pat didn't get on the phone to talk. She just sent me an email.

Hi, Jordy, The Hockney prints are a lot of fun. Thank you. It's something of a coincidence, or convergence if you like, that you sent me those. The one and only time I got a promotion, I rewarded myself by buying a Monet print. (The promotions at the Mercantile don't count, since I was working for Pops.)

That one time was back when I was about twenty-two and I had made my break for the wide world, as represented by Chicago. I was only there six months, and I hated almost every minute of it because I was too shy to get to know anybody. I felt like a farmyard hen who's been shipped to an egg factory, deafened by the cackling of a million other birds. The work I was doing was about as exciting as sitting in a cage waiting for the next egg to make its way down the tube. The only high point was getting promoted, from the mail room to the personnel department. In fact, it was like going from the bottom row of cages to the next row up, but it felt like such a triumph, to have someone not related to me tell me I had done a good job. It wasn't enough of a triumph to keep me there, but I did buy myself a print, to celebrate. I had forgotten that detail until your book arrived and reminded me. Pat

hi, pat, is the print the same one you still have on your wall?

i'm trying to picture you in chicago and i can't do it. after your description, all i can see is the little red hen carrying an attache case and scuttling around in confusion, which doesn't seem like you at all. i have a hard time seeing you anywhere but kilgore, but if i do manage a picture, you're ambling along completely lost in your own thoughts while crowds of people rush past, and you don't even notice when they bump and jostle you. jordy

Hi, Jordy, Just the opposite, unfortunately. I did notice and I couldn't get lost in my thoughts. That was the problem. I think only an urban person could not notice jostling. In a place like Kilgore, anybody you bump is probably somebody you know, and a collision would launch a conversation, starting off with how amazing it was that the only two people on the street could collide with each other and ending up a few miles away, on the price of cattle being driven down by the price of corn, or Gary Pilcher's daughter getting married.

And, yes, it's the same print on my wall. Why buy another one, right? However, I'm quite happy to enjoy the fruits of someone else's willingness to shop. Pat

One thing I didn't need to buy was any type of electronic entertainment system. I was still living with Mike, and the house didn't have room for any more gear. He had already added a TV to the kitchen and another to the bathroom so that he wouldn't have to wait for an ad break to leave the living room. He had also added a second amp, four headsets with twenty-foot cords and a whole spaghetti bowl of new wires and switches. The idea was that all four housemates could be in the living room at the same time, each enjoying his own individual choice of entertainment, maybe two of us hooked into the two TVs, one into the CD player and one into the cassette player or the turntable.

Mike had asked me once, in complete seriousness, if I thought he should add a second CD player because the other sound systems were so inferior in quality. I said I thought we could cope. Felipe and Barry were rarely in the living room anyway. Their social lives were at school. When they did come home, they retired to their rooms to sleep, to study or, once in a great while, to entertain a woman. Mike never brought anyone home. He just brought home new sound systems.

I quite often brought people home with me, women, but they came in pairs, and I never closeted myself in my room with them.

These visits were the only time all four headsets ever got used. June and her girlfriend Shannon and I would hook ourselves up to a movie on the VCR while Mike hooked up to something of his own, usually jazz on the CD player.

One evening I said, "Hey, Mike, why don't you watch the movie with us. It's supposed to be decent."

He looked surprised, like it was a radical idea to watch a movie just to be sociable and not because it was one he particularly wanted to see. His first reflex was to flip a switch to tune his headset into the VCR along with ours. Then he laughed and looked embarrassed. He flipped a different switch to send the TV sound to the four mammoth speakers, and we all took off our headsets.

I didn't really know Mike, even though we'd lived in the same house for a year and a half. We might talk about music and electronics or trade opinions about movies, but he never talked about his own life, and he never asked me about mine. If I did tell him about something that had happened to me, he seemed to hear but not listen, like I was background.

Then I struck it rich, and he tuned right in. I came home jabbering about my awesome paycheck, and soon after that I brought home the silver Civic. All of a sudden Mike seemed to think we had lots to talk about. He wanted to know what I was going to buy with all that money, and he started talking about what he was going to buy when he owned his own store. He seemed possessed by the idea of becoming the boss and not having to work for someone else ever again.

Once Mike started telling me about his plans, he could hardly shut up. He had the whole store laid out in his head, and its whole business plan. He could tell me how much capital he would need and which brands he would keep in his inventory and how they would be displayed. The picture was so clear, it was hard to believe the store didn't already exist. How was it I had lived with him all this time and he had never even hinted at this vision he carried around inside his head?

Maybe he thought I was a peon and would stay a peon my whole life. Maybe he thought I hadn't been worth talking to. Now, suddenly, I was a person who was going somewhere, and he could talk with me about his own plans for going somewhere. We were fellow entrepreneurs, at least in daydreams.

I hoped we might be able to build on that beginning. He'd let me in on something truly important to him, and maybe if I kept at it, we could become more than a Siskel and Ebert routine, two disembodied critics sharing a house. I tried branching out the conversation, to sports, politics, family history, women, food—anything I could think of that might qualify as a topic of universal interest.

What I discovered was that Mike had a truly comprehensive definition of the word "boring." If I asked probing questions about his family or his love life, he didn't get offended or defensive. He just drifted away into a yawn that encompassed his entire body, head to foot. Why on earth would anyone want to talk about that?

It didn't worry him when a conversation dribbled into aimlessness. He was just as happy to go back to his music. But it bothered me. Our other roommates rotated in and out, with the school calendar, but Mike and I were coming up on two years in the same house, and it seemed we ought to be a little more than two plugs who happened to be side by side in an outlet.

So I went on trying, and if most of existence didn't interest him, then I'd stick to the bit that did. One day, when I saw him phasing out and starting to scan his racks of CDs, I announced I was thinking of upgrading the sound system in my car and wanted his advice. Not that I needed four speakers and a better CD player, but I figured it would keep us talking.

And if talk just means words being spoken, then it worked. Within about two seconds, his mind was wide awake, zeroed in on the question, and he was pouring out more specifications than it had ever occurred to me to want. He even brought home an acoustic meter so that we could test my car and decide which kind of speakers suited it best and how to configure them. I managed to string the discussion out for a couple of weeks before I finally bought the system.

After the speakers were installed, I proposed a basketball hoop on the garage. For another week or so, we discussed pros and cons and brand names, and then I bought the hoop. After the hoop was put up, I said how about a rheostat on the living room light switch, and when we had our rheostat, I suggested buying a toaster oven to supplement the microwave. In time I realized I didn't always have to buy the things I proposed. I just had to suggest buying them so that we could converse about brand names and prices and whether they were worth the money.

Anyone seeing Mike and me through a window would have thought we were bosom buddies, yakking together over our cold cereal in the morning or over takeout pizza late at night. And it was true, we never ran out of things to talk about. If the conversation flagged, all we had to do was turn on the television and there would be some product whose merits we could debate.

Sometimes I tried asking Mike about his life, and he'd get up and say he was going to microwave some popcorn and did I want some? I never did find out much about him, not even whether he had brothers and sisters.

hi, pat, have i ever told you about my housemate mike? the one who had to have the circuits rewired to handle all the amperage on his sound systems? he's never been very sociable, but recently we've been talking more. it doesn't mean i know him, tho. i mean, with june i could know in five minutes that she's decent, but with mike, i know his shoe size and i know what products he thinks should be put at eye level in a store, but mostly i'm realizing you can have a million pieces of data about someone and still not know anything about him. like if he saw a raccoon in the road would he swerve to avoid it or swerve to hit it? j

Or keep driving straight, so as not to have to feel responsible for the outcome.

I suppose you could think positive and be glad he isn't a trial to live with, which some people who tell you everything might be. P

When spring came and the Ultimall software was actually released, I thought everyone at work would relax a little. Wrong. Instead of just plain frenzy and rush, we now had an overlay of anxiety and suspense, as if all of us were holding our breath, waiting for news. It's hard to hold your breath and rush at the same time, but that's what we tried to do.

The whole fate of the company might depend on the next few months. The product was out there, on the market. Would it fly? Would it bomb? Or would it wallow in some never-never land of mediocrity, selling just enough to keep the company alive but not enough to make the leap into the magical realm of "hot."

Guthrie's beard actually varied a few millimeters from week to week, I suppose because his side of the company finally had some serious action and he didn't have time to trim it quite as often. On the tech side, we were working as hard as ever, only now it was on the next phase of the product. The first phase was out of our hands. If it failed, the next phase might be wasted effort, but we had to keep at it. I think we all felt, superstitiously, that we couldn't slow down, that slackening the pace might somehow affect the karma of the company and cause phase one to fail. As if the World Wide Web really was a web and any little tremor of doubt would travel its filaments from end to end. Every brain wave in the company had to transmit power, energy, success and forward motion.

I didn't think Mips could possibly have a higher gear than what we had already seen, but apparently he had only been operating in his normal range. Now he went into overdrive. When we left at night he was still at his computer, and when we arrived in the morning, he was there ahead of us, and it wasn't clear he had gone anywhere in between. Sheer nerves were driving him. The next phase didn't yet have a specific deadline. He just couldn't make himself stop.

I asked him once if he had gone home the night before, and he said no.

"There's no way I can go to bed. If I try to lie still in the dark, my thoughts start accelerating, around and around, and pretty soon I've got mobile homes and cars and trees spinning up in a funnel cloud inside my brain."

One morning I came in a little earlier than usual and found him at his desk, flopped forward onto his keyboard, asleep. His arm and head were resting on one corner of the keyboard, and the computer was making a steady beep of annoyance. When I tried to slide the keyboard out from under his arm, he immediately woke up.

"What time is it?" he asked.

"Quarter to seven."

"Oh, okay. It's only been an hour then."

"How do you keep functioning?" I asked. "I'd be hallucinating by now, if I slept that little."

"This state won't last forever. One of these weeks I'll be sleeping ten hours a night and not even remembering a dream. In the meantime I'm getting a shitload of work done. I just go with this when it happens. I feel as though time has slowed down so much I can practically watch the instructions going through the processor one by one. Every step of logic is completely obvious."

"And the rest of us must seem mentally deficient."

He laughed. "I think it's more of a mental defect to connect with computers so easily. Like I must be missing some other brain functions."

He'd been sitting motionless ever since I woke him. He must have still been partly asleep. But now, suddenly, he jumped up and started pacing.

"Do you think I've overestimated human stupidity?" he asked.

"What do you mean?"

"Shopnotize. Can people really be suckered that easily? Or are we going to be bankrupt before the end of the year?"

I mumbled something vague, but he wasn't looking for an answer anyway. His brain was starting to centrifuge, spinning off thoughts.

"People think computers are magic, that they're adding a whole new level to human intelligence. But they're not. They're just multipliers. They take whatever people put in and multiply it by a million. Or a billion. So if you put in stupidity, you get a million times more stupidity. If you put in cleverness, you get a million times more cleverness. But it's still the same basic cleverness that a human thought up. Computers don't add anything, they just multiply. They don't think anything up. And they can't tell the difference between smart and stupid. To them everything is just a variable x that they multiply by a million.

"But then if you've got a million times more stuff, it makes it that much harder for humans to separate smart from stupid. That's what I'm counting on. That people will just be swept along. That they'll be so busy trying to take in that million times volume of stuff coming at them, they won't have any space left in their brains to be thinking about which of it is smart or stupid or good or bad.

"But what if I'm wrong? What if people are smarter than I think, and they see right through our program and say 'I don't need this'? Or what if they're stupider than I think and they aren't ready for it, they think it's too complicated? Or what if they just get stampeded in a different direction, and go back to shopping on Main Street? I've been working on this thing for six years. I've sweat blood, getting it to work, getting it right. And it's truly cool. There's nothing else out there yet that's half as good. But what if we've missed the wave? What if the time for this product was last year? Or five years from now? We're out there now. If it doesn't sell, we've got nothing more we can say to our investors about the wonderful future."

"It will sell," I said. "One way or another."

"Why do you think so?"

"Just a hunch."

Hi, Dr. J, Have you started applying to schools yet? You must be close to qualifying as a resident by now.

Not much news at this end. Fred bought a new pickup, so now he has three. Typical, right? Love, Mom

hi, mom, school's still on hold. the programming is fun and the $$$ are too good to quit. it's always possible the company could go belly up and then i'll bail out into college.

uncle fred would fit right in out here. except he might have to trade in one of the pickups for a convertible suv with a roll bar. love, j

Don't put school on hold for too long, unless you want all your classmates calling you gramps. Love, Mom

hi pat, don't show this to mom, because she'll have a fit. i'm not convinced i ever want to go to college. i mean, i'm making good bucks right now without it, so why blow 40k and go into debt when i wouldn't make all that much more than i'm making now? you've lived your whole life without a college degree and you haven't been warped by the lack. right? j

J, As the joke goes, it's not my whole life yet (I hope).

Also, it was because I was already warped by shyness that I didn't go. Somewhere deep in the Kilgore dump are the decomposed fragments of an acceptance letter from Berkeley. It's been over 25 years since that fork in the road and I can't begin to guess where I would be if I hadn't torn up that letter. But I wouldn't know you and Donna, since Kilgore was our point of connection. Today I am quite happy where I am and don't wish I'd gone the other way. On the other hand, there were a lot of not-so-great days getting here. So who knows? Pat

why did you tear up the letter? j

My mother had just died. Pops wanted me to stay with him.

i know that, but what did you want?

At that moment, nothing I did seemed to matter very much. My mother had wanted me to go to college, desperately, but when the time came, she wasn't there. My going wouldn't give her any joy, and my staying would make Pops feel better. So I stayed.

but what did *you* want?

You don't give up easily, do you? I'm not sure what I wanted. I suppose I didn't think about it. Not then.

As far as your decision, if what you want out of college is a ticket to a job, then you're right not to blow 40K on it, since you already have the job.

that "if" of yours suggests i could have some other reason for going to college besides getting a job. care to elaborate?

Where else could you find ten or twenty thousand single women
in one place? :) Alternatively, if you prefer the high-minded reason, what about "education for its own sake"? I know how you
will answer that one. For 40K you could buy enough books to
educate yourself thoroughly and still have 35K left over. So that
leaves the women. You will have to decide for yourself if they
are worth the other 35K.

For about five minutes, I was ready to contact the U.C. system
home page and ask for applications. Then I thought, no, if I go to
college, I'll just nose out all the lesbians on campus and fall in love
with them, one after another, and take frustration to a whole new
level. Better to stay where I am, only intermittently hopeful and so
only intermittently disappointed.

For a time, my dating efforts moved on from June's softball team
to some of the other teams in the league, the ones with the raucous
male cheering sections. The result was that June's team acquired a
new right fielder and a second pitcher, after two of the women I had
asked out on dates experienced a dawning of awareness and decided
they would feel more comfortable playing with other women like
themselves.

Their arrival caused a realignment on the team, as the new right
fielder lured the first baseman away from the catcher, who rebounded
into the waiting arms of the short fielder. When the dust had settled,
everyone seemed much happier, especially the short fielder. The new
pitcher was still odd woman out, but I could see that she was only
biding her time until the next realignment. To me, it all looked a lot
like high school, where each breakup set off a chain reaction until
everybody was paired up again. And just like high school, I was the
person off on the side, stuck in my infinite loop of futility.

It seemed I had a police-dog nose for lesbians. Just walk me down a line of one hundred women I didn't know, and whichever ones attracted me the most were lesbians. Guaranteed. The women themselves might not know it yet, but if we became acquainted, sooner or later I would find them pouring their tales of self-discovery into my ear.

They all loved me, too. Like a brother. I was the person they could talk to. I was the person who listened and understood and didn't freak out. We got along famously together, in all ways except one.

My pattern with women had settled into a kind of lunar cycle. I fell in love, she came to a self-realization, and afterwards she didn't know whether to apologize or thank me. She wanted to apologize but she was so happy, all that came out of her mouth was thank you thank you thank you, and how could she ever repay me. That's me, Jordy, the best friend a girl ever had. The universal catalyst.

At June's suggestion, I started going to an aerobics class. She thought my dating odds might be better there than they had been with her softball league, and statistically she was right. I was one of only two men in the class, but that didn't mean what it had meant on her team. If the health club had offered bleachers and a cooler of beer, we probably would have had a cheering section, too.

There were women in the class of every body type and quite a range of ages, and their unifying bond seemed to be a conviction that their legs were the wrong shape, a conviction with very little basis in visible fact. During floor exercises, rows and rows of legs went sweeping through the air, and from where I lay, sideways on a plastic mat looking up at them, I'd have said about ninety percent of those legs were just fine the way they were.

Between routines, we generally joked around a bit, or chatted, mostly trivia. The conversation was friendly and casual, easy, because we'd all just been hopping up and down and twisting ourselves into silly postures together, and because everyone knew the music would start up again in a couple of minutes so you wouldn't get into something deeper than you wanted. Two minutes seemed to be about the right amount of time for some of the women to slip in a mention of their availability, without too much riding on it, and another two minutes seemed to be about the right amount of time for me to ask them out, without it being any big deal.

If I could have fallen in love with just the legs themselves, I might have found a mate. During the half-hour stretches of pure sensation, our relationships were perfect. But then we stood up and put on our clothes and there were all the rest of our hours together, which were pleasant enough, but not memorable.

None of the women I met bouncing my way to cardiovascular fitness ever discovered they were lesbians. I wasn't surprised, because I didn't feel the slightest ache in my heart when I was in their company. My time with them only reinforced what was already a firm conviction in me, that I was doomed to perpetual futility. Maybe I had some quirk of poetic contrariness in my disposition, a longing for the unattainable. Or maybe I'd been imprinted, like a baby duck first seeing its mother. Or maybe it was all just a prolonged and unlucky coincidence, one of those statistical anomalies that make people believe in destiny. Whatever the explanation, psychology, biology or chance, at that moment in my life it seemed like an inescapable pattern, that the women I wanted would not want me.

I was barely twenty years old. I was not ready to settle for pleasant but unmemorable, not yet. Not when I had loved someone the way I had loved Reba. Maybe when I was forty, I would consider settling for pleasant.

chapter nine

As summer headed into fall, we still didn't have a definite take on the future of Ultimall. Guthrie's beard had grown a whole centimeter, and the rumors were flying. Since the bosses weren't talking, the rest of us picked up every speculation and played volleyball with it until it either burst and vanished, or hardened into a certainty. As the days shortened, the hardening certainty was that the sales figures for our product were stuck at okay—nowhere close to hot.

On October 29, Mips and Guthrie called everyone together for a company meeting. It was the anniversary of Black Tuesday, the stock market crash of 1929, which may have been coincidence, but I was more inclined to think they picked the day intentionally. We gathered upstairs in Guthrie's office, the only space apart from the computer room that was big enough to hold twelve people.

With a somber look on his face, Mips handed each person an envelope and told us not to open the envelopes until he and Guthrie had had an opportunity to explain the situation. Then Guthrie took the floor, coming around to lean against the front of his desk so that he was right in the center of the circle and not behind a barrier. He cleared his throat.

"As all of you know, we have not been selling large numbers of our software package. The problem is not our software. The problem is that the Web is not really set up to handle it yet. When a few more of the big catalog companies come on board, it should take off. The question is whether we can survive that long.

"The decision about our future will not be made by fiat. All of you will have a vote. At this moment, it appears we have two options, which I will outline, and then we will choose.

"Option one is that we struggle along as we have been doing and hope that the product takes off before every last penny of the company's worth is gone. Option two is that we close up shop now, and Ultimall, Inc., ceases to exist. If we choose option two, each of you will receive the current value of your share of ownership in the company. That value has been calculated based on the situation as it stands today, October 29, and is in the envelope we have given each of you. Don't look at the information yet. First, you should hear a few more details about option two. Mips, would you like to take it from here?"

Mips took over Guthrie's spot in front of the desk. He was silent for a moment, which was somewhat strange for him, and then he started to grin, which was even stranger, under the circumstances, and when he finally did talk, he talked much more slowly than usual, almost like an ordinary person.

"First of all," he said, "the end of Ultimall does not mean you will be out of a job. Your job may or may not be here in Sunnyvale. It may not be as much fun as it has been. But you do still have jobs, if you want them. The second detail is that only a portion of your equity will be paid in cash. I'm afraid you must take the remainder in the form of shares in the meg-amoeba that is proposing to buy us out for an amazingly large sum of money."

We had all been so tense with dread, it took a moment for his meaning to sink in. When it did, a couple of people burst into tears, the way you do when the cavalry comes charging over the hill at the end of a corny movie. We all ripped open our envelopes and pulled out the slips inside. The paper in my hand looked like the one that came attached to my paycheck, a neat row of numbers in boxes, but when I came to the last number, the value of my share of the company, I had to count the zeroes twice, and even then I couldn't believe it. I looked around and saw that my mouth wasn't the only one hanging open.

I couldn't even buy a beer yet, not legally, and I hadn't done anything that any other grunt couldn't have done, and here I was having to count the number of digits after the dollar sign. What did a person do with money like that?

I mean, I knew what you did with a couple of hundred dollars extra every week. You bought a basketball hoop. But a few hundred thousand, plus stock? I was going to need a broker. Maybe an accountant.

Did I quit my job and sail around the world? Did I buy a house? A Porsche? A speedboat? Did I hire a cook and a maid?

I decided a good start would be to pay off my mother's student loans.

When I suggested paying off the student loans, Mom said, "They're low-interest loans. You could invest the money and get back more than I'm paying in interest."

Maybe I already had an accountant.

I thought she would be jumping up and down when I told her my news, and she did jump up and down, for about thirty seconds. Then she reverted to practicality and started talking about investments.

"Since when do you know so much about investments? We've never had anything but debt."

"Since Pat," she said.

It turned out Pat did have some investments, nothing huge, just what she had saved from her pay, but she was definitely an ant and not a grasshopper. Until Mom came along, Pat had simply put her savings in the bank. She kept the books for her father's store because someone had to, but she didn't like the task. With her own money, she didn't care enough to spend any time looking for a more profitable place to keep it.

Now my mother had taken over the planning for both of them. Mom had spent too much time broke to be indifferent about money, and when she finally got the chance to manage assets instead of debts, she was as happy as could be, almost as happy as Pat was to let her do it. As a consequence, she could instantly explain to me why it was more advantageous to collect the half-percent difference between the interest paid out on her loans and the earnings coming in from any sensible investment.

Within hours, she had a plan worked out for me. I should take the whole fortune, put it into mutual funds and use the income to go to college. I felt like the kid in *Mary Poppins*, being dragged to the bank to put my tuppence somewhere safe and sensible.

I didn't want to be safe and sensible. I wanted to celebrate.

"Let me buy you something," I said. "Something major this time, not just a CD player."

"We don't need anything," she said.

"I could buy you a bigger house."

"I don't want a bigger house. It just takes longer to clean."

"How about a new pickup?"

"My pickup is running fine."

"A satellite dish?"

"We don't need one."

"There must be something you want."

"I want your future to be secure. So put the money somewhere safe and I will have what I want."

"Mom, you're being a drag."

She wouldn't budge.

That night I got an email from Pat.

> Jordy, There is something I'd like, if you are still determined to buy us something. Pat

> pat, i am still determined, and it had better not be a new roll of duct tape that you want. mom makes me crazy. it would serve her right if i bought a yacht and shipped it to her ups. what is your something? j

> Not a yacht, please. The nearest open water is the Great Salt Lake and even that is a few hundred miles away. I was thinking we might travel somewhere, England, or Italy. Not for too long a time, about two weeks. I wouldn't want to leave the dogs or the Mercantile for any longer than that. We had already planned a camping trip for next spring. You could surprise her with some plane tickets instead. Make sure they're nonrefundable, and then we'll have to go. :) P

> done. j
>   p.s. which do you prefer, knowing the language or driving on the right?

> Language, I think, since neither of us has ever been out of the U.S. before.

That was all I could get them to take. They refused even to stay in fancy hotels. They would be more comfortable in small B&Bs, they said. No theater, no London, no shopping at all. They wanted to head straight for Wales and the Lake District and go tramping through the countryside. Apart from the plane ticket and the rental car, it was hardly going to cost more than their camping trip would have.

If they wouldn't spend my money, I would have to spend it myself. I traded in my Civic on a brand-new Acura. I bought a connoisseur-quality entertainment center, even better than Mike's. I bought a racing bike, skis, roller-blades and a camera. I bought two really nice jackets, one soft brown leather, the other a Mariners warm-up jacket with Griffey's number on it. Then I hit the wall.

It was mile twenty, and my glycogen had just run out. I walked into a store to look for some court shoes, and I saw ten thousand pairs of shoes, stacks of shoes, linked lists of shoes, multidimensional arrays of shoes, wearable objects with every imaginable degree of cushioning, arch support, heel stability, width, length, color and advertising hook. I suddenly found myself thinking like Pat. I already had a pair of shoes.

I was ruined. For the first time in my life, I could spend money without counting it, and the thought of shopping made me nauseous. Ultimall and Mike had ruined me. For a year and a half, I had spent sixty hours a week shopping. Trying on outfits. Searching for bargains. Comparing colors and tailoring. Trying on more outfits. Taking advantage of computer-assisted accessorizing. There was no permutation of the shopping process that I had not experienced.

Anything I missed at Ultimall, I had hit with Mike. After my year and half of virtual shopping, I had had a year of the real thing. We had driven the length of El Camino looking for one particular model of programmable coffee-maker. We had spent hours browsing shelves of CD-ROMs. We had stood at the acoustic center of a room full of stereo speakers and compared each of twenty pairs with every other pair. We had taken advantage of free trial offers for cell phones, cable networks and home-delivered bottled water. We had read product reviews in magazines and debated buying decisions late into the night. Shopping was the only topic Mike was happy to talk about, and by now I had said everything I could imagine wanting to say about it.

Since I had no stamina left for buying small things, I decided I should blow a big wad all at once, by buying a house. That was what people did, wasn't it, the moment they could afford it?

At the real estate office, the listings and prices gave me a serious reality check. For a quarter million or more, I could buy a little ranch like the one I was living in, shoebox bedrooms, shag carpet, a sliding glass door onto a patio in the back and a wide paved driveway into a carport. Something really nice, a house up in the hills, would cost more than I could conceive of paying for a place to sleep. I had thought I was rich, but it seemed a lot of people in California were a lot richer.

Crossing one living room to point out the rheostat, the real estate agent caught her spike heel in a loop of carpet and as I caught her elbow to stop her fall, I had this sudden vision of myself as a home-owner, leaping across the room to save myself from the lawsuit she would bring if she fell. Other visions followed—plumbers and roofing contractors, tax forms arriving in the mail, insurance salesmen at the door, neighbors complaining if I didn't keep the lawn mowed. Did I want to be Joe Suburb, wearing a chef's apron adorned with bathroom jokes, flipping burgers on the backyard grill?

I rented an apartment. One bedroom on the third floor of an almost-new complex with a pool and an exercise room, and no lawn to mow or shrubs to trim. I bought a futon couch and set up my entertainment center, and my castle was ready for habitation. It still looked bare, though, too many blank white walls, so I steeled myself and bought more stuff, chairs and pictures and some kitchenware. I hadn't realized how many objects it took to make a space look occupied.

I couldn't tell if Mike was regretful or relieved at my departure. I knew he was a little sorry, because he insisted on coming to my new place to make sure I had the entertainment center arranged in the most acoustically perfect way, and he repeatedly offered to help me with any other electronic equipment I might buy in the future. But I was quite sure he was relieved as well. With me gone, he could go back to listening to his music and be left in peace, no one bugging him with questions.

My own feelings were mixed, but I thought that relief was uppermost. After two and a half years Mike and I still weren't friends, not what I would call friends, and I finally had to concede that we never would be. I had made a connection with him, by buying things, but it was the connection of a tow-bar. We had moved in tandem, always at a rigidly exact distance apart.

For the time being, I continued to work at my job, mostly because I didn't have something else I wanted to do. Artie had quit immediately and moved to Oregon to live in the woods, but the others planned to stay. Like me, they enjoyed programming and didn't quite know what else to do with their time. I figured, if I quit, I would probably spend my days playing on my own computer, and I knew I could learn more working with Mips than I would on my own.

We found out after the buyout that Mips had been the keystone of the whole deal. The agreement wouldn't have gone through if he had not signed a contract to stay on for three more years. The amoeba wanted the product, but particularly wanted him, because he was the man who would have the product fully up and running sooner than anyone else. It wasn't fully up and running yet, even though it had been released and was on the market. Apparently this was standard procedure with new software. Get it out there, get a buzz going about how hot it was, then worry about filling in the details.

The buyout had gotten a buzz going all right. It certified that what we had done was real. Now that we were hooked up with a corporation that could actually distribute a product, the project became a lot more serious. We moved to a different office park because our work force expanded from twelve to fifty-eight in two months.

We had whole new departments—documentation, customer service, marketing and personnel—but even with fifty-eight people, we were just one tiny division of the larger corporate structure.

Not long after the move to the new building, June followed Artie's example and left. Shannon was moving to Santa Cruz to work as a massage therapist, and June had decided to go with her. She could have commuted from there, like a lot of people did, but she thought, why bother, and it was hard to argue with that view. Right away she found a new job and a basketball team for the winter season, so she was happy. For my part, I thought the walls of our new building must be hollow because fifty-eight people weren't enough to dampen the echoes.

It wasn't only the building and the people that had changed. The work had, too. Instead of "Let's try this," there were formal specifications for every part of the program. Stacks of memos circulated from office to office, documenting every move we made. I was still a peon, status-wise, and even I exchanged memos sometimes.

It soon became clear that our program was just one small feature of a much larger electronic-shopping concept under development by the corporation as a whole. We were no longer creating new programs. Our task now was to adapt the existing program to fit the larger structure. Even the name, Ultimall, was abandoned in favor of a yet-to-be-determined name that would reflect the new configuration.

One of the numerous memos, early on, presented an outline of the overall vision in a tone that was, I think, intended to be inspirational. As it happened, Mips was standing beside my desk when the memo came up on my screen, and he read it over my shoulder. Nothing in the memo was anything he didn't already know. Maybe he was just curious how the news was being presented to the working masses.

"Conventional local retail stores, both small independent stores and chain-affiliated superstores, are rapidly becoming obsolete," the memo informed us. "Their distribution of goods is inefficient. Their labor costs are enormous. They waste time the consumer does not have. They represent an outmoded system, and sooner or later they will inevitably be replaced by a streamlined system of centralized warehouses with computerized ordering and inventory, and mechanized packing and shipping, all of it accessed directly by the consumer by way of electronic communications.

"By eliminating the huge and unnecessary labor expense of local retailing, this centralized system will be able to deliver a much higher volume of goods at a much lower cost to the consumer. Efficiency will be multiplied, and the American workforce will find that it has been freed from millions of man/woman-years in low-skill-level jobs in the retail sector. Our system, when it is fully implemented, will be able to service 80 to 90 percent of the retail purchasing needs of the American consumer . . . "

Mips and I looked at each other, and I think we both had the same thought. We had definitely been swallowed.

Along with all the other changes, the amoeba had budgeted an administrative assistant for Mips so that every second of his time could be devoted to flights of genius. Mips said he didn't need an administrative assistant, but the amoeba insisted. So Mips hired a woman with a degree in philosophy and asked me to take turns with him staying late and teaching her how to write code. He said if he had a real assistant, he would end up spending all his time going to meetings and drafting memos, because that was what people with administrative assistants did.

"How can I think with someone sitting outside my door waiting for me to tell them what to do?" he complained.

He didn't fully trust the people the amoeba had shipped in to help us.

"They all have degrees in CS," he said.

The business about CS degrees was just symbolic. The fact was that half the original group of programmers at Ultimall had had degrees in computer science.

Inexperienced as I was, I found I was now part of Mips's inner circle, along with the two graphic designers, Teresa and Sam, and the "new hire," Rodney, who had gotten "my" office in our old building. I had an office now. It had no windows and was barely big enough to hold the gigantic potted plant that had defined my virtual office in the computer room, but it had a door and four walls. I would rather have been back in the computer room. The company had metamorphosed, way too fast. Instead of a vessel bound for the Spice Islands, it felt like a conveyor belt.

Before the buyout, Mips had given us vague, impossibly ambitious targets and dared us to try and hit them. Since there were so few of us, he said, the product must be stripped down, lean and mean, only the most essential and interesting features included. Consumers were too busy to learn how to use a thousand different features anyway. Just give them a game that was simple and fascinating, chess or checkers or a deck of cards, a dozen rules and a million different ways the game could play out.

The amoeba had changed the game. Our game was too simple, it said. Consumers wanted features, it said. More, always more. The more the better. And more features meant more code, which meant more programmers, which meant more memos and specifications, because programming seemed to work like a game of telephone: the longer the chain of programmers between one end of the product and the other, the more every detail had to be spelled out so the message didn't get garbled.

Our targets were now defined at great length, in writing. The amoeba didn't believe in impossible targets. It knew exactly how many lines of code the average programmer could write in a day. That was our target, and we sank to meet expectations. With Mips and his crazed vision leading the way, I had written half again that much,

June and Artie had written almost twice that much, and Mips himself had been in Griffey Jr. territory, three or four times the average. Now there was no inspiration, only perspiration. I felt as if I had been hitched to a peddler's cart, piled to the point of toppling, and my only goal was not to tread on the heels of the person in front of me.

Mips tried to hold us together—the old guard—to preserve a guerrilla squadron of creative anarchy amidst the plodding accumulation of code. It didn't work. The weight was too great. The amoeba simply spread itself glutinously, smothering everything in its path by sheer bulk.

At the time of the buyout, Mips had signed on for three years, and it soon became clear that at three years and a day, he would be gone, off to a place where he could start from scratch again and make another killing. My plan was to try and stick it out, too, and hope that wherever Mips went, I could go with him. I also hoped it wouldn't be in California.

Even through sunglasses, California was starting to bleach my eyeballs. I was no longer too busy to notice where I was living. On an expedition into the unknown, mundane details don't matter. On a conveyor belt, you start noticing the texture of the rubber and the noise of the rollers.

I remembered how Mom had started to hate trees. At the time, I had wondered how someone could hate something as benign as a tree. Now I was starting to hate the sun. It was there, day after day, like a vacant stare in that blank blue sky. I longed for rain. I longed for the smell of decaying leaves, and fungi and moss. I longed to hear water dripping. I started driving out to the coast, in the hope that it would be foggy. I haunted Big Basin and the damp green shadows among the pillars of redwood. But always I had to come back down out of the hills, to the hundred-mile grid of sun-baked suburbs around the bay, the desert of red tile and tan stucco and gray pavement, the paper-dry ornamental vegetation in tidy squares and rectangles and the army of cars in precision formation marching north, south, east and west.

Mips had developed the habit of prowling among the offices of his inner circle, appearing at odd moments and hovering or pacing while he talked. He had always had trouble sitting still, but this was different, more like caged behavior. For him, the worst part was losing control of the large design. Until now, the program had been the actualization of an idea he carried around whole in his mind. It had been coherent, all its parts tightly interlocking, no awkward protrusions to grate on the inside of his skull.

That coherence was long gone. The amoeba did its large design by committee, in the belief that an individual could not possibly think up all the things customers might ever want to do with its software. And they were right, the committee did think up a dizzying multitude of new functions to add. The result was ugly, ungainly, huge and confusing, but it did have a lot more functions.

For Mips, the transformation was painful. The program had been his passion. Now he had to sit back and watch as his simple, elegant nucleus was engulfed, buried under a blizzard of Post-its from committee brainstorming sessions.

"I'm sleeping ten hours a day now," he said to me one day, as he hovered just inside my office door. "There's no reason not to. Subtract the meetings, and the work they want me to do doesn't even take until lunchtime."

"Why don't you tell them you could do more?"

"Why should I bother? Why push myself just to double the number of loads I dump in the landfill? You remember what I said once about hoping people would be too swamped by volume to be able to separate smart from stupid? Well that's their whole design principle. They just pile on anything, smart or stupid, because some customer somewhere might want it. So I guess I got what I asked for."

"You got the millions to go with it," I pointed out.

"True."

Mips used to talk endlessly about software design. Now he talked about nothing in particular, because he had nothing he wanted to say about the program. He couldn't even talk about ideas for other software, unrelated to Ultimall, because any ideas he talked about, the amoeba could claim it owned. So he hovered and jittered and talked about *Star Trek* or chaos theory, or asked about my life.

"How do you like it, being so rich all of a sudden?" he asked.

"I like it a lot," I said. "I can buy cool stuff I've never had before. I don't have to worry about money. I'm free to do whatever I want."

"And what do you want to do?"

My mind went strangely blank, and I realized my other answer had been a reflex, unthinking, an expression of what I had always assumed it would feel like to be rich, back when I wasn't. It was only part of what I actually felt at the moment. I also felt a little as if the north pole had mysteriously disappeared. I was well provisioned, in no danger of privation, but lost.

Until now, I'd never had to think about what I wanted because it was obvious. A good job. Plenty of money. A nice place to live. A woman. Check . . . check . . . check . . . And?

I couldn't quite bring myself to tell Mips the only item left on my list was finding a woman. That didn't seem like a goal, exactly. Love should be something that came along when you weren't thinking about it, when you were aiming at something else. But what something else?

"I don't know," I said. "Maybe I'll just stay here adding my plastic bags to the landfill and racking up dollars until my net worth clicks over to another zero on the end."

Mips laughed, practically a cackle. "Your net worth. Now there's a concept to think about. You, Jordy, summed up in one round number at the bottom of a balance sheet. Arithmetic is so much easier than philosophy."

It would simplify life, for sure. Just define myself as a number and then watch that number get bigger and bigger, the digits clicking over like the readout on the gas pump.

Why didn't I quit, like Artie and June? I had enough money to do whatever I wanted. But what did I want, if it was not to keep working and earn more money?

The first twenty years of my life had been molded by the inflexible assumption that I would have to earn a living. Now I had a living, pouring into my bank account every month like overflow from an oil well.

Should I move to the city, where the streets had sidewalks and people walked on them? No one walked on my street in Sunnyvale. Sometimes people jogged, or roller-bladed, but nobody walked. It was too slow.

Maybe if I had been in love, I could have seen the bayburbs for what they were, a paradise with a rheumatism-free climate and a left-turn lane everywhere you needed one. But I wasn't in love, not with anyone who loved me. I owned a hundred CDs, a hundred women's voices, honey and smoky bourbon and clear lemon ice, all yearning for love, but no one yearned for me.

I kept right on working the same long hours I had back when the company was operating in a controlled panic. At least if I was working, I didn't have to watch couples strolling hand in hand, couples gazing into each other's eyes across restaurant tables. Now I needed my job, needed it to distract me. If I quit, I would only have more free hours to watch other people who were happily mated and loved the perpetual sunshine. Besides, I was making too much money to quit.

Instead of poetry, my longings poured themselves into code, floods of code, way beyond the company's targeted average. I had a knack for programming. Not genius, like Mips, just a mechanical ability to crank out routine code at a high rate of speed. I beat every deadline by weeks. Every time I started thinking about following Artie's example and retiring to a cabin with a dog, the company would raise my salary another notch. I had started playing tennis, and I'd bought a secondhand Ford Bronco for the drive to Tahoe in the winter, and even then I was banking a large part of my salary.

Some of the other programmers were annoyed with me, like I was making them look bad. I wasn't trying to make them look bad. It wasn't my fault if they were happily mated and wanted to go home in the evening. I would have preferred a warm-blooded companion myself, but a keyboard was better than total solitude.

The trouble with paradise is that you can't leave. I had it perfect. Nice apartment in a nice clean neighborhood, two cars, an oversize graphite tennis racket, a state-of-the-art home entertainment center, a great job with a health plan, a retirement plan, even a dental plan. My investments were perfect, three top-performing mutual funds, plus my shares in the amoeba. I lived in a Shangri-la—a Mediterranean climate in easy reach of the ocean, the mountains and an ultra-cool city, San Francisco. There were women all around me, beautiful women, tanned and athletic. If I couldn't find one here, I couldn't find one anywhere.

There was nowhere for me to go. I was at the pinnacle. Anything else would be a step down. No other job would pay as much. No other climate could be as pleasant. No other location could have so many desirable features. No other population could have a higher percentage of attractive and available women. There was no sane reason for me not to continue on my present course until I reached retirement age.

So what do you do when your life is perfect and you have started hating the sun?

chapter ten

hi, pat, have you heard of a theory called karmic realignment? or a place called cloudwater? i'm not entirely sure what i'm doing here, but i liked the name. and it's foggy most of the time, which is good. sunnyvale has started feeling like a solar food dryer. i didn't used to mind so much, but lately the sun has seemed relentless, like isn't life just wonderful and isn't it the cutest final touch, to have a big yellow happy face pasted up in the sky all the time?

i've only been at cloudwater a couple of hours, but i already feel better. i look out my window and all i see is mist and gray ocean swells. the ocean here is really cold, and you can pretty well plan on the fog to come rolling in every day, like the tide. it's great.

all the buildings are made out of natural materials, stone, wood, glass, tile, with everything nontoxic and super energy-efficient. it's supposed to be a model for simple, low-impact living. i have noticed one little flaw in their concept, which is that it cost about fourteen million to build the place. so it will need a little refinement before it's the next model t. but the idea is good.

the low-impact part is really just background. the main point of coming here is supposed to be personal growth, self-realization, what not. or that's what the piece in the chronicle said. that story is how i got here in the first place. i'm looking around, thinking i need a change, and right in front of me, in the lifestyle section, is a big feature on cloudwater. i thought, okay, why not, maybe it's a sign. i know mom would see a reason why not—the place is outrageously expensive. but it's only ten days, so i won't be bankrupt.

we're supposed to think of ourselves as seekers, not students, all of us together examining our habits and feelings and beliefs, trying to sort ourselves out. there are nineteen of us in this session. apparently there always has to be a prime number, eleven, thirteen, seventeen or nineteen. i don't know what they do if one person gets called away to a dying relative. maybe they keep a backup seeker on the staff, like a utility infielder.

the first thing we did when we arrived was gather in the big common room, with our luggage, and then each of us came forward, very ceremonially, to dump everything electronic, our cell phones, watches, beepers, laptops, into a big pile to be locked away in a storeroom while we're here. the idea is to start freeing our minds from the clutter of modern life. i thought that was kind of inconsistent, though, since one of their big hypes is all the sophisticated computerized controls that help make their buildings so energy efficient.

luckily i had brought both my laptops, so i could make a big fanfare of dumping my pc onto the pile and know that i still had the powerbook stashed away in the bottom of my duffel bag. there's no phone in my room, but the jack is still there, so here i am. i figure it's only in my own room and no one has to know about it. i've shut off all the sound effects, to keep from messing up anybody else's realignment. jordy

Hi, Jordy, I suppose as long as your emails keep coming, it means you haven't been expelled for breaking the rules. Or would it be a karmic incongruity to expel someone?

What are the other people like? Pat

i don't know much yet. another rule is total silence, outside the guided workshops. they consider small talk pernicious and don't want us falling into habitual chat about "what do you do, where do you live, etc."

i did get some impressions, though, when we were shedding our electronic gear. as near as i can tell, there are two other young, high-paid geek types like me, and almost everybody else is white, midlife, and probably overscheduled. for the midlifes, it seemed to be a truly religious experience to throw aside all battery-powered objects.

i peg the other two as geeks, because when they put their laptops onto the pile, they looked like mothers leaving their babies at day care for the first time. it's the way i would have looked, if i hadn't had the powerbook stashed away. probably it means the three of us are the ones who need this training more than anyone. j

hi, mom, i'm sending this from a place called cloudwater, up the coast north of the bay area. it's a training center, with workshops on personal growth, spiritual exploration and so forth. the idea is to take some time free of distractions and think about what really matters in life.

i hope it will be useful, but if nothing else, it will be a

vacation. it doesn't cost all that much more than a nice resort where all you do is lie on the beach and get fed. love, jordy

Jordy, A vacation sounds good, and if you get something useful out of it, all the better. I trust you're smart enough not to get sucked into anything phony.

One of my co-workers here has become a workshop groupie, and I'm guessing she's spent more money on three-day feel-good sessions than I spent getting a college degree. Whenever she starts feeling bored or down, she goes off to get a booster shot of wisdom in seven easy steps, no homework. Then she comes home, and both she and her life are exactly the way they were before. I know you've got more sense than that, so I'm not really worried. Love, Mom

hi pat, mom's been warning me not to find this place too wonderful, as if i'd go into it like a wide-eyed baby and swallow anything they tell me. j

J, Maybe you should go into it like a baby. I've never met one who wouldn't spit out anything it didn't want to swallow. P

The food, at least, was so utterly plain, I didn't think anyone could dislike it enough to spit it out. No salt, no seasonings, no sugar, your basic beans and rice, plus a short list of allowable vegetables.

Before our first meal, a very serious woman wearing vegetable-dyed cotton stood up to explain the underlying philosophy of the meals at Cloudwater. Her message had more or less the form and timing of Grandma's "For what we are about to receive . . . " except that she didn't thank anyone.

"Elaborate cookery is a form of clutter," she said. "A distraction from the essence of life. We learn to crave the overstimulation of chocolate, and so lose our appreciation for the subtlety of rice. Simplify the diet, and the palate will begin to notice the smallest nuances of flavor. To the uncluttered palate, a pinto bean is as different from a navy bean as chocolate from vanilla . . . "

When she finished speaking, the rule of silence was resumed. We all unfolded our napkins, picked up our forks and began educating ourselves on the nuances of beans.

The problem with silence was that it left me nothing to do but watch and think. As I looked down the long table at all of us silently chewing our simplified diet, I flashed on Grandpa and me standing beside a feed bunk, watching a group of weaner calves. The calves had been methodically chewing some bland but scientifically calibrated ration, and I couldn't stop myself from wondering if the uncluttered existence of cows and chickens gave them a fuller appreciation of life's essence.

I tried to shut up my thoughts. I knew they were counterproductive if I was here to learn. But then I'd look down the table at the row of jaws rhythmically chewing, and I'd start thinking about the feed bunk again. Maybe the room around me was completely silent, but in the privacy of my brain, my better and lesser selves were having quite a lively dinner conversation.

In the morning, after a silent breakfast of unsweetened oatmeal, we gathered in the room called the Commons to await the arrival of the person who was to be the guide to our seeking. Nineteen chairs were arranged in three nested curves, three, then five, then eleven. More prime numbers. We sat down and waited. The only sound in the room was our own breathing. The floor was cool gray stone, the walls cream-colored plaster, the beams overhead reddish fir. All the windows were above eye-level, letting in light, but offering no views to distract us.

After several minutes' wait, hearing only the tiny sounds of silent people, I felt my scalp begin to prickle. I glanced up and saw that a man had come into the room, from behind us. He was dressed in undyed, loose cotton clothing, and as he walked across the room, his sandals made no sound.

He sat down cross-legged on the floor in front of us, facing in the same direction we were facing, as if to say by his posture that he was a seeker with us. His one was the prime number that completed the pattern. He remained silent for quite a long time, and the prickles swept across my scalp in waves. Then he began to speak, slowly.

"My name is Elam. I have been, and always will be, a seeker. A seeker after the essence of life, which is ineluctable, inexpressible, yet unmistakable. All who come here with open hearts are welcome to walk the path I walk."

My immediate reaction was that he did not have to walk anywhere, and that it didn't matter what he said, so long as he kept talking. His voice had the rich golden tone of a baritone sax, and he used it like one, his phrases rolling out like long, lazy, introspective jazz improvisations. If he had just kept his back to us and gone on talking, I'd have followed him anywhere, soaking up every word he said, filling up the dry hollow inside me.

Then he turned around to face us, and something in me balked. I felt as if I knew him or at least had seen him somewhere before. I couldn't place him, though. I was quite sure I'd never known anyone named Elam, but maybe I had met him in a situation where I didn't learn his name. The one certain thing was, he made me uneasy.

The voices in my head started up again: You're being stupid. Why pay a whole bunch of money and then refuse to learn anything?

But the guy gives me a bad feeling.

Just listen to what he has to say. What's the harm?

His voice, that's what. The guy could sell the devil a fur coat.

He can't sell you anything against your will. And how far into the ozone can you go in ten days?

Pretty far, according to Mom.

Okay, then try Pat's approach. Put it in your mouth, see how it tastes, and then swallow it or spit it out.

That I can do, I thought, and I began to relax. But I still wanted to know where I'd seen the guy before.

Elam had blue-gray eyes and what seemed like an unchanging half-smile of serenity. His manner was not in the least pushy. I thought he seemed like a tree with very, very deep roots, outwardly softspoken and gentle, but a hurricane could not topple him. To argue with him felt futile, because he made you feel as though you were arguing against the tao itself, the universal being whose nonresistance is irresistible.

He rarely tried to use logic to persuade. In fact it was his avoidance of attempts to persuade that was so persuasive, as if his beliefs simply were, in the same way that the universe simply is, with no need for justification. He made logic and reason look like the tools of the weak and unenlightened, proof a priori that the arguments they defended must have shallow roots. After my years working with computers, whose persuadability was in exact proportion to the perfection of the programmer's logic, I thought this new way of thinking might be quite restful.

As an opening exercise, Elam invited us to take a few minutes to become thoroughly acquainted with our own bodies.

"Let us begin at the top, the center of sight and thought, the place of illumination," he said. "Lay your hand on the crown of your head. Feel the perfect curve of the bone, its strength . . . Now feel the energy of the mind inside, and its fragility, which that shield of bone guards from harm . . . Move on and introduce yourself to your face . . . "

His voice rose and fell, slow and soothing. Led by his words, our hands wandered dreamily over our bodies, feeling our collarbones, the points of our elbows, the pulse at the wrist, breasts and testicles and the indentation of the navel, the elastic band of the Achilles tendon.

"It is a miracle, is it not? Every bone and muscle is a miracle," he said, and we sighed in contented agreement.

"Your body is the universe—trillions of cells, each unique and each living in harmony with the others to create a balanced whole. You do not have to tell your cells what to do. They already know. And so it is with all the other levels of being in the universe. You yourself are a cell, which knows in its being what it is . . .

"We squander energy, thinking that the world is a place of problems to be attacked, that we must somehow 'take action.' The simple, beautiful truth is that harmony and abundance are the natural state of the universe. We will come to them, not by struggle, not by effort, but by simply letting them happen. And your part in this process is simply to be the perfect unique individual that you are."

His voice felt like languorous tropical waves, gently rolling us free of gravity until we floated warm and weightless inside our own selves.

" . . . Consider your breathing," he said. "Oxygen is the flame of life, and the deeper each breath, the brighter the flame. Try taking a deep, deep breath, slowly. Do you feel how the body expands and grows light? Awareness of breathing is the first element of self-awareness. The more you can focus your attention on your own breathing, the more perfectly you will be conscious that you are alive. Remember, any moment that you allow your attention to be diverted by the noise in the outside world is a moment of self-awareness that has been lost."

He fell silent, and the only sound in the room was the slow rise and fall of our breathing.

> hi, mom, i've made it through my first day, and i don't think you
> would say i've been sucked into anything. we spent the whole
> day learning how to breathe properly, which was very restful,
> but not likely to breed fanaticism.
>
> it does make me think about things i've never thought about
> before—practicing energy conservation in the largest sense,
> not stressing ourselves over things we can't change, like the

balkans. so maybe it will be both a vacation and useful. love, jordy

In that case, it will be a bargain. I'm glad it's going well. Love, Mom

hi, pat, i haven't decided yet what i think about this place. i've always thought it was a sensible piece of evolutionary design that the brainstem and vagus nerve took care of our breathing so that the rest of our brain cells could give their full attention to the tiger that was about to attack, or the deer we were stalking, or inventing the wheel and the plow and the flush toilet. but now it seems that our higher brain can also make improvements in our breathing, if we set it to the task.

i did feel like i was expanding my lungs a bit, and maybe that meant my brain was getting more oxygen, but i couldn't figure out why my brain really needed more oxygen if our whole goal was to empty it of thought. j

Hi, Jordy, I suppose it could be a kind of spiritual goal, to simplify your life and clear your mind to the point that it can be wholly occupied by the task of regulating your breathing. Theologians could have a long debate about which is closer to the divine, that perfect simplicity or the extraordinary complexity of thought and imagination that leads to the creation of flush toilets, among other things. Pat

The second day followed the pattern of the first, oatmeal eaten in silence, then on to the Commons and Elam's arrival. For an hour he sat facing the front of the room, silent, joining us in our breathing. Then he turned around and said it was time for the next step.

"As the air we breathe is the flame of life, so the foods we eat are the fuel. Every bite that enters your mouth will diffuse through your body and influence every living cell. Tune into those cells . . . they know which foods will nourish your inner harmonies . . . they will tell you which foods are right for you, if you will listen . . . "

As his golden voice went on speaking, my mind began to drift, and I caught only fragments of what he said. What he said really didn't seem to matter. It was his way of being that was the message, his pure serenity.

" . . . you and every other human being are perfect, exactly as you are . . . learn to listen to your inner self . . . at every moment you will know what is right for you . . . this is the totality of meaning, to become your unique self . . . the universe asks nothing more, only that your life be the fulfillment of the true you . . . "

I floated on the slow, slow rhythmic rise and fall in tone, the pauses given to let each thought settle. His voice was like the breathing of a person in deep, restful sleep, and I felt lulled into a total absence of thought.

Then his voice stopped. For the first time since our arrival, we were invited to share ourselves, to speak our feelings, to ask questions.

No one said anything. The room was silent, except for the shifting of bodies into new positions, the squeak of a chair, here and there a cough. In the silence, I bumped back onto solid ground, abruptly. I could feel the edge of my chair pressing into my hamstrings. My brain woke up and with it my misgivings. My hand shot into the air.

"You need not raise your hand before you speak," Elam said. "This isn't a schoolroom, where one person knows the answers and everyone else is ignorant. All the truth that exists can be found inside yourself. The only person who can teach you anything is yourself. So speak up freely. Say whatever you feel your true self wishes to say."

"Um, well, I was wondering . . . What happens if a person's true self turns out to be, like, Jeffrey Dahmer? Or Caligula?"

Elam smiled, peacefully. "A man like Jeffrey Dahmer is a perfect example of a person who is not in touch with his true self."

His gaze moved on from me to find someone else who was moved to speak. I could feel a ripple of negative gravity spread out from where I sat, as if I must be seriously out of touch with my true self to imagine that anyone's true self could look anything like Jeffrey Dahmer.

A thin, anxious-looking woman on the far side of the room was talking now. " . . . I mean, how do we know if the vegetables we buy have been given all the minerals our bodies need? Also, I've been reading that hybrid varieties don't have as many nutrients, but when I go to the market, how can I tell which are the hybrid varieties? I am trying my best to get all the right nutrients. I take high-potency vitamins, and herbs and nutritional yeast, but I'm worried that might not cover everything. I've been reading about molybdenum, and I'm concerned that vegetables may not take up enough of it from the soil. Or maybe it wasn't molybdenum. It may have been cadmium. Or is that the bad one? Maybe I'm thinking of chromium. Anyway, I am very worried about the food supply in the United States. I don't see how anyone in this country can possibly get an adequately nutritious diet . . . "

> hi, pat, what do you know about hybrid plants? a lady in our workshop said that hybrid foods aren't as nutritious. j

> J, The only thing I know about hybrids is that they usually grow faster and larger than their parent strains. I suppose it is possible that each kernel of corn is allotted exactly x vitamins, regardless of its size, so that two small kernels will have twice as many vitamins as one large one. But that's an untested hypothesis. It is also possible that the amount of vitamins is proportional to size, and a kernel twice as big has twice as many vitamins. So I haven't helped you. You must ask a plant scientist. Pat

when elam was talking about it during the session today, he said there might not be any difference a chemist could measure. he said hybridization destroys the spiritual essence of the living being. j

Does this mean he opposes interracial marriage, on the grounds that the hybrid offspring will have lost their spiritual essence? P

i think he would say you are applying logic to a question for which it is the wrong method. i don't always go along with everything elam says. although i could listen to him talk all day long. his voice makes you feel the way i think valium must make you feel. not that i know, since i've never taken valium, but i assume it feels nice. a lot of the time i don't try to follow the words, because i get tangled up in quibbling arguments. i just listen to the voice and let my mind relax. it's very pleasant.

As we gathered for dinner that night, I could feel that people were trying to stay away from me. The place settings were at a fixed distance and silence was still the rule, so there wasn't much anyone could do overtly to avoid me, but I could feel it nevertheless. When I walked to my chair, I felt a small, involuntary recoil in the people on either side. The woman directly across from me, the one so anxious about mineral nutrients, spent the entire meal studying her plate, as if it were the homework assignment for the evening.

It wasn't my intention to bother people. I didn't stare at anyone or try to make them meet my eyes. But my eyes had to look somewhere, and I didn't feel like studying my plate, so I looked here and there around the table, trying not to linger in any one place too long. After a while I began to see how an outcast could get a reputation for having shifty eyes.

Then, as my gaze was sliding past one of the geeks, he looked straight at me, wagged his eyebrows and grinned, and I felt a whole lot better.

Later that night, I was about to start sending emails when somebody knocked on my door. I quickly yanked all the cords out of the wall sockets and stuffed the computer into my duffel bag. As I opened the door, I tried to look as if I were still partly lost in a meditative daze.

It was the geek, wire-rimmed glasses, whatever haircut, and skin undamaged by UV exposure. He immediately put a finger to his lips, as if he thought some ungoverned impulse of politeness might cause me to break the rule of silence. He glanced up and down the hallway, which was empty, then spread his hands, mimed typing at a keyboard and raised his eyebrows in a look of inquiry.

I gestured for him to come in and shut the door.

hi, pat, not only am i a hard case myself, i've now become a subversive influence on someone else. an enabler, i think they call it. one of the other seekers here, a guy named gavin, somehow intuited that i might be getting online. so now he's started sneaking down to my room to catch up on his own email.

probably it means i'm wasting my money here, since i haven't thrown myself into the process with my whole being. some piece of me insists on stepping back and analyzing things, not just going along, and i can't seem to change that. jordy

Isn't it the purpose of being there, that you're figuring out how to be your true self? P

well, yes, but i keep getting the feeling that some people's true selves are more true than other people's, and they're hoping

my current true self isn't my truest self and eventually i'll find a
truer one. j

Four days into the workshop, I finally figured out why Elam looked familiar to me, and things went from a slow drift downhill to a fast skid.

The topic of the day was mental clutter and how to clear it out.
"Take the newspaper," Elam said. "The daily news is the quintessen-
tial example of mental clutter. In half an hour, you can fill your mind
with a hundred pieces of information that have nothing whatsoever
to do with your own life. A hundred sources of stress that you can do
nothing about.

"The newspaper is other people's stories, not your own. Likewise
television. Movies. Novels. History. Biography. All of it is other people's
stories, and many of them are people who don't even exist."

His voice had underlined the "other people" and now he paused,
for additional emphasis.

"Perhaps these stories make you feel happy. Or sad. Or angry. All
of that is emotional energy wasted. There is only one story you need
be concerned with and that is your own. It is the only one you have
any control over.

"Perhaps one day you read in the newspaper that a certain baseball
team has lost a game, and you think you feel sad. But are you sad, in
truth? You have been reading about strangers playing a game whose
existence was arbitrary to begin with. Your own life has not changed.
The sadness you think you feel is a perfect example of a manufactured emotion, which has nothing to do with anything real."

I had been trying, at least some of the time, to keep an open
mind, but when Elam started talking about baseball, a swarm of
protests came leaping up in my throat and suddenly I knew why he
looked so familiar.

It wasn't the man I had seen. It was the beard. Guthrie's beard, down to the millimeter. The natural man, living his real, true, self-authentic life. I'd seen Elam each morning for the last four days, and his beard hadn't changed a millimeter. It was the same perfect 1.95 centimeters, all unruly straggles down the neck shaved clean. As if, having discovered the exact length of beard that expressed his true self, he had also found some miraculous way to halt its growth.

My own spiritual growth came to a halt then and there. When Elam invited each of us to share some moment of deep emotion from our own lives, I talked about how crushingly disappointed I had been when the Seattle Mariners lost in the playoffs.

Elam looked at me, hard, and I suspected that the real emotion happening in his real life was furious irritation, but he refrained from expressing it. It wasn't in his manual of appropriate phrases to tell me I was being a pain in the ass, or even to say that my example of a deep emotion looked pretty damned shallow. He stared and I stared back, and neither of us said anything, and nothing that was real right then made it anywhere close to daylight.

I think he knew that if he questioned the honesty of my choice, he'd have me right back in his face saying who the hell are you to tell me Griffey's game-winning home run last night was a piece of clutter and I'm a stooge if I feel happy about it.

hi pat, i really am wasting my money now, because there's nothing the guy can say that i won't argue with. i feel like a complete alien here. everyone else seems to feel that their lives are being transformed, that they finally understand themselves and accept themselves and feel at peace. but what if a person doesn't want to sit around contemplating the nameless, infinite it?

i look around at all of us with our fat bank accounts and our lexus or whatever out in the parking lot, paying this guy big bucks to tell us it's okay to be complacent, that there's not a thing we can change in this world except our own attitude, and all we should be thinking about is our own lives. i guess i don't find my own life so overwhelmingly fascinating i could never get bored thinking about it, and i don't buy elam's idea that reading the newspaper and getting pissed off about something like homeless people is just a way of avoiding my own issues. or if it is, then i guess the people we call heroes, like martin luther king, must have had a shitload of issues.

i came here thinking i might get some ideas about doing something, and all they want to talk about is how okay it is not to do anything.

am i just a constitutionally misaligned person, that i can't deal with this place? jordy

Hi, Jordy, If you're right about all the other people there, that they're in midlife and chronically overscheduled, then it probably feels like paradise to be told to sit still and do nothing. But the place does sound a little coercive, in its peaceful, passive way.

I'm not sure misalignment is the right word for an aversion to entities that want people to line up, fit in and not ask questions. Armies, for instance, or computer databases. Churches. Cemeteries. I'd say argue away. I know the town of Kilgore and I found out a lot more about each other when we started arguing than we ever did when I was quietly going along minding my own business.

And as a side point, if you were being fully cooperative, I wouldn't be getting any mail. Pat

I wasn't actually expelled from Cloudwater. An action that definite would have contradicted its fundamental operating principle, that what is meant to happen will happen, if you simply let it. And perhaps it did, in fact, because I was clearly not meant to be there. To me, the place felt like a sensory deprivation chamber, and for everyone else, I was probably a low-grade irritant, like a housefly buzzing and banging against the window, trying to get out.

On my last day there, I broke the rule of silence. Not in any big way. But enough. At lunch, I had just dug my fork into the mound of beans and rice on my plate when I felt a balloon of air gather itself deep in my lungs, vibrate up my throat, and push itself out between my lips in a long, mournful "*Mo-o-o-o-o-o-oo*."

Every person at the table turned to stare at me. Gavin had a hand over his mouth, suppressing a laugh, but everyone else looked shocked and outraged. I shrugged in apology. I knew what I'd done was infantile, and I hadn't planned it. It just came out.

The silence was palpable. Not the peaceful, cud-chewing silence of self-acceptance. This was the silence of people who are furious but don't know what to do about it.

Elam knew what to do, however. At lunchtime, he ate with us, and in keeping with his role as the guide to our seeking, he led by example. He did absolutely nothing. It was as if I had done nothing, as if I did not exist, in fact, or at least the sound I had made did not exist.

In that moment, I could see exactly what Cloudwater was all about. It was about ignoring real reality and living in a reality created by your own will. Anything unacceptable did not exist. You didn't need to explore the world or life or other people. You simply created a reality out of those things whose existence you chose to acknowledge, those whose existence would not disturb your own serenity. And maybe Elam preached self-acceptance, but it came with a gigantic string attached, that your self first had to be acceptable to his view of the world.

In that moment, I ceased to be a seeker and became an outside observer, and it did wonders for my own serenity. I ate the rest of my meal contentedly, as I would eat the local cuisine in a foreign country. I did not have to fit in. I was just a visitor here.

That night I was midway through composing an email when there was a knock on the door. I assumed it was Gavin and went to let him in, without even exiting the message.

Instead of Gavin, I found myself facing Elam. In a reflex of guilt, I looked back over my shoulder at the Powerbook.

Elam didn't say anything. He just looked at the computer, with a kind of patient sorrow, like a person of perfect virtue confronting inescapable evidence of human weakness.

Finally he asked, "What do you think would be appropriate in this situation?"

"I think probably I should leave," I said.

He nodded. He was silent for a moment and then said, "I think that would be best."

I began to gather up my things and put them in the duffel bag.

"You may wait until morning," he said. "I didn't mean immediately."

"I did."

hi, mom, i expect you'll be relieved to hear that i did not fall in love with cloudwater. in fact, i was telepathically encouraged to leave, because my discontent was making it hard for other people to enjoy serenity. so i won't be going back for annual booster shots.

i can't say it was even a vacation. but to look on the bright side, i've eliminated one potential future from consideration. love, jordy

Dear Jordy, Speaking of potential futures, have you considered

simply looking for a different job? There must be companies
who still offer a challenge to your brain. Love, Mom

does your job offer a challenge to the brain? love, j

As much as a crossword puzzle. It's nothing innovative or mind-
expanding, but the time passes pleasantly enough. That's plenty
for me right now. Love, Mom

If I came home to a woman I loved and two dogs, maybe it would
be plenty for me, too. I thought about getting a dog, at least. But
what was a dog going to do all day in Sunnyvale?

When I got back to Sunnyvale, I felt as if the world around me had
been containerized. The sun glared down and ricocheted off pavement and plate glass. The occasional dog was leashed, to ensure it did
not soil the sidewalk. The town was clean, spacious, orderly and empty
of people. All the people were in containers, in houses and offices and
shopping malls, or else in cars or on bicycles transporting themselves
as rapidly as possible from one container to another.

I fled to San Francisco, in search of streets that were alive and air
that was damp and misty. I found myself standing in front of Nieman
Marcus, staring at a coat that cost two thousand dollars.

But at least the streets were inhabited. Most people were hurrying,
but a few were strolling. I joined the strollers, gazing through windows at leather handbags and boots, coated aluminum cookware, crystal, Cuisinarts, then espresso bars, sushi bars, vegetarian cafes, then
VCRs, cameras, skateboards, a bookshop, an art gallery, silver jewelry, T-shirts and team jerseys, evening gowns, sportswear.

I glanced down an alley, saw what looked like a pile of trash and
secondhand clothes, and then realized it was an old woman asleep,

curled up among her possessions. I continued on, past CDs, imported olives and pasta, home computers, men's sport coats, then a man sitting in a doorway, with a coffee can for spare change and a sign propped against his knees: "I don't drink, smoke or do drugs." A beggar with a resumé, to prove he was worthy of our compassion.

I passed rugs imported from Nepal, specialty coffees, a toy store, then another beggar, this one making no claims about his lifestyle. Probably he should have. His upturned Giants cap was having much less success than the virtuous coffee can. Probably he was too passive. He was slouched in a corner where one storefront was inset from the next. His sign said simply, "Anything you can spare. Thanks."

He had a good location, though, next to a confectioner's shop that poured gusts of chocolate-scented air into the street every time the door opened. I stopped in front of the window and gazed at the chocolate—silver trays of bonbons, hand-dipped in imported dark chocolate, laid out in elegant tiers, gorgeous, almost like jewels or fine handicrafts. Thirty-two dollars a pound. Forty dollars a pound. One bite cost a dollar.

I glanced at the beggar again, and my look must have given him hope. "Some change, mister?" he said. He didn't sound like he expected success. Probably that was why he wasn't having much. Ours was a nation of free enterprise. A man must believe in himself. He must sell himself. No one wanted anything to do with losers. Their failure might be catching.

I didn't have much change, so I pulled out a couple of ones and tossed them into the cap. If I had thought he would light up with gratitude, I was wrong. His expression didn't change. He said, "Thanks, mister," as indifferently as he had asked for money.

I couldn't tear myself away from the chocolates. Not that I wanted to eat any. I just felt mesmerized. The cost of a pound of these chocolates would probably buy a two-month supply of beans and rice. With one hazelnut truffle, you could open your mouth and swallow six meals in a bite. My stomach started to churn.

The door of the shop opened, and a woman came out. She was exquisitely dressed, a pale cashmere sweater, pearls and gold. Her figure, her skin, her nails, every inch of her announced that she might be past forty, but she had not let herself go. Her hair looked like a shampoo commercial. She was very slender, all the bones of her face sharply outlined. A faint, tasteful whiff of her perfume accented the smell of chocolate that swept through the doorway with her. In her hand, she carried a bag from the store, forest green with gold lettering.

She glanced at the beggar, and her mouth curled in distaste. Then she glanced at me.

"You would think people like that could find a more suitable place to park themselves," she said.

"Such as where?" I asked, politely.

"I don't care where," she said. "I just want to be able to do my shopping without stepping over drunks."

Something snapped. I think it was the phrase "do my shopping," as if she had been buying bread and milk.

"Do you actually need those chocolates?" I asked.

"Need? What do you mean, need? It's my sister's birthday, so yes I need . . . " She started edging away from me.

"That guy would enjoy them more than your sister will. Your sister is probably worried about getting fat. Why don't you give him a couple?"

"What are you talking about? He's drunk. What would he do with chocolates? Are you crazy?"

I leapt forward and snatched the bag out of her hand.

"What are you doing! Give that back—"

I pulled out the gold lettered box and yanked off the gold elastic. "You can spare a couple, can't you? A tithe for the poor . . . "

The woman tried to grab the box away from me.

I pulled off the lid and held out the chocolates to the beggar. "Here, take a couple."

He was scrambling to his feet, trying to get away from me, too.

"I don't know this guy," he said. "I had nothing to do with this. I don't want any trouble . . . "

The woman snatched at the box again, and it slipped out of my hand. The precious chocolates scattered across the pavement.

"What do you think you're doing?" the woman shrieked. "You had better pay for those!"

The beggar had collected his cap and the rug he had been sitting on and was hurrying away.

Suddenly I didn't feel furious any more, just sick and stupid. What was the point?

"I'm calling the police," the woman said. "Don't let him leave," she added, to the half dozen passersby who had stopped to stare. She went back into the shop.

I followed her inside and shoved a couple of twenties at her. "Here, buy yourself some fucking chocolate."

I walked back out of the store and down the street, slowly. None of the people watching tried to stop me.

What was wrong with me? I had just dumped two months' worth of food into the gutter and for what? What did I know about the woman, anyway? Maybe she was thin from cancer and not from a health club. Maybe her sister had lost her job and needed consolation. Maybe her husband had left her for the maid. Forty-dollar chocolates didn't necessarily make your life perfect. I should know.

I gave notice the next day. I had no idea what I was going to do. I only knew I had to get out of this place.

"What could we offer that would make you stay?" Mips asked.

"A different planet," I said.

He laughed. "I'll be right behind you. In seventeen months and twelve days."

"You could skip out on your contract," I said. "There's bound to be a loophole."

"None that isn't plugged with a big fat stock option."

When I called Mom to tell her about my decision, her first question was typical: "What exactly are you going to do next, now that you've quit this job?"

"I'm rich," I said. "I'm taking early retirement."

"You're twenty-two years old. You don't have a career to retire from."

"Why do I need a career at all? Maybe I'll grow orchids and work on my tennis backhand."

"Be serious. You can't work on your backhand for the next fifty years."

"Mom, I don't know. Okay? I can't think about fifty years. I'm just thinking about right now. And for right now I've been thinking I might do some traveling."

I hadn't been thinking that, but the moment I said it, I thought it sounded like a great idea.

"Where will you go?"

"I'm not sure. Maybe Latin America. I've heard it's cheap to travel there."

"It's cheap because it's poor. I'd have thought you'd had your fill of fleabag apartments by the time you were in third grade."

"All the best baseball players are coming from there," I said.

"I'm not surprised. Start chopping sugar cane when you're eight years old, you build up a lot of arm strength. And a lot of motivation to find a different line of work."

"Then maybe I'll come fleeing back to Sunnyvale and kiss the pavement outside my apartment. I just want to try something different for a while. You remember how you got sick of green in Portland. Well maybe I'm just sick of honey-gold stucco and sunshine."

She was quiet for a minute. Then she asked, very tentatively, "Are you sure you're okay?"

"I'm fine, Mom. I'm just a little restless."

Her intuition was working fine. She knew that all was not well with me. But I didn't want to talk to her about it, and she couldn't force me. In my present state, I wanted someone who would go out and get drunk with me and ask no questions, not someone who would sit there nursing a glass of Perrier and hinting that I should get professional help.

> hi, pat, don't you think a person needs to do something totally irrational every once in a while? i suppose it sounds like a futile gesture, to go off traveling, the kind of thing old decaying rich families used to do with their useless sons, send them off on the grand tour in the hope that it would somehow make them less useless. but i feel as though i am on the wrong track and need something to knock me onto a different one, even something crazy.
>
> i know no rational person would say i was on the wrong track when i had a great job, unlimited future, huge amounts of bucks and a nice place to live. but i suddenly had this vision of myself middle-aged, trying to decide which of two very expensive sets of golf clubs to buy. that's not what i want to be thinking about when i'm forty. i want to be doing something that makes a difference. i don't want to end up as a rich old fat guy who fusses because a bird messed on the hood of his mercedes. or a rich old skinny guy who cooks a third-world diet on his multi-thousand-dollar professional-style stove and congratulates himself on having simplified his life.

it's like i've got to get out of this place because it's too nice. is that nuts? j

Jordy, I've done only one crazy thing, the sculpture, and it changed my life. Pat

chapter eleven

At first I thought I'd let the travel agent plan my trip, on the assumption she knew more about other countries than I did. But as soon as I mentioned Mexico, Guatemala, maybe the Caribbean, she started burbling on about which resorts had the nicest white-sand beaches. I said I wasn't looking for a place to lie on the beach. I could go to Santa Barbara for that. So then she said, not to worry, there was plenty of good shopping right near the beach. I said I wasn't looking for shopping either. I'd had my fill. I wanted to see places that were interesting. Different. Culture, if you like. She said in that case I'd be better off going to Europe. When I said I didn't want to go to Europe, I wanted to go to Latin America, she heaved a big sigh and said she supposed I could go see some Mayan ruins.

At that point, I told her just to book me the flights down and back, and a hotel for the first night, and I'd figure out the rest for myself. After I'd looked through a couple of guidebooks and done some poking around on the Internet, I went back to the agent and said I'd concede her the Mayan ruins, she could book that flight for me, too.

I didn't need any of Mom's grim predictions to know I was going to places that were poor. I had the TV news images, the descriptions in newspapers. In an hour on the net, I'd come across reams of bleak statistics. People earning in a year what I earned in a week. People who didn't have flush toilets. People who left school at age ten to start working.

But the images on TV are two-dimensional, and statistics don't have any smell. Statistics travel through the eyes to the brain; smells take a straight-line path to the gut. Once I got to Latin America, it took me about three days to decide on a new definition of what was real in a person's life: reality was what you could smell.

My first night I spent in the hotel the travel agent had booked. In the morning I woke up and looked out the window at a view that would never be called "too nice."

For an American, I had been poor enough, and Duane Selby had been a lot poorer. But compared to the neighborhood I was looking at, both he and I had lived like minor nobility. My hotel was barricaded behind high walls topped with broken glass, and beyond the walls lay an accretion of tin-roofed shacks the size of garden sheds, built from mud-bricks or plywood, a shantytown squatting on the oddment of land between the hotel wall and another concrete barrier in the distance. In the patches of dirt between the buildings, bony dogs and scraggly chickens scavenged for bits of garbage among the litter and weeds. It was my guess the people who lived in the shacks were familiar with every nuance to be found in a plate of beans.

The hotel was an American chain, the kind you could book by computer from the United States. It was a very clean, very well lighted place, tinkling with fountains, gleaming with polished chrome and glass, echoing with fine-leather footsteps on marble floors. I had felt like an intruder, checking in. Instead of an elegant leather tip-tap, my sneakers made rubbery little squeaks on the marble, announcing that I did not belong here. My backpack hung off-balance from the bellman's hand, bumping against his creased pantleg, and when I fumbled in my pocket for a tip, the crumpled bills fell out and landed on the floor. The desk clerk had looked me up and down, skeptically, and I thought that he and I were wishing about equally that I was somewhere else.

Even so, this was my world, this clean, efficient, modern American hotel, one of the field offices for the corporate management of the global economy. I was a player on that organizational chart. A very tiny player but, still, one who was situated on the plus side of the power equation. I could walk up to the polished reception desk, slap down my VISA card and wheels would start to turn. If I ate beans, it was by choice, probably because I was worrying about my cholesterol.

The hotel felt like an isolation bubble, ready to be dropped into place in any unsanitary spot where there might be some money to be made. It could have been anywhere. It could have been in Chicago, or Atlanta, except that here the ice machine displayed a large sign assuring me that the ice had been made from purified water and not from the water drunk by the people I could see out my window, seven stories below.

Before I left the States, I had reserved a rental car for exploring the countryside. But now I thought, if I went touring around the country in a nice shiny car, it would be the same as the hotel, me safely isolated behind glass looking out at a different world. I called up to cancel the car, packed up my stuff and caught a bus.

Two weeks and three countries later, the world outside was inside me, too, and I was curled up, fetal position, in a very inexpensive *pensión* in Guatemala City, alternately shivering, sweating and making desperation sprints down the hall to the toilet. For three days I told myself it was just the ordinary *turista* described in the guidebook and I could ride it out. On the fourth day, I wobbled over to the landlady's apartment and asked for directions to a doctor.

I must have looked moderately dreadful, because the landlady blanched and insisted on taking me by the arm and leading me to the doctor's office herself. After probes and cultures and several hours of waiting, the doctor told me it was more than just the ordinary turista; it was amoebic dysentery. Great, I thought. Why drive a Chevy when you can drive a Cadillac?

The doctor wrote out a prescription for Flagyl, then asked, in excellent English and with a distinct air of disdain, whether I had perhaps been traveling somewhere more rural, somewhere in the lowlands. His tone said clearly that I could not possibly have contracted dysentery here in a modern city, high in the mountains. When I said, yes, I had been to places that were lower, wetter, more rural, he nodded and almost tut-tutted, as if I had just told him I had been vacationing in a petri dish.

The Flagyl worked, but not instantly, so I spent two more days more or less immobile in my room. At intervals, the landlady came fluttering in with bottles of water and pop, and inquiries about whether I was taking my pills properly. In between her visits I lay staring at the gray block walls beside my bed and listening to the faint *McGyver* theme music and dubbed dialogue coming from her apartment.

After almost a week of fever and nausea, I found the first part of my trip had run together into a montage of images that were vivid but disjointed. Flies crawling on candies in a street vendor's cart. Dust outlining the snot on the face of a child peddling fruit. Decrepit, overloaded trucks and buses, grinding and downshifting up winding mountain roads, enveloped in clouds of black smoke. Those same trucks and buses flying full-speed down the hills, careening around hairpin turns and threatening to run oncoming traffic off into a ravine. The noise of a radio blaring in a cafe, a frenetic soccer announcer screaming *"Goooooooollll!"* like a person swept over a waterfall. Tiny houses with yards stripped bare of vegetation by chickens and goats. Children playing soccer barefoot in a dusty street, using any object that would roll. A garish billboard with a woman in a bikini caressing a car battery. A banner in a village announcing the installation of a potable water supply, the way Kilgore would announce its Fourth of July celebration.

The images faded in and out. What didn't fade was the memory of the smells. Some were peripheral, introductory—the fumes of city traffic, tropical flowers, the wet-plaster smell of fresh stucco. But the one that stuck, right down in the early-hominid part of the brain, was the smell of an open-air market. It was like life, in your face, in your lungs, through your pores—human bodies not washed too recently, onions frying, oranges, chili peppers, dog shit, the hot metallic smell of an electric motor, just-ground cornmeal and, over everything, the sweetish stench of meat hanging in the sun.

The smell brought back the place, a small town in the mountains, hours away from Guatemala City. The market was a miniature city built with poles and canvas and blankets. Rows and rows of stalls filled the central plaza and spilled down all but the narrowest side streets. Merging with the crowd, I had wandered through the market at random, not shopping, just taking it in. I passed baskets of fresh vegetables and racks of T-shirts, stopped to watch a man sharpening knives and scissors with a treadle grindstone and then moved on, past boxes of Frisbees and yo-yos, piles of hand-woven place mats and scarves, a woman frying tortillas and a stall selling dried beans, a dozen different kinds in open fifty-pound burlap bags laid out on the ground. Around me, the aisles were dense with people, two continuous streams of bodies moving past each other at a slow shuffle. The market was as jammed as a mall at Christmas time, but no one seemed to be in a hurry, no one seemed worried that a bargain might be gone before they got to it.

On the highways, the drivers were always in a frantic rush, as if every one of them had a wife in labor in the back seat. In heavy city traffic, they zipped from lane to lane, one hand on the horn. On two-lane mountain roads, they pulled out to pass in the face of an oncoming truck. They seemed blithely confident that a space could be found for three abreast and, strangely, they were right. All three drivers adjusted on the fly, and one slipped through the gap, with side mirrors missing by an inch.

But on foot, people seemed to have all the time in the world, to feel no need to hurry, push or squeeze through gaps. At lunch in a cafe, I could sit with a book for an hour, an hour and a half, and never feel a glare of impatience from the proprietor, never be prodded by the waiter, would I like my check?

Again and again, I met the same incongruity. Markets selling intricate hand-woven fabrics side by side with plastic yo-yos and souvenir baseball caps. A mass of brilliant purple flowers climbing the wall of a makeshift plywood shack. People with faces of ancient Mayan beauty dressed in cheap, mass-produced American-style clothing. Mountains that rose towering over my head, while my feet walked through litter, dust and goat shit.

I felt divided myself. At times I could travel quiet and unremarked—a passenger on a bus, a stranger pausing on a footpath to watch a farmer plowing with a walk-behind tractor. People noticed me briefly, occasionally smiled, but they were busy with their own concerns and not particularly concerned with me.

But when I came to places that were supposed to be "interesting," places with some claim to beauty or culture, all of a sudden I, too, was an object of interest. I became as conspicuous as a billboard, an American tourist, swarmed by people offering to sell me something, guide me somewhere or pose in native garb for a photograph. In the eyes of local entrepreneurs, I was a walking wallet. A family could live for a week on my pocket change.

Surrounded by the clamor of urgings, there was no way I could feel anonymous or peaceful. I stopped seeing the things that were beautiful, the faces and mountains. They receded into the haze, and all I could see were the dirt and the shabbiness, right in front of me, close enough to smell and touch. Sometimes I paid people a few coins to guide me or be photographed, sometimes I said no and passed by, but either way it seemed that the gulf between us was bottomless, that I could toss in coins forever, everything I owned, and never feel that less was needed.

I kept remembering a particular moment in a public market in Mexico, back near the beginning of my trip. I had stopped to look at a stall of toys made out of scrap metal—spark plugs, nails, rivets, wire, sheet metal—bent or cut to shape and soldered together to make cars, tractors and train engines. They reminded me of the clown commandos my mother had manufactured from her scavengings, and I was tempted to buy one.

As I was standing there, looking, a group of uniformed schoolchildren surrounded me and began asking me questions. Was I an American? How long had I been here? Did I like their town? Where was I going next? I answered their questions, as well as I could with the remnants of my high school Spanish.

Then one boy stumped me totally. If I was an American, if I lived in such a wonderful place, then why had I come to Mexico?

Because it's beautiful, I said. Safe answer, polite and reasonably true. But the boy persisted. Isn't the United States beautiful, he asked. Yes, it's beautiful, too, I said. Then why come here, he asked again.

Why had I come? The Rockies and Sierras, the Arizona desert, the coast of California, all of them are as beautiful as anything in Mexico. Did I come just so that I could look at people who lived in tin-roofed huts and be glad I didn't? Rich people come look at poor people so that they can be extra glad they're rich? Had I traveled several thousand miles just so that I could go home and bow down in front of my household appliances and emission-controlled cars and water faucets, and give thanks?

I almost canceled the last part of my trip. Surely I had seen enough goats and grubby children and mud huts to get the point, that I did indeed live in paradise and if I wasn't content, the defect must be in me. But I already had the plane ticket out to the ruins of the Mayan city Tikal, and it was the only place on my itinerary that the travel agent had thought was of any interest whatsoever. So I had just as well go see it.

Tikal was the first place I'd been where I was not constantly reminded of my wealth and good fortune. Not because I was any less wealthy, or the place any less poor. There just wasn't anyone alive to remind me.

There were plenty of ghosts. The whole city was one big spook house. Ghosts and tourists, that's all there were in this place.

The tourists I could see, posing for pictures next to a sacrificial altar or puffing their way up the knee-high steps to the top of a pyramid. The ghosts I couldn't see, but I could feel them walking around and whispering. They were as present and palpable as the costumed employees who made historical theme parks "come to life." It wasn't their choice to be here walking around, creating atmosphere. They had been well on their way to a peaceful oblivion, their city crumbling into the earth, engulfed and digested by the vegetation. Then people came along with machinery and chainsaws that unearthed the city, exposed it to the sun and the tourists, and woke up the ghosts to populate it.

I could feel them jostling me as I strolled through their public market. I could feel them turning irritably from a meal or a conversation when I walked into their living rooms. I felt myself intruding on their privacy. Why else would they have built these coffinlike interiors in the midst of tropical splendor, unless it was to hide themselves away?

Their living rooms gave me the creeps, actually. I felt pressed down by mountains of stone. The walls were thicker than the rooms were wide and the only light came from the tunneled doorways and a few narrow slits cut through the walls. The ceilings closed in over my head, crude corbeled arches, slab piled on slab, cantilevered inwards until the two sides met at the center. A thousand tons of rock had been piled up to make a room the size of a closet.

Whoever lived here had been a tycoon, for sure, commanding companies of slaves to drag and hoist those slabs into place. And what did he get for all his power and wealth? The privilege of living in a dark, damp tunnel, in the middle of a landscape where anyone with the wit to set up four posts and a square of thatch could live in a shady bungalow drenched in fragrant tropical warmth. Weird. But I suppose he had needed to do something to show he was important.

And now the ones who had lived under thatch were resting peacefully, digested into trees and vines, while the tycoons were stuck here on display. Their civilization was dead, but its body had been embalmed and laid out in public view. Would the tycoons have built these pyramids, monuments to the hope of immortality, if they had known that their role would be to stand around in Goofy and Mickey Mouse costumes while a foreigner forty generations into the future took photos of his girlfriend mugging beside the carved image of a god?

Other tourists climbed the pyramid, snapped their photos and descended, but I stayed on my perch, gazing down at the city as the sun dropped toward the horizon. Seen from the pyramid, the city was a different place from the one I had seen up close. Instead of a cluster of dimly lit, massively oppressive stone cells, it became a beautiful geometry of terraces, courtyards and stairways, a shifting pattern of shapes drawn in light and shadow. It seemed a place that had never really been meant for daily life, but only to be admired from a great height. I tried to picture the courtyards beaten into dust by human feet, but all I could see were the shaded green rectangles among walls of stone, the once-trampled dust now growing a carpet of grass that the feet of ghosts did not bruise.

Only a few times in my life had I felt an urge to pray, and it had always been in some moment of desperation: Please, god, let me make this field goal; Please, god, make her love me. At this moment, I wasn't desperate, but I did feel an impulse to say something. Not to ask a favor, just to be friendly. Like there was something alive here and I wanted to talk to it. Or maybe it seemed rude not to talk to it, because it felt so present. Like sitting in a room with someone and not saying anything. But what was I supposed to say? Hey there, dude, how's it going? *Nah,* nothing special, just checking in, saying hello, because I noticed you sitting there.

And maybe I was praying, in a way. If there was ever a place where a person could talk to thin air and not feel weird, this was it. Not that I actually said anything out loud. But with or without words, as I sat watching the shadows lengthen across the ruins, I began to feel a vague expectancy, as if I had just murmured to the cosmos, casually, that I wouldn't mind if something came along to change my life.

My reverie was interrupted by the sight of a woman scuttling across the courtyard below and launching herself up the steps of the pyramid as if she were running to catch a train. By the midway point, she had slowed a little, but she still climbed with a look of breathless haste. She was dressed in bright-colored, hand-woven cottons and had white flyaway hair, cut blunt with half a dozen swift chops of the scissors. She was carrying a string bag that appeared to be equipped for every contingency—umbrella, guidebook, camera, water bottle, snack food, raincoat, all visible through the mesh. As she neared the top step, I could see sparkly blue eyes surrounded by a web of wrinkles. She was in her sixties, minimum, but evidently her system was equipped with turbochargers.

She half-staggered from the last step onto the summit, then whirled and looked toward the setting sun.

"I made it!" she said.

She pulled a cushion out of her bag and flopped down beside me, panting. "My plane was late and I only got in this minute, but I thought if I hurried I could just catch the sunset. Isn't this place glorious? And horrible, too, if you think about it. All those slaves and human sacrifices. I never know what to think. Because it's so utterly magnificent, but so many people must have suffered miserably in building it. And the only one with his face on a stone is whichever brutal egomaniac happened to be king. Everyone else has gone to feed the worms.

"On the other hand, maybe that's not all bad. Do you think that's what they really mean, about the meek inheriting the earth? The pompous get petrified into granite, and the poor get transformed into dirt. And then into grapes and then into wine and then into you and me. I'd like to think that, but somehow it comes around to looking like a way to tell poor people to stop complaining and be glad they're poor."

She'd been watching the sunset as the words poured out, but suddenly she stopped and whipped around and looked at me more closely, with an expression of worry. "I hope you're not devout. Or I've probably offended you dreadfully."

I shook my head. "No, not at all."

In fact I was completely spooked because of the way she'd come flying up the pyramid, like a messenger with a reply to my petition, and because what she'd just said was so close to what I'd been thinking myself.

"I'm too confused to be devout," I added.

She burst into a smile. "Oh, thank goodness. Where there's

confusion, there's hope. Somebody who's certain of everything had just as well be dead already. What on earth do they have to think about? And what can you say to them, since everything is already decided in their minds? I didn't think you looked like that. And you're much too young to have hardening of the neurons. When you're my age, maybe, but not now. Although I hope I never start acting old, not if it means turning stodgy and giving up hope."

She pulled out her bottle of water and took a long drink. "*Whew.* I was dry. That feels better."

She looked at me again, curiously. "Are you a student?" she asked. I shook my head.

"No. Of course you aren't. You'd be in school. So you're what . . . on vacation?"

"I'm retired," I said. "I can do whatever I like."

"But that's marvelous," she exclaimed. "The world should have more people like you. And what do you like?"

"I'm not completely sure . . . "

"That's tremendous! That means absolutely everything is possible. Someone your age should not have ruled anything out. The whole of life is laid out before you, a positive banquet of possibilities."

She took another drink of water, then held out the bottle. "Would you like some?"

"No, thanks. I'm fine."

"My name is Breeze, by the way," she said. "What's yours?"

"McNeil. Jordy McNeil. I'm pleased to meet you, Mrs. Breeze."

She laughed. "Not Mrs. Breeze. Just plain Breeze. It's my whole name."

"Your parents gave you a single name? They must have been way ahead of their time."

The words were out before it occurred to me that it might be rude to comment on how old she was. On the other hand, she had been talking about it from word one, so she probably wouldn't mind.

She laughed again. "It wasn't my parents. I named myself. The names my parents gave me were a prison of dreary conventionality. My husband's last name was even worse. I shed them all years ago." She fished in her string bag until she found her wallet and extracted her driver's license. "See, it's legal and official."

In the photo, she was wearing a purple and orange scarf, rolled and tied into a Willie Nelson headband around her shoulder-length white hair. She was grinning broadly.

"Now you must tell me all the things you have in mind to do with your retirement," she said.

She had focused right in on my problem. "I don't have anything in mind," I said.

With Breeze, that wasn't a problem for long. She rapidly filled the vacuum with ideas of her own, dozens of them, offered helter-skelter like scatterings of birdseed for me to pick through. I could continue my travels to other continents. I could build my own house. I could take up yoga, or step dancing. I could learn to play a musical instrument. I could meditate and keep a journal. I could run for political office. The possibilities were endless, and in her mind's eye, entrancing, all of them, even when they were diametrically opposed to one another. But the best idea of all, the one she returned to several times, was that I should come to Seattle and work as a volunteer with the nonprofit organization she had founded.

"Which organization is that?" I asked.

"It's called the Whole World Center."

I was about to say I had never heard of it, but caught myself. "I don't know much about it," I said. "What does it do?"

"Our guiding principle is that no problem exists in isolation. Every social and political imbalance in the world is connected to every other imbalance. To preserve the environment, we must stop overpopulation, and to stop overpopulation, we must end poverty, and to end poverty, we must end economic injustice, which is impossible as long as governments are controlled by the people who benefit from the injustice. It is useless to heal one illness in isolation. All of them must be healed at the same time, or else our efforts will be futile. Do you see?"

"I think so . . . "

I could see the concept, but I thought its application would be beyond the modeling capabilities of all the world's computers combined.

Her eyes were glowing. "I know what you're thinking. That it's impossible. That I'm a hopeless dreamer. As if one small organization could solve all the world's problems at once. But don't you see, they have to be solved at once, or the ones left unsolved just bring back the others. Nobody ever dares look at the whole situation, because it seems too complex, but that is what must be done. Our organization is meant to be a seed that will grow into a worldwide movement, millions and millions of people whose every moment is lived as a step toward healing. Every single person matters. What you do matters. You, Jordy, are the keystone of the whole process. If you choose to take action, you become a center of positive energy that will spread healing wherever you go."

"Really?"

Her smile was radiant. "Truly."

As the daylight faded, we climbed down the pyramid and walked back to the tourist compound outside the ruin. All the way there, Breeze went on talking with the bubbling exuberance that seemed to be her everyday mood. Her ideas did not exactly lead from one to the next in a coherent progression. They came flying out in all directions, like popcorn with the lid off. One minute she was stopping to identify some plant beside the path, and the next she was sputtering about some one of the multitude of injustices to be found in the human landscape, and all of it was fascinating and vitally important to her, whether the subject was the toxins emitted by the roots of a plant to eradicate competitors, or the toxins emitted by a corporate smokestack in pursuit of profit.

At the hotel, she exacted a promise that I would join her for dinner, and when we sat down together later, her conversation resumed almost midsentence, as if the intervening hour had been a pause for breath.

"Everything we do is a choice," she said. "For good or bad. Even toothpaste. Some kinds put bad chemicals down the drain. Others don't. Never mind into your mouth. So it's important to think about. Or toilet paper. If every person always uses two squares more than they need, it's something like five hundred million extra rolls every year. Just in the U.S. Don't quote me on the number. I'm not a mathematician. But it's something like that. And if everyone with a backyard used a clothesline instead of a dryer, we could shut down a couple of nuclear power plants.

"Or another thing. Think about marijuana. Do you know the real reason they don't want doctors to prescribe it? Because it would hurt the pharmaceutical companies. Nobody has a patent on marijuana. It's incredibly cheap. You can grow it anywhere. So no big corporation will make big profits off it, and it would compete with all the patented prescription drugs that cost a fortune. I was just talking to a friend who had to take antinausea drugs after chemotherapy. They cost something like thirty dollars a pill. You think that drug company wants to compete with a pot of marijuana on the window sill?"

The waiter brought a menu, which she glanced at absentmindedly, still talking.

"You always have to look at what's really going on. We should be writing our congressman. Well, don't get me started on that idea . . . "

Then suddenly her attention zeroed in on the back of the menu, where there was a list of beers, and she almost bounced out of her seat beckoning the waiter back to the table.

"La cerveza. No es Guatemala . . . " she began. She turned to me, in frustration. "I'm useless in Spanish. Do you know how to say they should serve local beer? Not American beer. That local products are better for their economy."

I made a try, but my Spanish was equally inadequate for making philosophical or political arguments.

"La cerveza de Guatemala. Es bueno. Por la economía. No la americana."

As I stumbled along, the waiter listened, polite but baffled. Finally he gestured for us to wait, hurried away and returned with the manager.

"There is some problem with the beer?" the manager asked.

"Oh, yes. Thank you," Breeze said. "I'm sorry to be troublesome. I just wanted to suggest that you serve beers from Guatemala. Not American beer. Or Mexican beer. It's much better for the economy of your country, to sell your local beer. And more interesting for your visitors."

The manager spread his hands in apology. "But the Americans always ask for American beer," he said. "Or else Dos Equis."

"But they shouldn't," Breeze protested. "Why do they come all the way to this country and then drink Budweiser? The local beer is just as good." She stopped herself abruptly, and then smiled, sweetly. "I know I'm asking too much. You have to have something American. But couldn't you have less American and more Guatemalan? It would make me so happy."

The manager smiled, too, still apologetic. "I don't know. I will try . . . "

"Thank you. I hope you will."

When the manager had left, she shrugged, laughing at herself. "I know. I know. It's such a tiny thing. But everything matters. That's the point."

"Now you'll have to come back sometime," I said. "To see if the menu has changed."

"I suppose I will."

In the morning, I met Breeze to tour the ruins again, and it was like keeping company with an electrically charged pinball. Breeze was never still, not for a single moment. If her body wasn't moving, her mind was. She wanted to inspect every tiny room, every passageway and terrace, every altar, every stairway, and all the while she kept up a running stream of commentary, which might or might not have anything to do with the immediate surroundings.

"Do you like this skirt I'm wearing?" she asked at one point, and before I was halfway through the word "yes," she was racing on. "I found it at a market. Eleven dollars, which is indecently cheap. I didn't say that. I didn't want to be insulting. But I didn't bargain, of course. It seemed immoral to try to talk the price down. Even if it's expected . . . "

She suddenly disappeared down a stairway into some dark cubbyhole in the stones. When she re-emerged, she was still pursuing the question of the skirt and its place in her personal philosophy.

"I don't know what to think about cotton," she said. "I know it's a natural fiber, but they use oceans of pesticides on the fields. It's one of the very worst crops. I wouldn't touch cottonseed oil for anything. But what else is there? Synthetics are mostly nonrenewable, and besides, I hate them. And you can't wear wool in the summer. I try to find organic cotton, when I can, but so often the colors are positively funereal."

She bent down to pick up an empty plastic bottle.

"They ought to have more trash cans," she said. "Although it's far worse at home, and we have no excuse. Our country is wonderful, but it's so infuriating, too. The world looks to us for leadership, and this is what we give them." She stuffed the bottle into her string bag.

"We should be exporting democracy and the Bill of Rights and better sewage treatment, and instead we're exporting junk food and plastic packaging."

For most of the morning, we zigzagged here and there, until we reached the far edge of the compound. There, in what seemed almost like untouched jungle, we came upon a path winding steeply up a wooded hillside. Breeze stopped abruptly and began rummaging through her bag.

"If this is what I think it is . . . "

She pulled out a guidebook and leafed through it.

"There's not much left of it, but I believe this is the tallest of the pyramids. Shall we go up?"

I looked at my watch. I was scheduled to catch a plane in the afternoon.

"I only have an hour before I have to catch the bus to the airport."

"Oh, an hour," she said. "That's plenty of time, if we keep moving."

She charged forward up the hill and I followed, laughing. "Right. Of course," I said. "Whatever was I worried about?"

On the climb, even Breeze lacked breath for conversation. The path wound steadily up, mostly through uninterrupted trees, but occasionally some giant stone slabs could be seen. Near the top, the woods opened out into a clearing, and the structure of the pyramid appeared. Much of it had collapsed and eroded away to dirt, but some of the walls and terraces remained.

At the top, we sat down on a crumbling ledge of stone to look at the view. For about half a minute, Breeze sat panting, not saying anything, but the moment she had regained enough breath to speak, she turned to me and said, "I've had an inspiration. I've thought of the job for you."

"You have?"

"It's the very thing. You know all about computers. And you have plenty of free time. You can go to work at Cyberplace. I'm afraid we couldn't pay you anything. And it's not in a very nice neighborhood. But that's the whole point, isn't it? The kids in nice neighborhoods have a computer in their own bedrooms, so they don't need somebody like you. I hope you'll think about it. You could make such a difference."

"This not-nice neighborhood is in Seattle?"

She nodded. "It's on the other side of the city from where I live."

"Does it really rain a lot in Seattle?"

"Oh, drat the rain! We get such bad press, and it becomes the only thing anyone thinks about. Not that it doesn't rain quite a bit. But you get used to it, and the city is so lovely. Most of it. After you've been there a while, you'll hardly notice the rain. Really."

"You don't understand," I said. "Rain is good."

hi, pat, i'm back in the land of the windshield sunshade. i'm not sure what i expected out of the trip to central america, maybe a new perspective, but what i did get in fact was something i could no way have predicted. in guatemala, i met the most amazing person. her name is breeze, and no i am not in love with her. she is almost as old as grandma. but she is so full of warmth and enthusiasm, and she makes you feel as if things really could change, if we just set about it. or at least she reminds you that they definitely won't change if we sit and do nothing. i think i am going to move to seattle and work with her organization.

do you think there are places that change the people who come to them? for a while, sitting up on the pyramid in the mayan ruin, i was feeling as if it might be changing me somehow. but then breeze showed up, and it turned out the change was outside, not inside.

i'm wondering, which do you think is more important, the

179

message or the messenger? sometimes i think about elam's way of being, how he seemed so totally integrated and consistent and peaceful, and i know his advice was probably very sensible, and then i look at breeze, who's all over the place and completely inconsistent, and i know she isn't realistic. but she's fun. so if it were you, would you listen to the person who makes sense or the person you like? jordy

Jordy, At the Mercantile, I listen to both, and everybody else, too. What was the change you thought the place had made? Pat

p, nothing, really. just spooking myself. i was thinking about all the work those people did, piling up tons and tons of stone just to get themselves a couple of hundred feet closer to the sky. they must have thought their god was right up there over their heads, almost in reach, if they could just pile up stones high enough. if they'd known you could shoot a rocket all the way to the moon and still find nothing but rock, nothing anywhere close to a god, they'd never have bothered, would they? i mean, why bother struggling and striving to get two hundred feet closer to something that might not even exist? even a pyramid starts to look pretty puny and futile these days. still, for a minute or two, i felt spooked, sitting up there, like the place really did mean something. but when breeze came along, i decided the portents might be different from what i'd been thinking.

it has occurred to me that one person cannot be in two cars at the same time, so perhaps i will sell one. j

J, I think your pyramid-building might be a sort of working definition of god—the entirely nonrational, non-Darwinian urge to be closer to the sky. Along with all the other marvels, Monet paintings, for instance, and volunteer work in nursing homes, that do nothing to ensure one's own survival or perpetuate one's own DNA.

Which of your cars do you plan to sell, since they are equally amusing but impractical? P

both. i'm buying a toyota.

Seriously?

yes.

Why?

it's a step in the right direction.

chapter twelve

For a while, I thought Seattle had been falsely advertised. I arrived there in July, and in the next two months it rained only three times. It made me wonder why on earth the Mariners played baseball in a dome. Somebody like Griffey should have the whole wide sky over him when he played.

When I told Breeze my worries, she started laughing uproariously.

"You're the first person who has ever complained about too much sun in Seattle."

"I'm not complaining," I said. "Just wondering."

"Relax. Summer is the dry season."

"In California, summer is the dry season, too," I said. "The trouble is, summer lasts about nine and a half months."

"This is not California. I promise."

In fact, I wasn't seriously worried, because in spite of all the clear, sunny days, the vegetation had a damp look. There was no honey color in sight, only deep coniferous green, and gray, and chocolate brown. During the summer in California, the wild vegetation settled into a peaceful doze and turned uniformly golden, like someone tanning on the beach. Here the grass dried out in irregular brown patches that looked reluctant and fretful, eager for this season to be over. I knew the clouds would come.

hi, pat, for the first time in quite a while i feel like i might be on the right track. i'm not feeling so miserable about not having a woman to be my "one and only." breeze makes you feel like you can love just about anything and you don't have to focus it all on a particular person. you can be in love with a leaf that drifts down and lands next to your coffee cup at a sidewalk cafe. just for a minute, maybe, but then you can be in love with a waiter who makes a joke, or with a 1958 thunderbird you see on the street, or anything at all. you can be in love every minute of the day, with a thousand different things, and you don't have to own any of them. well, that's not actually what she says. it's sort of my own interpretation. but i think it's the same idea. anyway, i'm really happy here.

breeze has a big house surrounded by huge evergreens and lots of shrubs. the ground in her back yard never dries out. it's all moss and ferns, and it makes the house feel like an animal's burrow, or an indian baby's cradle, tucked away in the shade. the house isn't exactly a modest little cottage, though, and it's right in the middle of a high-class old seattle neighborhood. she says it's an artifact from her former life that she hasn't mustered the strength of character to give up.

maybe sometime i'll find myself a place like that, but right now i've got two rooms over a sub shop in the university district. when the shop's open, i live in a sort of salami-meatball-provolone steam cloud, but i don't really mind. it's close to everything and right on a bus line, luckily. breeze told me i was positively forbidden to live out in the suburbs and commute by

car. partly philosophical, but she also said the traffic is so hor-
rendous i would be popping antihypertensive drugs before i
was thirty. here i can bus or bike to everything, and breeze has
my car stashed away in her driveway.

how is skipper? give him a hug for me. j

Hi, Jordy, I never thought it would happen, but Skipper is starting to slow down a little. He is almost eleven, so I should expect
it, and it is nothing drastic. But I always hope the signs of age
will hold off a little longer.

I'm interested that you like rain and huge trees. Donna
would climb the walls in a house that felt like an animal's burrow. Do you think we are imprinted with a habitat in early childhood, a landscape that will still feel like home when we are
eighty? P

i guess mom shouldn't have let me get my first look at life in a
place with trees and rosebushes if she wanted me to be happy
in the desert. i love it here.

When Breeze suggested I come to Seattle and work at Cyberplace,
she had neglected to mention an important detail. Cyberplace did
not yet exist.

At the moment, it consisted of a stack of computers in boxes, a
grant application that was temporarily delayed at some bend in the
pipeline and a tentative arrangement to lease part of an abandoned
warehouse. The whole idea had started when some company decided to upgrade its systems and offered to donate its old computers as a tax write-off. The processors were two generations out of
date, so they had zero resale value, but by donating them, the company recouped some of their remaining paper value and got some

good PR at the same time.

When I inquired a little further, I found out I was not just working at Cyberplace, I was Cyberplace. I looked at a copy of the grant proposal, and there was my name, listed as the person who would be "responsible for day-to-day management of the project." The application was dated about two days after I had told Breeze, yes, I was coming to Seattle. She still did not know when we would get the grant. The only things firmly in hand were the zero-value computers.

So instead of going to work at a computer training center, I spent the rest of the summer and the first part of the fall stuffing envelopes, running errands and racing around being a warm body at whatever trash-cleaning or playground-building event the Whole World Center had organized for that week.

Working with Breeze, I found out pretty quickly that Cyberplace was completely typical of her modus operandi. She would spot something, like a stack of old computers, that looked like a building block, and right away she could envision the structure that might arise around it, put together out of this person's presumed willingness to help, and that organization's possible willingness to donate money, and the odd landlord who might be persuaded to discount the rent on some long-vacant space. As it happened, a lot of her structures actually got built, maybe by the infectiousness of her optimism, or maybe because it took more energy to resist her than it did to say yes. There wasn't any system to her choice of projects. She just did whatever looked doable at the given moment.

hi, pat, my original purpose in being here has been postponed, but i'm finding plenty to keep me occupied. breeze gives you such a feeling that what you do matters. i don't know if i'll ever be as dedicated as she is, but she sets a standard to aim for. for instance, she'll spend endless amounts of time searching for clothing that's made from organic cotton and dyed with

natural dyes. i don't know if i could ever go to that much trouble.
j

J, She's lucky she doesn't have to shop in Kilgore. She might be walking around with no clothes on. When organic cotton finally finds a market here, we will know the world has changed. Pat

breeze isn't quite that absolute, luckily. if she can't find the organic cotton, she'll make do with something else, and she'll laugh at herself about the whole issue, which isn't true of everybody at the whole world center. some of them are so ultra-earnest in their good intentions, they make me want to streak the place or pass out cigarettes, just to shake things up. there's one guy who won't eat anything that wasn't grown in the state of washington. he also won't touch wine or anything of animal origin, including salmon, even if it came from washington. i think he's left with a diet of wheat, barley and apples, and whatever root crops he can find locally and store for the winter. if i pulled out a pack of cigarettes as a joke, he'd be out the door in a full-bore panic. he doesn't bug me the way elam did though, because he really cares about what happens in the world.

i guess that's what i like about the place, that people are so passionate about something.

When I bought my leather jacket, back in the Bay Area, I hadn't been thinking about the meaning or message in what I did, but now the jacket didn't feel right. Nobody at the Whole World Center said anything, but I could feel a subliminal shudder every time I walked in wearing it.

I didn't know what to do about it though. It wouldn't solve anything to throw the jacket away. The cow was already dead, and anyway, if she hadn't come into the world to make leather and meat, the ruling species wouldn't have let her come into the world at all. Still, I could see that the jacket offended some of the people I was working with, and even if I sometimes felt an itch to shake them up, that wasn't the way I wanted to do it.

My nylon Mariners jacket wasn't a whole lot better than the leather one. In addition to being synthetic, it symbolized all sorts of social ills—overpaid athletes and greedy owners, the legalized extortion of public money to build stadiums for private profit, the overglorification of celebrities, the loss of joy in the game itself. I spent a lot of time looking for an organic cotton warm-up jacket with the logo of the minor league club in Everett, but as far as I could tell, such a thing did not exist.

In the end, I reached a compromise. I bought an organic cotton blue jean jacket and hired a needleworker to hand-embroider an improvisational take-off on the Mariners' logo and Griffey's number. According to Breeze, hiring craftspeople was a highly positive way to spend money, so I could wear this jacket knowing I was sending mostly good messages out into the world.

It could be overwhelming, sometimes, trying to keep up with the pace Breeze set. I couldn't even hit the walk button and cross the street without noticing all those stopped cars, idling away fossil fuels. She never slowed down, never stopped thinking about consequences, and even when she was laughing at herself and granting herself forgiveness for hitting the walk button, her mind was already moving on to the next situation where something might be done.

Breeze seemed to be hooked into every progressive political network there was, and she knew about every problem everywhere, almost from the moment somebody realized it was a problem. I would pick up a newspaper and read an article about deformed frogs in Minnesota, and then I would find out it was old news to Breeze, that she had received a mailing weeks ago from a group demanding investigation of hormone-mimicking chemicals in the water supply, and another mailing from a group suggesting that the mutations were related to UV exposure and the depletion of the ozone layer. She had the phone number, fax number and Internet information for almost every government entity at every level, local, state and federal. Every day we sent letters to someone—legislators, newspapers, regulatory agencies, school boards. A lot of other organizations had the Whole World Center's phone, fax and Internet information, too, and we were at the center of a constantly multiplying number of action alerts, petitions to sign, and pleas for money and volunteers.

Still, frenetic as it was, this life suited me a lot better than meditation. If there was a defect in my character, I had no time to think about it, any more than I had time to tune into the harmonic responses of my cells as I wolfed down some Vietnamese takeout on the way to pick up flyers at the printer.

hi, pat, i guess i'm not going to be finding inner peace anytime soon. if breeze had her way, neither of us would ever sleep. i think she must lie awake at night calculating how many problems per hour we have to solve to stay ahead of the problems being created. i know it's crazy even to try. i'd have better odds trying to become the next mugsy bogues in the nba. still, i don't need any coffee to stay awake these days.

you remember once i asked you about message vs. messenger? back then the sensible message was to live my own life as a whole, happy person, but this morning the not-so-sensible messenger was fretting about living in a country with metal detectors in its public schools. as you see, the not-so-sensible has won out, because the person who was preaching inner harmony and self-fulfillment turned out to be kind of an annoying human being.

do you consider yourself a balanced, connected person? j

I haven't really thought about it. As a kid, I was odd, and then I was queer, and now I guess I am both odd and queer. Does that make me balanced?

Perhaps you could tell Donna that you are trying to do something about crime and poverty and the erosion of the Bill of Rights. Just to reassure her that you haven't moved to Seattle to work on your backhand. She'll be very pleased, you know. If she had become a tycoon at twenty-two, that's what she would have done. Set out to slay the dragons of injustice and stupidity. P

are you serious about mom? i've always thought the first words out of her mouth as a baby were "let's be realistic."

She learned those words the same time most people do, the day your umbilical cord was cut. P

hi, mom, i'm a little behind on the news. my life's been all over the place lately because the job i was supposed to be doing is temporarily on hold, waiting for funding. in the meantime, i've been helping out on all the other community projects at the whole world center. most of it doesn't tax the brain, but i hope it's useful, maybe making some positive change in the world.

i know this city would make you as crazy as portland did, with all the damp, drippy green, but i like it.

are you in charge of the dp department yet? love, jordy

Hi, Long since. Didn't I tell you? Maybe I forgot because it's not that big a change. I was already doing the work. Now I get paid for it, which is an improvement.

I'm glad you've found a place you really like, even if it is damp and crawling with vegetation.

By the way, Granddad is having a knee replacement next week, so you might send him a card. Love, Mom

I had a "Far Side" get-well card hanging around, one I had bought in California for no reason except that I had laughed for about five minutes when I read it and I figured someone I knew was bound to get sick sometime. I wasn't sure a Far Side cartoon was right for Granddad, though. When I showed it to people at the Whole World Center, half of them laughed and the other half said it was sick. I thought that sounded about right. The card might not be Granddad's style, but at least he would know it was from me.

Dear Granddad,

I hear you're going into the shop for repairs. Amazing, what they can do these days. Just walk in, give them your make, model and serial number and out you come, good for another hundred thousand miles. I'll expect to hear that you and Grandma have gone out dancing at the American Legion very soon.

Question, do you and the other gimps get to sit around at the parts counter and yak for a while before they wheel you in?

Love, Jordy

Hi, Jord, Granddad's knee is coming along in fine shape. He was very pleased to get your card. He showed it to me several times. He's not a letter writer, as you know, but he told me to say thank you for him.

I guess there must not be anything you need. It's very odd to feel so rich all of a sudden. Looking ahead to these years, I had always imagined I would be hoarding every penny to help pay for your college tuition. Now that I'm not, we have all these extra thousands to put toward retirement instead.

Are you still enjoying the green? Love, Mom

more than ever. the rains have started up, finally, and i love the sound of it. there's water everywhere, with the lakes and puget sound, and the streets and vegetation shining wet, and mist hanging over huge fir trees. in california, the sky looked like sun-baked porcelain, but here it looks soft.

A few weeks after the rain arrived, the money came through for Cyberplace. Breeze greeted the official notification with a huge look of relief and also some surprise. She confessed she hadn't been entirely sure we would get the grant.

In fact, she had thought all along that the odds were fairly low.

In uttermost fact, she'd just been taking a flyer when she asked the organization's chief money-hound to whip out the application in a spare moment.

She hadn't said any of this out loud, of course. Doubt became a self-fulfilling prophecy, she firmly believed.

Now she had the money, she had me, she had the computers, and the warehouse space was just as abandoned as it had been back in July, so we were go for liftoff.

chapter thirteen

With Breeze, liftoff meant she suddenly shifted the project from background to foreground mode, giving it her full attention, and Breeze's full attention was akin to a firehose. In about two weeks, she had a lease on the warehouse space and had recruited half a dozen more geeks-in-search-of-meaning to volunteer some hours each week. She'd also found a managerial type to keep track of the money, publicize the place and organize schedules and such, because she had surmised, accurately, that those of us who were comfortable thinking in machine code were likely to be a little random in our business habits.

The warehouse was in a derelict part of the city, south of downtown, in a sort of transition zone between residential and industrial neighborhoods. Inside, the space looked like the exercise area on Cell Block D, a big concrete rectangle with fluorescent lights overhead, wire mesh on the windows and paint peeling off the ceiling I-beams. There was no way to make the space look homey, and I thought the next best thing would be to make it strange. I bought some paint, and a couple of the other volunteers and I went to work redecorating, painting the walls orange and the I-beams black and metallic silver, alternately. We tacked up a lot of posters—*T2, Die Hard, Speed,* anything to make the place feel less brain-deadening.

Then I unpacked the computers and started setting them up on folding tables Breeze had scavenged from a church that was remodeling its parish hall. The whole time I was hooking up cables and plugging things in, Breeze was hovering, shifting the tables into new configurations and generally fidgeting with impatience. When I turned the first machine on, she came and stood behind me, watching.

From the moment I had heard about the donated computers, I had a feeling they might be more or less junk, and when I hit the power switch, I knew it for sure. Not that they didn't work. They did. But they were slower than death, and an order of magnitude too small to run any current software. If some company had gotten a tax benefit by donating the things, then I thought I should look into donating the empty trays from my microwave dinners. On top of everything else, the only applications installed on them were for business—accounting, personnel records, word processing—stuff that would put teenagers to sleep.

As I was sitting there, waiting a short eternity for one of the applications to come up on the screen, Breeze couldn't contain herself anymore. "Well, what do you think?" she asked.

I wasn't really paying attention when I answered. The application had finally come up, and I was clicking through it, checking it out.

"They're pretty much junk," I said. "Old, slow, and they've got no memory."

There was a silence, and I went on clicking, and then she said, jokingly, "Sort of like me, you mean."

Even though I knew Breeze was kidding, something in her voice didn't sound right. I turned around and saw that she looked completely deflated, in a way I'd never seen before. Her forehead was furrowed and her eyes had no sparkle, and her bright cotton clothes hung loose because her shoulders had sagged forward.

The computers were the tangible foundation for the concept of Cyberplace. Once they were on the premises at the Whole World Center, Breeze hadn't given them another thought. Now I'd told her they were junk, and she looked so discouraged, I thought the whole grand structure she'd built out of sheer belief in the possibility was going to collapse around us.

"I don't really mean they're junk," I said quickly. "They work fine. It's just that they're a little . . . out of date. But if we could get some different software . . . "

"Software," Breeze said. "You mean programs?" She sounded vague, like her mind didn't want to focus. "What sort of software . . . ?"

"For programming, mainly. And graphic design. Maybe some video games. The hitch is, the software would have to be as old as the machines . . . "

"And that's a problem . . . ?"

Her shoulders were still sagging, and I decided suddenly it was my turn for unfounded optimism.

"No. It's no problem at all. I'm sure there's a way."

"You think so?"

"Sure."

"And that's really all we need? To find some antiquated software?" She looked like a pot that had been put back on the burner.

I nodded, shrugged.

"Well, okay then," she said. "What do we need to do, go to yard sales? Secondhand stores? Run a classified ad?"

"I think it might be better to put out some feelers on the Net . . . "

"Of course! You're brilliant! It's the very thing. I knew I could count on you."

It seemed that optimism was as self-fulfilling as doubt, because in no time at all we had all the obsolete software we could possibly use. A few queries on the Net had triggered an avalanche of replies from people who had upgraded years before but couldn't bring themselves to throw their old diskettes and manuals in the trash. A couple of the programming languages were still in their original plastic wrap, sent in by people who had obviously hoped to do a lot more with their computers than they actually had.

By the first week of January, Cyberplace was ready to open. Organized classes wouldn't start until the end of the month, but for the drop-in tutorial part, Breeze and I both thought, why wait?

I had no idea what to expect. Our business brain, Lido, had done the PR via every low-cost method he could think of, from flyers on power poles to announcements in churches and rec centers. When I worried out loud that it might not be enough, that maybe no one would come, Breeze told me to stop being defeatist. She said electronic circuits were a magnet that worked on the human brain whether we liked it or not, and the kids would simply be swept in off the streets by the pull.

On the day of our opening, Breeze surprised me by saying she wasn't going to be there. Cyberplace was not her show, she said. She had no useful knowledge to offer, and she didn't think it would create the right atmosphere to have a hostess fluttering about dispensing charm and hors d'oeuvres. The kids needed to meet the people who knew something, not her.

The event wasn't exactly a stampede, but people did come, probably because the flyers and announcements had all made prominent mention of free refreshments and the chance to play video games. There were three or four mothers, but most of the crowd were kids, junior high, high school, even some from grade school. They wandered in, a few at a time, and drifted around the room, awkwardly, maybe grabbing some bites from the food table, talking among themselves and looking at the computers, but generally acting like they were at an art show opening, look but don't touch.

The other geeks and I had each settled in at a keyboard to run demos of some video games, the jazziest ones you could run with a slo-mo processor. After a while, some of the kids came and clustered around us, watching, but they kept a little space between us and them, like we were a different species, to be observed from a distance.

Unfortunately, neither I nor any of the other tutors were anything like the jovial, back-slapping emcee types who can get total strangers to relax and laugh. We tried, but every time one of us turned around and asked if anyone wanted to give the computer a try, the semicircle of watchers would back away a couple of steps. It looked as if the neighborhood was going to drop by, make a respectful, arms-length tour of our project and then depart, never to return.

Then I felt a little ripple of energy run through the room, and I saw that a new bunch of kids had come in, five of them. They were a little older, maybe seventeen or eighteen, and they slouched around the room with an air that said, So what's the big deal here? They ran their fingers over keyboards as they strolled past, casual, disdainful, ignoring the random beeps of response from the computers.

Everyone else in the room was much stiller than they had been, watching the five guys without watching them. Something was going to happen, but I wasn't sure what. Maybe the computers were about to get smashed as a random amusement. Or maybe the five would stroll back out again, dismissing us, and pull the rest of the crowd out after them. Or maybe they would stay, and then what?

I kept on clicking, generating missile whines and engine roars and explosions, just so the room would be a little less quiet. The five guys continued their circuit of the room, and everyone else pretty much stayed where they were, trying to look interested in our demo without for a moment losing track of what the five were doing.

When they reached the far end of the room, the five guys stopped and stood for a while near a couple of the computers, half checking them out, half just hanging there. They still had a look of contempt, like they wanted us to know that they knew that these were a pretty sorry bunch of machines, like even the sorriest public school had equipment better than this and they wouldn't even be here if there were anything of any interest whatsoever happening anywhere else on the planet.

But then one of the guys sat down at a computer and started fooling with the mouse. He still had a sneer, like all he was doing was checking out how sorry this salvaged box of scrap really was. Still, he checked it out pretty thoroughly, and then one of the other guys sat down at the next machine and started fooling with it. The other three hung over them, watching, making jokes, heckling a little, but they didn't leave.

Pretty soon, some of the other kids drifted away from the circles around the tutors, sat down at keyboards, and started making some tentative pecks and clicks. A couple of them even stepped across the barrier space to look more closely at the screen in front of me and ask a few questions. And then, gradually, as more and more electronic whines and beeps and explosions went flying around the room, bouncing off the concrete and I-beams, multiplying into harmonic reverberations, the place started to feel like it might actually be alive.

I was pretty well occupied, explaining something to a couple of the youngest kids, so I didn't notice right away when the room went quiet again. But then I got a feeling that the kids weren't paying attention anymore and I looked up. I looked toward the door and saw that another group of guys had come in, four this time, and they had the same slouch and same what's-the-big-deal air as the first five, but it was clearly not "hail fellow well met" between the two groups.

For a minute the new guys just hung near the door, surveying the room, and I had this goofy feeling that I should be hearing a rattlesnake buzz on a guitar in the background, like the moment after the saloon doors swing open, and then everyone would start diving under tables. In fact what happened was that the kids at one end of the room seemingly melted away, leaving a row of computers available.

There was another little pause, as the four new guys glanced at the vacated computers, but they didn't move from where they were. Instead, they kept hanging there, looking sideways across the room at the first group and I was thinking, this room is way too quiet. But I didn't think it would be the best plan for me to hop up and start shaking their hands and saying, "Welcome to Cyberplace, have a doughnut, why don't you?" So instead I did the only thing that came into my mind, which was to ignore the fact that the two kids at my computer were paying absolutely no attention to me, turn back to the monitor and launch myself into a world's-most-boring-science-teacher drone about the file manager and how to set up a directory and all the neat things you could do by dragging file names here or there.

My back was to the door, and I didn't have Larry Bird peripheral vision so I couldn't see exactly what was happening, but I felt a change in the room. Then I realized that the four new guys had slouched over into the edge of my field of vision and were checking out the open computers. Although they continued to act bored and disdainful, they stuck around. Gradually, the sound effects started up again, and then some conversations here and there, and the place went back to feeling almost normal.

The next morning, I told Breeze about the opening day dynamic, the groups of guys coming in, the moments of tension and then everyone adjusting into equilibrium, and as I described the trajectory, her expression followed the same path, tension and worry until I got far enough along for her to know everything had worked out, then relief and a kind of vindication.

"We picked that location intentionally," she said. "It's a kind of no-man's land. You go a few blocks this way or a few blocks over there, and you're in a neighborhood, but that particular spot isn't part of anything. Some economic development money has been going in, helping start up a couple of manufacturing projects, but that's about it. The whole idea was for us to be like the city buses, neutral. Nobody's an insider, and nobody's an outsider. Anybody can ride."

Amazingly, Cyberplace did come to life, slowly but steadily. Breeze, of course, was determined not to be surprised.

"What did you expect?" she asked, when I gave voice to my amazement.

"I don't know," I said. Maybe five anxious tutors hovering over one forlorn baby geek, and the rest of the room an echoing shell with a circle of screensavers haunting the perimeter.

It was my own burb-nerd-with-a-dental-plan bias, I suppose: if a machine wasn't state-of-the-art then it was complete crap and why would anyone want to bother? No one could possibly be that desperate, right?

But the fact was, the kids seemed more pragmatic than desperate, and if someone was going to dump a perfectly good load of stuff in their backyard, then they were going to take advantage of it. Sure, maybe life was harsh, and maybe there were a lot of people in the world who had it a lot nicer than they did, and maybe it made them fairly pissed off sometimes, but they weren't just going to sit down on the curb and boo-hoo about it.

> hi, mom, my real job has finally started, and i think it's something right up your alley. (actually i'm still doing about a thousand different things and can hardly keep up with them all, but this one is my favorite.) the whole world center got a grant to set up a computer job training center for teenagers using a lot of outdated desktops some company donated. the center is in a lousy

part of town, and i'm not sure how much job training we really expect to accomplish, but i think the underlying idea is that any hand holding a mouse isn't holding a gun. also, if we can make the center a cool place to be, which school isn't, then maybe a few kids will spend less time on the streets, and some of them might get hooked and learn something.

anyway, guess who's now working as a volunteer tutor? i know it's not very practical, but i hope it might do a little good. love, jordy

Computer training sounds like a good use of your brains, and I'm glad of that. A lot better than coasting along in neutral. It was never clear to me what you did at the Whole World Center, and I didn't believe you'd be happy for long if you weren't doing something tangible.

I hope you'll be a little bit cautious, though. It's terrific that you want to help kids from tough backgrounds, but don't expect them all to turn nice overnight, like a movie, and don't be trusting to the point of foolishness. Love, Mom

hi, pat, mom's worrying about me, as usual. i'm not totally stupid and naive, the way she seems to think i am. cyberplace (that's the name breeze gave it) is about the coolest thing i've ever done. it's not like we've created a hive of budding computer geniuses. a lot of the kids just sit around like zombies, playing games, letting themselves get drugged by electronic manipulations instead of chemicals. but there are a few who have decided they want to run the computer instead of letting the computer run them, and those are the ones i work with.

these kids and i almost come from different planets. they know people in jail, people who have been murdered. for them, getting into a fistfight barely registers as an event worth mentioning. i can hardly imagine their lives, and i doubt they can imagine mine, but we can all talk about computers. a computer is like a haven for them. it sort of has some human qualities. it can interact with you and talk back, in its way, but it doesn't have any emotions, so it doesn't have any warped emotions. it can't get violent or cruel in a way that hurts.

there's one really smart kid named spider. (i don't know why it is that everyone i meet lately has a weird name, but so it goes.) anyway, he came in the first day, and i thought for a while he might be planning to smash the computers to bits, just for the fun of it, but it turned out he was actually a little interested, as long as nobody tried pushing him. he's only seventeen, and he dropped out of school a while ago. i heard him tell one of his buddies that his classes were the equivalent of reading out loud from the telephone book, just something to keep him occupied and out of trouble for six hours a day. i'm pretty sure he belongs to a gang, tho he doesn't tell me about it. we only talk about computers.

i think spider could be a really sharp programmer. some of the other kids are pretty good, too, but he's like, snap, a shark. i'm only half way through explaining something and he's saying, 'okay, man, i got that, now what?' his teachers must have been pretty dim not to latch onto him, because he makes me feel like, hey, teaching is a piece of cake. i guess he probably had an attitude, tho, and the teachers were part of the system so he wouldn't let them past the attitude. whereas me, i'm harmless, just a skinny little geek he could break in two, and if he doesn't want to come to my class he doesn't have to. so far he's been coming every afternoon, and yesterday he asked me how hard it would be to design a video game. j

Hi, Jordy, You may call me a mother hen, but I hope you will be a little cautious. I worry that you may be a little too kind for your own safety sometimes.

I've been thinking about what you said about computers being safe because they have no emotions. I think dogs are safe, too, but for opposite reasons. A computer is all language and no love, while a dog is all love and no language, and somehow that makes both of them safe. It's as if the combination of language and feelings is what makes humans such a dangerous species (and such an interesting one).

Skipper is getting quite arthritic, a little prematurely, I think. He can't jump into the back of the pickup anymore. If I remember right, though, I had to lift my old dog Lulu into the truck for five years before she died, so I hope he may keep going the same way. Pat

give skipper a ten-minute belly rub for me. j

Early on, I'd had this idea that I might get to know some of the kids who came to Cyberplace. They weren't all that much younger than me, and I hoped we might find something more to talk about than data structures. But I realized pretty quickly that wasn't going to happen, because they weren't coming there to talk to me.

For them, I think, Cyberplace was this weird anomaly, a sort of pod that had touched down in their part of town with a clutch of geeks inside. And that was how they treated it. Like a mobile exhibit from the Pacific Science Center, another world with different rules that they could step into for a while. The place really was like the city buses, open to everyone, and part of that neutrality depended on me and the other geeks being like the guys in a uniform with a name tag. We were the curators, the reference librarians, more or less a bunch of walking CD-ROMs that the kids could reference when they got stuck.

A couple of times I tried to get beyond that role. The kids' conversations were going on right there, within three feet of me, and a lot of the time they were completely mundane, just kidding around, nothing I couldn't have been part of. One time some of the younger boys got going on a gross-out contest about sandwiches, about the weirdest, most disgusting combination of edible products you could possibly put between two slices of bread. Peanut butter and pickled cabbage. Banana, ketchup and pepperoni. Anchovies, celery and strawberry jam. Cheez-whiz and chocolate syrup.

"Bologna and marshmallow creme," I said.

And the conversation stopped dead. It was like one of the computers had said something.

I was thinking, What's the problem? We really do belong to the same species, even if we grew up on different planets. Can't we just act like human beings? Am I that weird?

But then I saw one of the thirteen-year-olds glance across the room at some of the older guys, the ones that usually arrived in multiples. And that quick, uneasy flick of the eyes made me step back and look at the whole scene from the outside, and I saw this little bubble where all these different groups could coexist for a while, before they went back outside to deal with whatever they dealt with in the rest of their lives.

And I was one of the control rods, dampening any reactions before they chained out of control. As long as I was talking about electronics, I was a buffer. I could even kid around, make jokes. About electronics. But I couldn't cross over into ordinary life, not with anyone.

I had spent hours in conversation with Spider, teaching him computer languages, working out his ideas for a video game, and then just once I tried to talk to him about something else, something unconnected to computers, and right away he pulled back and a hood came down. This room was one world and his life was another, and he didn't want them getting confused. Just one simple question about his parents, what they did, and he didn't come back to the center for three days. Maybe he could talk about his life, with his own crowd, even when he was in this room, but the room itself was something separate, and I was part of the room, not part of his life.

Even so, I loved the place. It felt real. The kids were real, not some hypothetical legislator or bureaucrat who might or might not read another indignant citizen's letter. It didn't matter that I wasn't everybody's pal. What mattered was that the kids loved the computers, enough to wrestle with them, enough to keep coming back. Computers were consistent. If you put some effort in, you saw a predictable result. Maybe that was the appeal, more than anything else. If the way to keep the whole place running smoothly was to dissolve my real self into the persona of the hypergeek, then so be it.

And it wasn't all bad, being socially nonexistent. The kids might not know anything at all about me, but I learned quite a lot about them, because they just went on with their lives, all around me, and I could watch and listen without anyone seeming to take me into account. Not that I got a whole picture. It was more like channel surfing as their conversations moved past me or started and stopped in alternation with the stops and starts in puzzling out some keyboard problem. But I did hear enough, the startlingly casual mentions of this person strung out, that person busted, someone else knocked across the room by her boyfriend, to know that rough as I thought I'd had it, I'd actually had it pretty easy.

For a while I'd thought, well, I grew up poor, with a single mom. I'd taken my share of abuse. Maybe we can relate.

But I began to understand that Mom and I had never been poor. Not this way. We'd been broke, and that was different. Mom had grown up in a family that owned something, that had expectations out of life, and even when she didn't have a cent in the bank, she never lost the attitude that she could get somewhere if she worked at it. She could overlook the small stuff, like secondhand clothes, because she had her eye on a bigger prize.

But what if there wasn't any bigger prize? What if you looked around and saw two different worlds, a world of people who drove nice cars and owned houses and believed in their bones that effort would be rewarded, and then another world, your own world, of brutalizing ugliness and very little evidence that anyone you knew ever got out of it?

Sure, my mom belonged to a demographic that got hated in the abstract, but on the other hand, she had the choice to hide or lie. She didn't have to tell her employer or her landlord or the guy who reads the meter. She could twist herself into a knot and pretend to be just like everyone else, if necessary. Maybe that wasn't a great choice, but at least it was a choice. And on top of that, her being in that box didn't say anything about what other boxes she might be in. As a queer, she might be rich and Catholic and half-Chinese, or she might be a lily-white Methodist sales clerk, and those would be the things most people noticed first, unless she decided to be pointedly truthful.

As for me, I was in the default box, the one that's assumed until you put a check mark somewhere else. Maybe my mother was an asterisk, but I was a straight white male, and I'd reached an age where people had pretty much stopped inquiring about my mother.

The kids at Cyberplace, though, most of them fit in boxes that they couldn't lie about or pretend were something else, and that would be the first thing anyone noticed about them, whether they liked it or not, and they were boxes that came with a whole string of corollary boxes, like money and education and probability of being questioned by the police. It seemed to me that a lot of the kids had developed this permanent air of not expecting much, of being on guard against the next insult or disappointment. Not that they never laughed, never kidded around. They did, all the time. But there was always an underlying caution, like "Okay, this is fun, but where's the catch?"

And yet they were so regular, too. One minute they'd be talking about a neighbor's house getting raided by the police, the next minute they'd be talking about clothes or the Sonics or a mother on their case about grades. And as I sat there listening to them joke and laugh and horse around, I thought, it's no wonder the human race has spread over the entire globe, because we're the species that can create normality out of any situation, play checkers in an air raid shelter or take our cat to the South Pole.

Some nonrational part of my mind must have known that if something seriously bad was going to happen to me, it would happen when the sun was shining. The sun and I just didn't get along, not if we were in the same place for too long.

In June, the sun slid out from behind the clouds and showed no signs of sliding back. Right then, I should have known enough to be on guard, that the coming summer would not be my season. By July, the lawns were turning brown, and longtime residents were commenting that such weather was not normal. Wherever an untended patch of grass and weeds baked dry in the sun, I caught the smell of Kilgore and California. I tried going to a baseball game, but the Jell-O-green turf in the Kingdome was worse than the desiccated weeds outside, and on top of that, Griffey was in the middle of a slump.

Unlike most people, who rushed outdoors in this weather, I kept right on working. If anything, I worked more. All the other tutors at Cyberplace had planned vacations and were delighted when I said I could fill in for them while they were gone. Fewer kids came into the center in the summer, but the ones who did come were the diehards, and I wanted to be sure someone was there for them.

Then, late in August, a front blew through and the weather turned chilly, almost like autumn. The air was abnormally clear, magnifying distant objects, creating the illusion that I could count the individual shingles on a house on a hillside half a mile away. I was working full time at Cyberplace and squeezing extra projects with Breeze into cracks of time around the edges. There was no mush in my days. Everything required chewing. I liked the chill in the air. I could feel my blood rushing into action to keep me warm. Summer was ending, and soon enough the rains would start up again.

But summer wasn't quite over yet. The air was cool, but the sun still smiled down, a villain biding its time. It had waited almost three months for the right day, and now the day came.

On the phone, Breeze was breathless, as usual. "There is the most wonderful project we might be able to help with. Can you spare an hour or two to check it out with me?"

The project was a new day-care center located in a neighborhood where Breeze felt more comfortable with a man along, even in daylight. The neighborhood looked ordinary enough when we got off the bus. The stores and houses were a little shabby, but it wasn't as if there were gangs of skinheads or people doing drug deals on every corner. The day-care center itself was downright cheerful, freshly painted in robin's egg blue and daffodil yellow.

According to the director, the center needed more funding, more supplies, more aides. Breeze said she would pursue any contacts she could think of. When we left, she was bubbling.

"It's so hopeful to see a resource like this in a neighborhood like this. We absolutely have to make sure it succeeds. Do you have any time to volunteer as an aide . . . ?"

"I don't know . . . " I didn't see how I could fit it in, unless I gave up one of her other projects.

"At least think about it. This place is truly special."

But which of her projects wasn't special?

At the bus stop, she kicked at a pile of trash in the gutter and shook her head. "There's always something more," she said.

I barely glanced at the trash, because my eye had been caught by a figure I recognized. Halfway down the block, on the other side of the street, Spider had just come out of a store. He stopped, looked up and down the street, then started walking, slowly, in our direction. He was alone, and the way he moved made me think of a hunter in the woods, not that he was searching for something, but he seemed hyperalert.

I said to Breeze, "There's someone I want to say hello to. I'll be right back."

The moment I started across the street, he saw me, and it seemed to me that he hesitated, but then he kept on coming.

"Hey, Spider, how's it going?" I said.

He shrugged. "It's goin'." He smiled a little but he looked confused, as if he wasn't sure how to behave out of our normal context. "Cool jacket," he added.

I was wearing the blue jean jacket with the hand-stitched Mariners logo. The needleworker hadn't been strictly literal in her interpretation. She might have started off making letters and numbers but she had ended up making wildly twisted shapes that looked like creatures from a B monster movie. I thought the jacket had turned out pretty cool, but Spider's was a lot better, and I said so.

His had started as a real baseball warm-up jacket, but the original Mariners logo had nearly disappeared under a collage of custom adornments, glued on, sewn on, drawn on or pinned on—skulls, snakes, Spiderman comics, chains, rings, cartoon characters drawn with a laundry marking pen, a photograph of Shawn Kemp driving to the hoop and an array of scrawled messages that collectively added up to "Don't mess with me." It looked like a scrapbook, or a leg cast with six weeks' worth of graffiti on it, except that none of the messages were goofy. Once he turned to look up the street behind him, and I saw a large, hand-painted cobra, hood spread, coiling up the back of the jacket.

Like most guys, Spider was a lot taller than I was. My eyes were on a level with his collarbone and the blue Magic Marker message: "Life sucks. Get used to it."

He seemed strangely shy and uneasy talking to me, even though we were on turf he obviously knew and I didn't. He kept shifting his feet and looking around, but he didn't leave, so I kept talking. I figured it might be my only opportunity for a conversation with him away from Cyberplace.

"You live in this neighborhood?" I asked.

He jerked his head left. "Over a few blocks."

"Do you follow the Mariners?" I pointed at what was left of the logo on his jacket.

He shrugged. "Not really. This was my mom's idea. She likes Junior. I'd have bought a Sonics jacket. Baseball's like little old ladies playing croquet."

"So Shawn's your man."

He grinned. "He's, like, dry ice. Touch him, you get burned."

"They gonna win this year?"

"Maybe if your man breaks his leg."

"My man?"

"Michael."

"Oh, right."

It had been a while since anyone had made that connection to my name. When people at the Whole World Center heard the name Jordan, they thought of spirituality and power spots, not professional basketball.

"You play yourself?" I asked.

He grinned again. "I can dunk, easy."

"I can too, with a stepladder. Trouble is, it takes too long to set up."

He laughed, and I noticed that his feet weren't shifting around quite so much.

"Actually, football is my game," I said. "I played in junior high."

"No way."

"Sure. I was a kicker."

"For real?"

"Yeah, but not for long. One season. The whole school only had about eighty kids, so anyone with a Y chromosome could be on the team."

"What kind of school only has eighty kids? Were you, like, caught dealing or something?"

Now I laughed. "It was a regular school. The whole town only had about a hundred people. Well, not really. I'm exaggerating, but that's what it felt like. Kilgore. You can find it on a map, exactly halfway between nothing and nowhere."

"How did you get out?"

"My mom had a connection."

"That figures."

In my head, I was trying to figure whether I might somehow, some-day, have a connection for Spider. He was plenty sharp, but what company was going to hire a high school dropout with a cobra on his jacket just because I said he was sharp?

"Listen, I've got to go," I said. "I've got a friend waiting for me over at the bus stop. But I'll see you at Cyberplace, okay?"

The minute I said that, his feet started shifting again, as if he had remembered we were out of context and it made him nervous.

"Yeah. Okay. You shouldn't be hanging around here anyway. There's something going on . . . "

"What do you mean, 'something'?"

He shrugged. "Don't know for sure. I'm not in on it. Just some people acting edgy, like something's going on . . . "

He was glancing around now, and all of a sudden his face got a look, like he wished he were elsewhere.

I'm going to have that look in my mind forever, because everything that happened after that went so fast, the tape couldn't catch it all. I felt somebody moving behind me, fast, like a basketball move, and then I heard a car accelerating, hard, and then gunfire, but nothing like a .22 popping prairie dogs or even the crack of a deer rifle. This noise was continuous, like a regiment opening up, but all from one point, an accelerating point, as if the regiment were firing in a wave. The wave reached us, and my legs were cut out from under me, as if I'd been tackled hard at the knees. As I fell, I felt something hit my head and the street vanished.

chapter fourteen

Somebody was pumping helium into my head. The top of my skull was trying to expand, detach itself, float away. My head throbbed, but distantly, from behind cushions of cloud.

Something else was throbbing, too, even farther away. My legs.

Voices were murmuring behind the cloud. "Considerable trauma . . . swelling subsides, we'll know more . . . possibly can reconstruct . . . flight arrives in three hours . . . "

My body started shivering, uncontrollably, and suddenly I was crying, uncontrollably.

"Anesthetic is wearing off . . . the trembling and crying are entirely normal . . . caused by the anesthesia . . . "

A hand took mine. "Jordy?"

I opened my eyes. Breeze. She looked old and haggard.

Her face blurred a little, then cleared, then blurred again. I closed my eyes and opened them again. Clearer, but something was strange, like I had a patch over one eye. I closed one eye. The image narrowed a little, but I could still see. I opened the eye, closed the other one, and the image widened a little, but still the same, like a patch over the right side.

"My eyes are weird . . . " I said. "I can't see to the right."

"A bullet nicked the back of your head. They don't know yet, whether the sight will come back. Swelling or something."

"Spider," I said.

"What?"

"Where's Spider?"

"What spider? What do you mean?"

"Where is he? Is he okay? Spider. I was talking to him."

Breeze looked away from me. Her mouth was trembling. "You mean Curtis," she said. "The boy in the jacket." She still wasn't looking at me.

I watched a drop form, slowly, slowly, sap from a cut stem, and slide down her cheek. She didn't say anything.

"He's dead?"

I'd said the word. Breeze's words now came in a rush. "He died instantly," she said. "Before the ambulance got there. He never knew what happened to him. It was so quick. I'm sure he never knew."

No, he knew all right.

And what comfort is it to die quick when you're seventeen years old?

He hadn't wanted to be there. He'd been headed elsewhere and would have gotten there if it hadn't been for me. He wouldn't have been standing there, in the wrong spot, if I hadn't stopped him and made him talk to me. If I hadn't been such an eager, wriggling, simple-minded puppy dog, insisting on friendship, insisting on kindness. As if our friendship would be a new beachhead in the struggle against injustice and misunderstanding. As if I could make the world kind just by believing in kindness hard enough.

I closed my eyes and felt my own tears sliding out of the corners of my eyes and along my cheekbones. Not from the anesthesia, these ones.

I found out facts later. No one else had been killed. Four other people had been wounded, one of them a gang leader, apparently the target of the shooting. Probably he was the basketball move I had felt behind me. The weapon was an assault rifle, several hundred rounds a minute. Police said it was a miracle more people weren't killed. The specific reason for the shooting wasn't known. Just "something going on."

I was asked some questions, but not with any suspicion. They just needed to confirm that I was an innocent bystander.

When I woke the next morning, Mom and Pat were there. Mom said they had been there the night before, but I had been sedated into oblivion by the time they arrived. Now that I was awake, Mom started talking about all the different possibilities for my recovery. It was like an involuntary reflex in her, to consider every possible future alternative and what should be done about it. There was a chance I'd get the rest of my sight back, she said. They'd know more when the swelling went down, she said. As for my knee, the doctors could replace it, just the way they'd replaced Granddad's. As soon as the surrounding bones and muscles had healed enough, I could go ahead with the procedure.

Over and over, she laid out all the likely scenarios, until she started to sound like a CD on auto-repeat. I'm sure she was trying to cheer me up, to get me looking ahead with hope. Probably the doctors had told her I would heal faster with a positive attitude.

But I didn't want to have a positive attitude. I didn't give a shit about my knees or my eyes right then. Life was unjust, and it seemed like an inevitability that out of a random spray of bullets, the six with my name would shatter a kneecap and a couple of leg bones while the six with Spider's name would leave his brains on the sidewalk. I'd already won the lottery once, at Ultimall, and now I had won it again.

I couldn't explain to Mom, what had really happened. She would say I was being irrational, that it was pure chance and not a cosmic pattern that had sent bullets directly into Spider's brain while I just lost a few replaceable parts.

Anyway, my head still felt like a balloon from all the painkillers, so even if I had thought she would understand, I wouldn't have been able to organize my thoughts into a coherent explanation. It was simpler just to lie there and let her talk on and on about the practical details of medical care.

Her mind was on my health insurance. Had I taken out an individual policy when I left the company?

"Of course I did," I said. "It's genetic. I couldn't help myself."

"I'm glad my genes are good for something," she said. "I thought you must have, since the doctors are already talking about reconstructive surgery and where's the best place . . . "

"Was my ambulance a Rolls Royce?" I said, cutting her off.

"What do you mean?"

"Nothing. Never mind. Probably Breeze has been bugging them about my care. Did you meet Breeze?"

"She was here when we arrived last night. This thing has hit her really hard, you know. She thinks it's her fault, because she asked you to go there with her."

"Her fault? It's not her fault. It's just the way the whole goddamned world works. Bad luck. Bad timing. Pure randomness."

Randomness that somehow keeps falling into patterns, like quantum mechanics. Each time a collision knocks you left, it ups the probability you'll go left the next time, too. Spider had passed through way too many losing shifts in probability ever to get back onto the winning side of the curve.

How can you talk to anyone about a feeling that makes no sense? Spider's death had left a hole in me that any rational person would say was totally out of proportion. I didn't even know him. I knew his hero was Shawn Kemp, but Shawn Kemp was a hero to half the seventeen-year-old boys in Seattle. Lots of the other kids at Cyberplace were sharp, and they all needed a boost as much as he did. But my heart had picked him and attached itself, like he was my little brother, and now fate had picked me to have a hand in his final roll of bad luck.

I couldn't let go of it. His face was in front of me, with that last look of "I knew this was coming sometime, but I wish it weren't now."

That minute played over and over, the way he had grinned when he said he could dunk, the way his disbelief at my having played football gave way to amused acceptance when I said I was a place-kicker, the way he thought a school with only eighty kids must be a reform school, and then that last question, "How did you get out?"

The pain in my legs and my head felt like something outside of me, something that passed through layers of gauze before it reached my brain. People kept coming into my hospital room, testing my eyesight, checking the dressings on my legs, discussing with Mom the options for the reconstruction of my knee. I watched it all with complete indifference, as if my body were a CPR dummy. Sometimes the manipulations hurt, but I didn't care. Physical pain was simple, something I could grit my teeth and endure.

I could locate physical pain. My knee hurts. My head hurts. I couldn't locate what I felt about Spider. It was everywhere. My whole being hurt, and the only time I escaped was when some sharp particular pain in my body diverted my attention for a moment.

I didn't read the newspaper stories about the shooting. I didn't need to see that piece of history from anyone else's point of view. The only part of the paper I looked at was the sports page.

And then one day the sports page announced that Shawn Kemp had been traded away, was leaving Seattle. Another squabble among multimillionaires. Two elephants get into a tiff and a million ants get trampled. You learn to keep your loyalties fast on their feet, ready to shift at any moment, like the modern military.

In a few days my blurred vision cleared completely, but I still had that blind patch on the right side. The doctors said my legs were healing as well as could be expected. The shattered joint could be replaced, but they recommended that I wait until the muscles around the joint and the bone in my other leg had healed. They said it was important to begin rehabilitation soon after the installation of the artificial joint. Their explanations expressed their earnest concern that I be kept fully informed.

I just shrugged. "Okay. Whatever you say."

Maybe they were hoping my mind would heal, too. I'm sure I didn't look to them like a patient who would bring the appropriate zeal to his rehabilitative therapy.

Mom was at a loss. "You really were very lucky," she kept saying. "The doctors tell me they can get you sixty to seventy percent of normal function in the knee. And you can see, well enough. The rest may come back, in time. You'll be able to do everything you did before. You weren't a professional athlete or a mountain climber. Granddad is back riding horseback, and if a manmade knee can stand that, it can stand almost anything. You have every reason to be hopeful."

I shrugged. "I know."

I really wished she would stop telling me how lucky I was and what a wonderful future I had ahead of me.

Mom wasn't totally obtuse. She did mention Spider's death a few times.

"You knew him a little, didn't you?" she asked.

"A little."

"He was a student at the training center?"

I nodded.

"Were you close friends?"

I shook my head.

"Still, it must be a shock that he was killed."

I nodded.

"And so senselessly."

I turned my head away and stared at the wall, which was painted a therapeutically cheerful pastel.

Pat had had to return to Kilgore to work, but Mom stayed on until I was out of the hospital and settled at Breeze's house. She had asked me if I wanted to come back home while I recovered, but that was definitely not what I needed right now. Besides, Breeze had offered at least twenty-five times to look after me, and I think Mom guessed that her eagerness was more than generosity, that she wanted the task as an atonement.

Looking at the situation with her habitual objectivity, Mom could see that her own best attempts to comfort me were only making me feel worse. She was not the right person to help me. Perhaps Breeze was. So after exacting a promise that I would stay in close touch and tell her immediately if I wanted her to come to Seattle again, she flew home.

When I got my laptop hooked up, I found an email from Pat waiting for me. At the hospital, our conversations had been very short. Most of the time, Mom had been talking, going over her worries and plans one more time, and Pat wasn't the sort to push herself into a conversation. In any case, I hadn't felt much like talking myself.

Her email was short, mostly asking how I was.

Skipper seems to know something isn't right with you. He trots into your room and whines, but he won't settle down beside your bed, the way he always has. He comes back out and hovers near me, as if your room makes him uneasy. I suppose he is picking up on our uneasiness, but it's a little eerie, even so.

I've decided to hire an assistant manager for the Mercantile, so perhaps soon I will be able to get away for visits more easily. Pat

hi, pat, i used to wonder why you never did anything but run a grocery store, but right now i feel like it doesn't matter what a person chooses to do, because the world is going to decide everything anyway. j

I had thought Mom's insistent planning was bad, but Breeze's remorse was a lot worse. She wouldn't stop apologizing, and I got really tired of telling her it wasn't her fault. She waited on me like a maidservant, and she practically begged me to be demanding and temperamental so that she could scurry around being obliging. The only thing I wanted was to be left alone, but Breeze had never been able to leave anything alone, not if she thought it needed fixing, and I was conspicuously in need of fixing, with my leg bones pinned in place and half my head shaved and garish pink scar tissue where the lesser wounds had closed up.

All I could think about was how much I wanted to be out of there, to be alone and on my own, taking care of myself, with no one telling me how sorry they were, how terrible it had been and how lucky I was, considering everything. I didn't want to talk about what had happened, and even less did I want to talk about how well I was healing. I wanted total blankness. For the hours I was awake, I watched television, or played video games. Especially I played video games because they focused my attention—busywork for the brain, blotting out all conscious thought.

I steeled myself to be polite to Breeze, even though she was driving me nuts. Objectively, I knew I owed her gratitude for taking care of me all these weeks, and I repeated my thank-yous like a mantra. But I was frantic to be away from her, and I raged at my own bones and muscles for needing interminable weeks to knit themselves back together.

I didn't want to be around anyone I knew, not Breeze, not the other people at the Whole World Center, not Mom. I wanted to feel nothing, not even kindness, because that seemed like the only way not to feel pain.

To make matters worse, Breeze kept prodding me to talk. It was an article of faith with her that traumatic experiences must be talked about or the emotions won't heal. She urged me to get in touch with my fear and pain and rage, to give vent to them so that my life could move on. She didn't have the faintest understanding of what was happening in my head. She wanted me to talk about the pain of my injuries, my rage at the maiming of my body, my fear at having come so close to death, my grief at the death of someone I knew. She could identify and categorize each emotion, just the way I could say my knee hurts. But I couldn't categorize what I felt, any more than I could fix boundaries on the open ocean. All I could do was keep myself watertight, so that I would stay afloat. She was trying to knock holes in my hull, to let the ocean in, and all my spare energy went into fending her off. Barraged by her good intentions, I pulled myself in tighter and tighter, keeping my eyes fixed on television and computer screens, while my mind circled in and in on a single idea—to get away.

⚘

In October, the doctors unpinned me and told me I could start, slowly, putting weight on my legs. My muscles had atrophied so that I looked like a wizened old man from the thighs down. My left knee throbbed steadily, and I could not bend it at all, and the doctors had fitted it with a brace to ensure that I didn't try. Still, I was upright and walking and that was all I cared about.

The doctors said we should talk about scheduling the knee replacement. I said I needed a couple of days to adjust, so they gave me several pages of exercises and a page of appointments with a physical therapist and told me to call when I was ready to schedule the surgery.

"Don't leave it very long. It will only get harder," they said.

I had had eight weeks of immobility to make my list, so when the time came, I could run through it fast. I talked to my landlord and spent an hour with an account manager, making some financial arrangements. With Breeze's help, I took my car to the nearest Toyota dealer and traded it in on a new one, same model with an automatic transmission, so that I could drive with only one working knee. I drove to the department of motor vehicles to pick up permanent plates. I paid all my bills and stopped by my bank to get a load of cash. I typed two letters to send by the postal service—email would arrive too fast. I told everyone I knew that I was headed over to the Olympic Peninsula for a few days to get my head clear. Then I packed up my clothes and laptop, dropped the letters into a mailbox and headed out onto I-90 East, three thousand miles of open road.

Dear Breeze,
Here's the key to my apartment. I've headed out to be on my own for a while, no ties. You can take my stereo, CDs, TV and anything else I've left and give them

away to whoever you want. The landlord knows I've split, so you can leave the key with him after you've taken everything that looks useful.

Jordy

Dear Mom and Pat,

I'm going to be out of touch. I don't know how long, but you don't have to worry about me. I haven't killed myself or anything like that. I just need to be alone and simple for a while. Perhaps I will get a dog.

Love, Jordy

chapter fifteen

The interstate was perfect—dry, smooth pavement precisely bounded by lines, every mile engineered to be exactly like every other mile, every grade and curve leveled and straightened to allow rapid, uniform flow of traffic. It was exactly where I wanted to be, detached and frictionless, gliding past a landscape kept distant by woven wire fences. Nobody knew me, and nobody wanted to know me. I could walk into a service-plaza restaurant and know that it would look exactly like every other restaurant in its corporate chain, that the food would taste the same, that the staff would greet me with indifference, that neither people nor objects would reach out to entangle me.

The interstate was a world unto itself. Its whole goal was not to be where it was. It wanted no complicating connections to the places it passed through, and neither did I. I wanted anonymity, solitude and constant movement, so that no adhesions could form. The highway and I were in perfect accord.

I noticed almost nothing of the landscapes I passed. Sometimes there were trees and sometimes there weren't. Sometimes the road climbed or descended. Sometimes it was level. Twice, around Chicago and Cleveland, I had to concentrate on the traffic. The rest of the time, I was on autopilot. I noticed only how hard I had to press the gas pedal to maintain my speed and when I needed to buy gas or use the headlights or windshield wipers. I popped aspirin and ibuprofen steadily to keep the ache in my legs endurable. When the pills were insufficient, I pulled into a rest area to stretch and walk around. For five days, I ate, slept and drove without talking to anyone not paid to wait on me.

Then I hit the ocean. Or rather, I hit Boston and a chaos of badly designed highways and unruly drivers that forced me into awareness for a time, long enough to ricochet north onto a different interstate that tracked the coast. In Maine, the interstate and the coast parted company, and I stayed with the coast until nothing remained ahead of me except Canada or the Atlantic. I ricocheted again, back inland a couple of hours, and fetched up near a lake, really a large pond, in a town smaller than Kilgore.

Wooler, Maine, was the bleakest place I had ever seen. In Kilgore, the bleakness had come from the vast expanses of emptiness, from feeling oneself tiny in the middle of boundless open space. This landscape was neither vast nor open. It looked closed in, scraggly, harsh and tormented, as if gray rain could fall forever and nothing would grow from the frost-heaved granite except lichen and moss and a dark, twisted coniferous forest. It was the sour and stunted poor relative of the Pacific Northwest, no majestic peaks and towering Douglas firs, just heaved humps of rock and stingy earth, murky bogs and crooked evergreens hunkered together into impenetrable thickets of gloom.

The town looked as poor as the soil. Along the coast, I had passed through town after town of stately and prosperous white clapboards, but the stateliness and prosperity had shriveled a few miles inland. Here I saw only small, nondescript pitched-roof boxes with cheap siding painted mud brown and pea green and rust red. One box, flat-roofed, appeared to be a general store. Another, shoebox shaped, was a diner, so I stopped to buy lunch. People glanced at me as I stumped in and then returned to their own conversations. From the stray words that escaped the general murmur, it appeared that all the conversations concerned hunting.

The waitress greeted me with a menu and one word, "Coffee?" I considered asking for tea, then changed my mind and turned my cup upright. I thought she looked mildly annoyed, as if I could have saved her an unnecessary conversation by turning my cup upright the moment I sat down.

The menu had been typed on a typewriter with a very old ribbon and was encased in a sleeve of plastic, aged yellow. I hadn't seen a sandwich for a buck seventy-five since I left Kilgore. When the waitress came to take my order, she didn't waste any words on what was already obvious by her presence. She just stood beside me holding her pad until I asked for a BLT. She returned with the sandwich, later with the coffee pot, but emphatically never asked whether "everything was all right."

By the time I finished eating, I had decided to stay. I wanted exactly one thing, to be left alone. Since I couldn't live at an interstate service plaza, this town seemed like the next best possibility.

On my way out, I asked the waitress what was the closest daily newspaper.

"Bangor," she said.

Bangor wasn't exactly next door.

"Would it list rentals out this way?"

She shrugged. "Might."

"Would the store have a copy of the paper?"

She shrugged again. "Might."

For one hallucinatory moment, I wanted to ask her if god existed, to see if her reply would be the same. But I was thinking of staying, so instead I asked her if she knew of anyone with a place for rent.

"A hunting camp, you mean?"

I shook my head. "Not for hunting. Just some place quiet and out of the way, with heat for the winter. Nothing fancy."

She thought for a minute, then told me to try asking at the store. "Mahlon Cadwell has a little place he's always talking about renting out. It's not much more than a camp, but the road's plowed in winter, and I think it might have power. You'll have to ask him if it's really for rent. And even if he says it is, I wouldn't feel too certain until you've moved in and he's taken your cash. Mahlon's always talking about doing one thing or another, so you never know if he's really going to until he does."

I was staring at her, wondering how a person could go from "Coffee?" and "Might" to giving me a complete real estate listing and character reference in the time it took to pay my check.

Later, when I thought about it, I realized I had finally asked a question whose answer wasn't self-evident. At that moment, though, the completeness of her information made me reconsider my decision to stay. I had misjudged this place. It was no relation to an interstate service plaza. And if Mahlon Cadwell was someone who "always talked about doing one thing or another," how soon would I be "the little lame fella doing something or other out in that shack of Mahlon's?"

Yet for some reason, I felt no uneasiness. The waitress was so matter-of-fact in her description of Mahlon Cadwell, no clucking disapproval, no motherly concern. As if everyone had peculiarities and you simply took them into account when you dealt with a person. As if people didn't change, so it would be a foolish waste of time to send in missionaries or psychiatrists. As if a neighbor's unreliability was just a fact to plan around, like a snowstorm or a bad back.

I decided I could live with having an identity, if identity was simply an unarguable fact.

Mahlon Cadwell expended more breath talking in the first minute than the waitress had in our whole encounter. Most of his talk went around and around the same circle of indecision. He wanted to rent out the shack, but then again he might want it himself for a night or two during deer season.

After what the waitress had told me, I figured I had better pin him down or look elsewhere. "I need it now," I said. "I can't wait until after deer season."

Mahlon circled a little faster, but still the same track.

"If you like, I can pay the rent in cash," I said.

The circle unrolled into a straight line. He guessed it wasn't worth keeping the place empty the whole winter just for a couple of days in hunting season. He generally went to his brother's hunting camp anyway.

"You want to go look at it?" he asked.

"That would be good. What time would be convenient?"

"Right now's convenient. Sandy can handle things for an hour, can't you?"

The woman at the cash register shrugged in acquiescence. "I'll be handling things all day long, once deer season starts."

Now that his mind was made up and we were in my car driving out to look at it, Mahlon had a lot to say about what a sweet little place his shack was.

"It's got power and water. No phone, but you said you didn't want anyone bothering you anyway. Heat's a woodstove. Two cords will keep you the whole winter. There's no backup, so you can't go away overnight, but you weren't planning to anyway, were you? My brother cuts firewood. I can lean on him to bring you a cord this week, before hunting season. Otherwise you wouldn't see any for a month. The driveway's a little narrow for plowing. You might want to leave your car out near the road once the snow comes. There's a wide spot you can keep clear for parking. My wife's brother-in-law does the driveways out that way, so we can set him up to do yours. He won't charge much, not for that little parking space at the end. Don't suppose you're looking for a snow machine? He's got a little one for sale, just right for starting out. He'd give you a good deal . . . "

I shook my head. "My knee doesn't bend. I couldn't ride it anywhere that wasn't flat and groomed."

Mahlon hadn't asked me anything about myself, but mentioning my injury opened the door.

"How'd you get that knee?"

All of a sudden I could feel the flood that would rush in to swamp me if I told him.

"I cracked up on an ATV," I said.

He nodded. It seemed to be the kind of answer he expected.

"I thought they could fix those things nowadays."

"Usually they can. Mine was different."

"Hit your head, too?"

I nodded. "I quarreled with a tree. The tree won."

He smiled a little, and the realization hit me. I could say anything I wanted. I could be anybody I chose to invent. I could become garrulous about this new person and never breach the seawall that protected me from pain.

"You're a long way from home, aren't you?" he said.

"Three thousand miles."

"What made you pick Wooler? Most people would say there's not much here."

"I want peace and quiet."

"You'll find that, anyhow," he said. "You doing something in particular with it?"

What did a person *do* with peace and quiet?

"I'm writing a book."

"Really? What about?"

"Philosophy. The nature of existence. God. All the big stuff."

I was going to be a topic of speculation no matter what, so I had just as well give them some good material.

"Are you an authority?" Mahlon asked.

I shook my head. "If you're an authority, you have to give reasons for what you say. I can say whatever I want."

Reason would have told me not to rent Mahlon's place, but I had already made up my mind before reason got a chance to state its case. By the time Mahlon sang out, "Turn here," and we bounced from a narrow dirt road onto a two-wheel track with thigh-high weeds scraping the bottom of my car, I was already in residence.

The only good thing about the shack was its surroundings. It sat in the middle of a hundred-acre piece of woods, and the back window looked across a pond and a marsh punctuated with tree skeletons and a couple of huge bird's nests. There wasn't a single human artifact in sight.

The shack itself was nothing much, a twelve-by-twenty shed with asphalt roll roofing and plywood siding that was starting to delaminate from too much weather and too little paint. The exterior looked ancient but the interior was only half-finished. The walls were papered with insulation facing, aluminum foil decorated with "Owens-Corning" and paragraphs of installation instructions at evenly spaced intervals. The floors were plywood underlayment adorned with a tattoo of nailheads at four-inch spacing until about the middle of the room, where the builder had either run out of steam or run out of nails and just tacked the last sheets down along the edges. In one corner was a bathroom with a curtain for a door. Both kitchen and bathroom had been equipped at the salvage yard, creating a showroom of outdated decorator colors—an avocado sink, a mustard refrigerator and a

Wedgwood-blue toilet. Windows are expensive, so there were only two, both small. The ceiling wasn't yet insulated. Mahlon said this was good, because the heat from the woodstove would melt the snow off the roof and I would only need to shovel the lower edge, along the eaves.

The room was furnished with a card table and two folding chairs, a stuffed armchair, a metal-frame bunkbed, two packing crates as side tables and some kitchen shelves made from boards and cinder blocks. Here and there on the silver foil walls, nails were hammered into the studs to serve as hooks, but nothing was hanging from any of them. Apart from the furniture and appliances, the place reminded me of our house in Kilgore six months before it was ready for us to move in. Judging by the amount of dirt ground into the soft plywood floor, the room had been in this same state for a good long time, years probably.

I asked Mahlon what he wanted for rent, and he named an amount considerably lower than what I had paid for my cubbyhole with three roommates in Sunnyvale. I must have looked surprised and doubtful, because he hurried to add that it included all the utilities.

My impulse was to leap and close the deal, but I made myself pause. I was remembering what the waitress had said. If I leapt too quick, he might think he'd been too quick to sweeten the offer and back out of the whole deal. I hemmed and hawed and made another circuit of the room and finally said I guessed I'd take it, and he seemed as eager as I was to get the bargain sealed in cash. He even stayed half an hour to help me carry my stuff into the shed.

It was only later, when I bothered to scan the Bangor paper, that I discovered I could have picked from a number of full-size houses with finished floors and walls for not a whole lot more rent. Maybe Mahlon guessed I'd get around to looking at the paper, because early the next morning I awoke to the sound of a truck backing down the driveway and dumping a pile of firewood near the door, and later that day, someone else appeared with a tractor and Bush Hog to flatten the weeds and brush in the driveway and front yard, and later still, someone else arrived to fix a small problem with the gas stove that Mahlon had neglected to mention, and it became more and more clear that I was not the one who had most cleverly disguised his eagerness. Having snared me, Mahlon was doing all he could to make sure I stayed.

He needn't have tried so hard. His shed was exactly what I wanted. I didn't want "Two bedrooms with fenced yard on quiet residential street." I wanted no phone, a P.O. box, and someone else's name on the utility bill. I wanted my entire previous self, Jordan Frederick McNeil, to be cut loose and left to drift away. I wanted my world reduced to one small place, a shell to keep me warm and two windows looking out on woods and a pond. I had all I needed, right here. The store in Wooler sold food and gas, seven days a week. In the next town west, I found a laundromat and a one-room public library, open three afternoons a week. Two towns east there was a bank, and that was the outer limit of my orbit. I wanted as little to do with human beings as possible.

When Mahlon Cadwell realized I wasn't going to duck out of our agreement, he stopped looking for ways to put me in his debt and just collected my cash. No one else bothered me either. The people I met at the store and the library were neither friendly nor unfriendly. If I talked, they talked. If I was silent, they were, too. Mostly I was silent, and when I did talk, it was all pure fiction, about my ATV accident, about how I had studied philosophy at the University of Washington, about how my father was in the state department so I had spent some time in Latin America, about how I had gotten a grant to pay my living expenses while I wrote my book. I made up stories at random, whatever came into my head, as long as it was not the truth.

One day the librarian asked if I would like to come to a potluck supper and slide show by a local naturalist. I declined, promptly, and no one else ventured any invitations after that.

I was surprised to find how quickly a day could pass doing absolutely nothing except feeding myself and keeping warm. I had never used a woodstove before, and I discovered it could occupy me for hours. Every morning I spent forty-five minutes nursing the fire back to life, poking in a couple of sticks of kindling, watching the slow spread of orange as air fanned the coals, the first small finger of flame curling around a stick and slowly spreading until the fire was strong enough for me to add a log, the fire retreating as the bulk of the log dampened it, then flaring up again as the log itself caught fire, then another log, another retreat, another resurgence, until finally the heat began to spread to the iron of the stove and out into the room.

I managed my woodpile meticulously, stacking it in square even rows, knocking snow and sawdust off each log before I carried it inside, removing the logs one by one in an orderly system, so that I always left an exact forty-five-degree slope at the open end of the stack. When the snow came, I managed it as meticulously as the woodpile, and each new storm kept me busy for hours. I shoveled a whole interstate network of pathways, to the woodpile, out to the end of the driveway, around the house, down to the edge of the pond. Every path was three feet wide, with neat vertical walls, a boulevard through the snow.

Everything I did took extra time, because of my knee. I had to figure out how to load the stove, how to pick up logs, how to shovel snow, all without bending my leg. For the first weeks, until my muscles strengthened, I had to pause often to rest. Then, with time, the relearned motions became automatic. The pain in the joint was a constant in my existence, something I simply endured and got used to and gradually almost stopped noticing because it was always there.

I was mesmerized by minutiae. I could sit indefinitely in front of the open doors of the woodstove, waiting for a log to burn through and tumble in a burst of sparks. Mahlon had said I would burn twice as much wood with the doors open, so I had told him to have his brother bring me twice as much. The last load didn't come until after the driveway snowed shut, so Mahlon lent me a wheelbarrow and I had an extra job, hauling the pile a barrow at a time down my shoveled pathway from the end of the driveway to the yard. From the look on Mahlon's face, I knew he thought that my leaving the woodstove doors open was a lot stranger than trying to write the definitive book about god.

I didn't particularly care what Mahlon or anyone else thought, as long as they left me alone. There wasn't anyone in Wooler I wanted to know. I wasn't sure there was anyone anywhere I wanted to know. My life now was simple and clean, nothing to think about except snow and ice, fire and food, and getting dressed in the morning.

I was sleeping a lot, twelve or fourteen hours a day, most of the hours of darkness. The daylight hours slid past me without a sound. I shoveled and poked the fire and sat in the armchair beside the window, watching small movements of branches and marsh grass in the wind. Sometimes I saw birds, a big black raven or crow quoting Edgar Allan Poe from the top of a dead tree, or a flock of tiny fluttering gray ones busy in a bush. For days after a big ice storm, I listened to the rifle cracks of trees shattering.

My power went out for a week or so during that storm, but it didn't matter much, just a few added steps in my routine. I kept one saucepan of ice on the woodstove, to make drinking water, and another in the fridge, to keep the food cool, and I used the woods as an outhouse and stored my little bit of frozen food in a trash can outside the door. After a while the power came back on.

I paid no attention to the calendar, but I could identify weekends by the whine of snow machines on a trail a quarter of a mile away through the woods. At first I had gone to town once a week, but I began to stretch it to two and sometimes three. In between I saw and spoke to no one. I was taking books out of the library, but more often than not I didn't get around to reading them before they had to be returned. They all concerned people, one way or another, and I was not interested in that subject. I didn't need diversions anyway. The days simply slipped past, and I was never bored, not when the moving shadow of a windblown branch could keep my mind in a meditative dream for half the afternoon.

I didn't have to compel my mind to blankness here, or keep it crammed with a high-speed carnival of stimulation. It drifted of its own accord, like a leaf on a meandering lowland stream. At the end of the day, I could not identify a single specific thought that had arrested its drift for as much as a moment.

From the lights and plastic Santa Clauses in town, I knew that holidays were being celebrated, and when the lights and Santa Clauses went away, I knew I should add another digit to the date on the checks I cashed. That was as much as I needed to know about the world of human beings.

One morning I noticed that the rising sun had crept north enough to touch the front of the shed as well as the side. At noon, if the day was still, a hint of the sun's warmth could be felt, softening the bite of late-January air on the skin of my face. For the first time, I felt a slight ripple in my drift.

I looked at the braided throw rug I had bought to lay beside the bunkbed and decided I wanted a dog. No conversation, no demands, just a second body being warmed by the same allotment of firewood.

On my next trip to town, I looked in a phone book and found the nearest animal shelter. It was a forty-mile drive, and for most of the forty miles, I drove on autopilot, my mind imagining a dog. I hadn't expected to feel so eager, but now that the dog was an immediate prospect, I kept finding my speedometer inching up toward seventy on a humpy two-lane blacktop and I had to tell myself to slow down before I hit a patch of ice and totaled the car. What kind of dogs would they have, I wondered. And how would I know which was the right one? I had a partial picture in my mind, of a silky black and white coat and alert brown eyes. But what if no dog matched my picture, or all of them did?

When it came to the point, the decision was made in a moment, and no prior calculations mattered. I walked into the animal shelter, and every dog but one came tearing to the front of its cage, leaping and yapping. The one dog hung back, away from the barrier, sitting quietly. He was huge, the size and build of a Great Dane, but with a thick black coat like a collie or German shepherd. His eyes were fixed on me, not pleading, just watching intently for some sign of hope. When I stopped in front of his cage and stuck my fingers through the mesh, he stepped forward cautiously, as if his hopes had been raised and dashed too many times already and he wasn't going to risk enthusiasm again.

I filled out a form proving my fitness to have him in my care. The form was examined and approved, I paid my forty dollars, and the dog was handed over to me. Sitting in the passenger seat, he was taller than I was, his head almost brushing the roof of the car. The manager of the humane society said she had named him Bear, and I decided she had hit on his true name.

Bear was too big a dog to spend the whole day lying at my feet, so with me peg-legged and him bounding, we tramped a trail across the frozen pond and marsh and into the woods on the far side. I walked at a slow and measured pace, *da-dum, da-dum,* sticking to my path, while Bear galloped in zig-zags, sniffing, marking and returning to report.

As the days lengthened, our walks lengthened. Each day our tramped-out trail extended into a new stretch of woods, sometimes crossing a snowmobile track or passing a hunting camp or even a plowed road. I began to sleep a little less, ten hours instead of twelve or fourteen. Bear came with me in the car and slept beside the bed and rarely made a sound, just one deep bass *woof* if we encountered any living creature on our walks.

I taught him to retrieve a Frisbee, which he soon mangled, and to catch kibbles I balanced on his nose. He was not particularly alert or quick to learn, but he was quiet, strong and boundlessly good-natured. He liked me, and if he had any other thoughts, he kept them to himself.

Late in February, the nightmares began. Over and over, I woke at three in the morning, sweating and unable to fall asleep again. Bear had been hit by a car. I had left him at a kennel where the keepers teased him. He had been stolen from my car and sold to an experimental laboratory. He had eaten poisoned bait in the woods. The nightmares were clear and detailed and frighteningly real. I could see his body lying limp and bloody in the road and feel myself trying to run toward him, a scream strangled in my throat. I could see him dragged out of my car and shoved into a van with wire mesh over the windows, and feel myself running down the road, trying to overtake the van, but each step was hard labor, and the van slowly, slowly pulled away, with Bear peering through the mesh in the windows. I saw him in the woods, happily dragging a hunk of meat up out of the snow and gnawing on it, and then I saw his body spasm, take a few staggering steps and fall to the ground in convulsions, and I was running toward him, feeling the snow drag at my feet, and hearing a scream that sounded like it was someone else until I awoke and found the muscles of my throat constricted but no sound coming out. Each night the dreams were different yet the same, and I couldn't stop them coming.

I dreaded going to bed and started looking for ways to put it off. I checked out stacks of airport novels and stayed up later and later into the night, reading. I read silly English mysteries where murder is a painless and amusing brainteaser. I read hard-edged science fiction where all the characters are a compound of cynicism, ice-blue alloy metal and caffeine. I read action thrillers where lone everyman cops outwit vast organizations of seasoned, well-armed criminals engaged in treason at the highest levels. I read anything I could find that had no connection to my own life, anything that might keep me awake until I was exhausted enough to stay asleep until dawn.

In the daytime, I walked with Bear for hours, until my knee was throbbing, trying to tire myself out. I went to town as little as possible. I couldn't leave Bear alone at the shack, but I didn't think he was safe in the car, either. The nightmares felt like a warning. Even in daylight I was tormented by thoughts of what could happen to Bear if I was careless. I never left the car unlocked if he was in it. Whenever I could, I kept him with me on a leash. Most stores didn't allow dogs, so I stopped going into them. I still had to buy groceries, but other than that, I didn't need anything anyway. At the laundromat, I left my clothes to their fate and took Bear for a walk around town, one circuit for the washer, another for the dryer. At the library, I just scooped up the next foot-and-a-half stretch of books from the mystery or sci-fi shelf and then stood looking out the window toward the parking lot while the librarian stamped them for me.

Then one day in the grocery checkout line, I overheard two people talking about pet dogs being stolen out of cars and backyards and sold in Canada as training bait for fighting dogs. From the moment I heard this, it was as if the grocery clerk had gone into a time warp. I hadn't thought it was possible for a human being to move that slow. When she finally collected my money, I grabbed my bags and ran for the door. Out in the parking lot, I found a man in a checked hunting jacket peering into my car, talking to Bear through the crack at the top of the window. He smiled at me and said, "Nice dog," like he was just being friendly, but what else was the guy going to say, now that I was there. I said, "Stay away from my dog," and got out of there.

I started buying canned and frozen food by the boxload so that I could go a month without leaving the shed. My clothes smelled a little by the time I got back to the laundromat, but I figured it didn't matter since I never saw anyone. I put on a clean set for the trip to town. The rest of the time I didn't bother.

At the store, I tried to avoid getting entangled in a conversation with Mahlon. I handed him the rent and said I had to get on with my shopping. He was always inclined to chat, so I had to be almost rude to get away, but I couldn't endure to stand and listen to meaningless yammer while Bear was out in the car. If I hadn't come along when I did, that guy in the hunting jacket could have slipped a coat hanger through the cracked window and had the door open in fifteen seconds. I would have liked to leave the windows shut tight, but I didn't dare, not with the sun getting stronger every day. I had heard that a dog could die in a closed car, even when the outside temperature was close to freezing.

I planned my shopping down to the last detail so that I could whip through my list without a pause: cases of canned peaches and pears; boxes of spaghetti, cereal and rice; pounds of cheese; chicken pot pies; cans of chili and stew and spaghetti sauce; cookies, crackers and potato chips, and a giant bag of dog food. I could be in and out of the store in fifteen minutes, and I hoped that no one would get into my car in that amount of time.

After shopping, I stopped by a pay phone and called the library. The librarian would collect my next order of books and have them ready and waiting so I could duck in and out in just a couple of minutes. At the bank, I used the ATM and didn't have to leave my car at all.

I was walking more and more, hoping that physical exhaustion would bring unbroken sleep. Even so I had the nightmares. If I stayed up until two, I woke at three. If I stayed up until three, I woke at four. Only when the sky began to grow light would I fall back asleep for an hour or two and not dream.

It was April now, so there wasn't much to do with firewood, and nothing at all to do with snow, other than watch it melt and run rivers everywhere. I was walking for hours every day, but now I kept Bear on a leash in case there might be traps or poison. The marsh had become a lake, so we had found a new circuit around the water on trails and logging roads. Underfoot, the ground was either slush or mud, hard going. I would come home worn out with my feet and legs soaking wet and caked in mire, but even when I was exhausted, I didn't sleep well. My mind kept racing and racing, not with any particular thought, just with a general feeling of dread.

It occurred to me that I didn't know how old Bear was. Big dogs don't live as long, I knew. Great Danes barely made it to nine or ten, and for all I knew, he was close to that. Also, I was worried about his hips. I thought his gait might have changed a little, and I knew that some large breeds had trouble with hip dysplasia. I wasn't sure it was good to make him walk so many hours.

I tried cutting back our walks a little, but then I didn't sleep at all, so I went back to four or five hours a day. I watched the way he moved, but I couldn't tell for sure if his gait had changed. I had to hope he was okay, because I couldn't leave him behind.

My stack of books didn't last a month, so finally, in desperation, I plugged in my laptop and started playing video games in the evening to keep myself occupied until I was tired enough to sleep. I was needing less and less sleep, it seemed. Most nights, I slept only three or four hours. If I stayed in bed longer, the nightmares would come.

Often now I dreamed that I had left Bear in the car with the windows closed, in the sun, and something had happened to detain me. I couldn't get back to the car to let him out. People were talking to me and I was screaming at them that I had to go, I had to let my dog out of the car because the sun was killing him. But for some reason, I couldn't get away, because they wouldn't stop talking. They kept talking and talking, and maybe I was too polite or maybe they were holding me somehow, but I couldn't leave as long as they were talking and they wouldn't stop, even when I screamed that I had to get back to my car.

The next time I went to town, I stopped at the pay phone first and called Mahlon and asked him to put together my grocery order so that I could just pick it up. I parked near the door and we carried the boxes out and loaded them into the car, and I paid him there in the parking lot for the food and my next two months' rent.

He asked if everything was okay out at the place and I said it was fine. Then he asked how the book was coming and I said fine. It looked as if he might be ready to settle into a conversation, so I said I had to go, ducked into my car and headed for the library.

For the next few days, I walked for six hours, seven hours, eight even. My leg hurt all the time now, but I was used to it. I almost got a kick out of it, realizing that I could just go on walking and walking and the pain didn't matter. I could ignore it, because it was always there. I didn't even bother with the aspirin and ibuprofen any more. Let it hurt. I could ignore it. People walked across Antarctica on frozen feet. Their fingers and noses turned black and fell off. This was nothing.

Walking, my mind was blank, fixed on nothing but the next step, the uneven rhythm, right leg almost normal, left leg rigid, right leg striding with a hop up onto the ball, left leg swinging forward stiff in a half-circle, right with knee bent swinging forward, left rocking straight like the arm of a metronome, over and over, a thousand times, a million.

chapter sixteen

I'd been out walking almost eight hours, and the sun was low in the sky, shining straight into my face, as I returned to the shack. I had my head bent away from the light, watching where I stepped, and I was nearly yanked off my feet when Bear suddenly barked and bounded forward. The leash slipped out of my hand, and he galloped ahead.

I could see a person sitting on my front step, but the front of the shack was in deep shadow and I couldn't tell who it was. I hoped it was a Jehovah's Witness, or an insurance salesman, someone I could get rid of fast and never see again. More likely it was Mahlon, which would be a nuisance. No one had bothered me for months, but now that the weather was getting warmer, people might start thinking they ought to be more neighborly. I didn't want anyone to be neighborly. The whole reason I'd chosen this place was that people seemed to leave one another alone. I hoped that wasn't going to change just because the snow was gone.

I walked forward, slowly, squinting into the sun. When I reached the shadow, my eyes adjusted. I stopped. The person on my step was Pat.

Her hand was stroking Bear's head, and he had turned all friendly, the exact opposite of my own state of mind.

"What are you doing here?" I said.

She didn't answer right away. Her hand kept stroking the dog, but she wasn't really paying attention to him, because she was looking at me. Finally she shrugged. "I wanted to see you."

"How did you find me? Did you put the FBI onto it or something?"

She shook her head. "No."

"What gave you the right to come here? I told you I wanted to be on my own."

I felt sick inside and furious with her. Right before my eyes I could watch the last six months crumbling away, wrecked.

"Is Mom here, too?" I asked.

Pat shook her head again. "Just me."

"Why the hell did you come, when you knew I didn't want you to? I thought I made it pretty clear. I don't want you here. And for sure I don't want Mom here."

The worst thing was, my damned dog was practically curled up in her lap, like she was quadruple alpha dog.

"Why did you come?" I repeated.

Pat wasn't looking at me anymore. She was looking down at Bear, rubbing his ears, then she was looking off at the remnants of my woodpile, so intently I thought she must be counting the logs.

"I guess I missed the email," she said finally. She kept her eyes on the woodpile.

I'd been standing still and stiff, looking at her, but now, all of a sudden, my knee felt raw and ragged, like I'd walked a million steps with two rough splintered ends of bone grinding against each other.

"I really don't need this right now," I said. "I was getting along fine, until you showed up. But I suppose you thought you could be the white knight, riding to the rescue."

I needed to sit down soon or I was going to pass out.

"I didn't come here for your sake," Pat said.

"What do you mean?"

I was getting dizzy, from nausea. I wished I had a walking stick to steady myself.

"Could we go inside?" she said. "I'm cold from sitting, and you look like all your blood just got called away to an emergency."

When I moved, the grinding in my joint sent white-hot pain shooting up and down my bones. Pat had waited where she was, but after a couple of steps I staggered a little and she came and took my arm to steady me.

"I seriously don't need this right now," I said. "I've been walking fine for months."

"I gathered that," she said. "The people at the store said you walk twelve, fifteen miles every day, any weather."

"How do they know what I do?"

"You think people in a town like this don't know what you do? Probably somebody six miles from here takes his dog out and sees your tracks."

"Nobody has ever said anything to me about seeing my tracks."

"I think they've gotten the message that you want to be left alone."

"If they can get it, why can't you? I was feeling fine, and now I feel like shit."

Inside the house, I sat in the armchair with my leg stretched out, and the pain receded to its normal throb, no shooting knives. Pat sat on one of the folding chairs, and Bear immediately laid his head on her knee, as if that was the place of honor.

"Christ, you've even stolen my dog," I said.

"You stole mine, so it's fair enough. Skipper still watches for you, every day."

"He does?"

She nodded. "Whenever a car drives in, he picks up a stick and runs to meet it. As soon as he finds it isn't you, he looks completely downcast and goes off and lies down with the stick between his paws."

This time the pain was a giant starburst right in the center of my gut, burning outward in waves, forcing itself out in tears. I bent forward to hide my face, and the waves swept through me, rising from the center and pouring out and out and out.

Someone else would have come and put her arms around me, but Pat didn't move. Instead I felt Bear pushing his head in close to my face, nosing me, and I went on bawling like a baby until I was drained dry and only a dull, flat redness remained.

"How did you find me?" I asked. I was stirring two pots on the stove, chili and corn out of cans. Pat had offered to cook dinner so that I could keep the weight off my leg, but I said hell, no, the leg had had weight on it for the last six months and it could have weight on it tonight. It hurt a lot worse than it had for the last six months, though.

"Through the animal rescue," she said.

"Do they find missing persons, too?"

"No. But you'd said you might get a dog, so I thought I might find out where you were that way. I had to invent a pretty good story to get the shelters to tell me anything."

"Are you saying you guessed I would come to Maine and started calling animal shelters here?"

She smiled. "I'm not clairvoyant. I tried a lot of other states first."

While we were eating, I heard the whole tale. She and Mom had been searching since January. First they had asked Breeze if I had left any credit card bills so that they could get my card number and track down my address. But I hadn't. Then they had called all the state motor vehicle departments with a phony inquiry about my registration. But I hadn't changed my plates. Then they had gone to the phone lists on the Net and called every single Jordan and J. McNeil on the lists. That had taken a long time, because there are a lot of J. McNeils in the world. Then they had called power companies, with some phony story about a problem with a bill. But my bill was in Mahlon's name. Finally, they had moved on to the animal shelters.

"You must have racked up quite a phone bill," I said.

"Not too awful bad. We changed companies a few times, to take advantage of introductory offers. But the number of people I've lied to would fill a town bigger than Kilgore."

"Why didn't you call the police and have them look?"

"You're legal age. You said you wanted to be alone. We weren't going to call the police."

"Did the shelter tell you where I was?"

"No. Only that you had adopted a Great Dane mix. Once I knew that, I came out here and drew a circle on a map and started cruising general stores and diners."

"What, have you been going around asking everyone if they knew a guy with a bum leg and a Great Dane?"

She smiled. "Not directly. I had an idea people might not talk if they thought I was nosy. I'd just chat a little and mention that I'd seen a guy with a dog as big as a Shetland pony, and they would either say 'Huh?' or they would start talking about all the big dogs in their neighborhood. I hit Wooler and people said, 'Must have been that dog of Jordy's,' so I went down the street and asked someone else for directions to your place."

"You're persistent," I said.

"I spent years chipping rock. This was nothing. Especially since there were two of us."

It struck me as odd, suddenly, that Pat was the one who had come to find me.

"Why didn't Mom come, instead of you?"

Pat hesitated and looked away.

"That's complicated," she said. "I wanted to come. And we both thought she might be . . . too complicated. For you, I mean. I'm not so close to home. But she could be here tomorrow, if you want her to come."

"No," I said, really fast.

Pat didn't say anything, and after a minute I asked, "Did you tell her you found me?"

She nodded. "She needed to know you were all right. But she won't come see you unless you want her to."

"Why should I believe that? I didn't want you to come, but you did anyway."

She was quiet for a long time. She was staring at my clothes hanging on nails, the way she had stared at my woodpile.

"Donna is thinking about what helps you," she said finally. "I was thinking about myself."

"What do you mean?"

She was quiet once again, and I almost expected her to get up and start folding my shirts, she was staring at them so intently.

"There was another time when I let someone vanish out of my life and didn't do anything. You know about that. Alma Rose. She didn't want me to find her, and I took her at her word. You can't push people into things, so I didn't try. I just set to work hammering on a rock. And maybe I'm not sorry now. Because of Donna. But you don't . . . "

Her voice caught, and she stopped. Now she was staring at the wall, like she was reading the installation instructions on the insulation.

"When you lose a lover, there's the chance you'll find someone else and move on. But you don't move on to another kid . . . I know you're not my kid . . . You're not even a kid, for god's sake . . . But . . . "

She stopped again.

"It's different. For Donna. You're her son, no matter what. But with me, you could vanish. I could be left behind. Somebody you knew once. That feeling was too familiar, and I couldn't stand it this time."

She smiled suddenly. "Lucky Jordy. I was stupid twelve years ago, and now you get to suffer through my learning curve. You can tell me to go to hell, you know. I just wanted to be sure I got told to my face this time."

It was a strange feeling to discover I had been living on my own private asteroid. I mean, I knew Mom would worry about me, because that's what mothers do, and I guess I thought Breeze might worry a little, too, because she worried about every single problem on the planet. But it hadn't occurred to me that Pat would be so bothered. She never got bothered about things, or she didn't seem to. But if I had thought about it, I would have realized that a person had to be fairly bothered to spend years carving a sculpture of someone who had ditched her, and if I had thought a little further, I might have realized that my hitting the road could call up some hard memories for her.

On the other hand, this was totally different. I wasn't her lover. I was just her step-kid. How could she be anywhere near as bothered about my leaving as she had been about Alma Rose? A person couldn't go to the library and find shelves of poetry written by parents to their children. Never mind their stepchildren.

And yet here she was, about a thousand phone calls later, sitting on one of my folding chairs.

Pat wasn't looking at me. In fact she hadn't looked at me once the whole time she was telling me she wouldn't go to hell unless the order came face to face. She was looking down at Bear, rubbing him behind the ears, and his head lolled against her leg in total capitulation.

Pat's concentration on the dog was intent out of all proportion and I realized suddenly that I hadn't said a word since she had told me I could kick her out if I wanted.

"You don't have to go," I said. "To hell or anywhere else."

She let out a long, long breath, but she still didn't look at me.

247

That night, instead of nightmares, I woke up with a strong hard-on, which was unexpected and also awkward. One feature of a metal bunkbed is that every little movement travels through the frame from one bunk to the other and every little sound gets amplified by all that metal tubing. I lay still to hear if Pat's breathing was steady. When I was sure she was asleep, I brought myself off, quietly, trying to quell any involuntary movements. I twitched a little, in spite of myself, and then held my breath, listening, but the breathing from the upper bunk didn't change.

The whole episode was strange. I had been doing myself every few days, out of habit, but it was pretty much like brushing my teeth. Hygiene. I really hadn't been thinking about women, or sex, for months. More accurately, I hadn't been thinking about anything for months, and "anything" included women.

And it wasn't as if I had suddenly started fantasizing about my stepmother. She was close to fifty and built like a good sound oak tree. Nor did I imagine that she had been fantasizing about me, an undergrown cottonwood sprout of the wrong sex. And yet I could not escape the sensation that old Freud was sitting there watching me jerk off with a really annoying smile on his face.

It was clear to me I had no desire to crawl up to the other bunk. Yet it was equally clear that my waking up was not a pure coincidence. So what was going on?

My knee was hurting like a bastard, and for the first time in weeks I thought I was going to need some pills or I would never get back to sleep. I slid out of bed and found my way by feel to the bathroom. I couldn't find the pills by feel, so I pulled the curtain closed and turned on the light. Ibuprofen, I decided. It did more long-term damage, so it must be more effective. I swallowed a couple of pills, switched off the light and started feeling my way back to the bed.

"Jordy, you okay?"

Had she been awake the whole time? But I could hear her breathing now, and it was different, awake-sounding. The light under the bottom of the curtain must have waked her.

"Just getting some ibuprofen. My knee's a little sore."

"It should be. They're going to think your muscle tone is amazing when you start your rehab."

I froze, halfway to the bed.

"Is that the real reason you've come out here?" I said. "All the other stuff was so much baloney, wasn't it? That's really why you're here, to talk me into getting my knee fixed. An emissary from Mom, bearing common sense."

There was a long silence. I could hear little metal creaks coming from the woodstove and gurgles from the refrigerator and Bear snoring on his rug, but not a sound from the bunkbed. Finally she sat up.

"Are you wide awake right now?" she asked.

"You could say so."

"So am I."

She climbed out of her bunk and slid to the floor. As she did, a whole string of bizarre images flashed through my head—she had grabbed me by the shoulders and was shaking me, like a troublesome six-year-old; she had ripped off my shorts and pulled me onto the bed with her; she had thrown a coat over her nightgown and put on her boots and stormed out the door.

In reality, she did none of those things. She simply walked over and stood beside the window, leaning against the casing and staring out into the darkness. There was no moon, just faint stars, so I couldn't see her expression.

"You can do whatever you want with your knee," she said. "I may think you're a damned fool if you leave it the way it is, but it's your knee. I didn't come here to talk to you about your knee."

She went on staring out the window. The outlines of trees were humps of black against the lesser black of the sky. After a while I needed to get the weight off my leg, so I sat down on the edge of the bed.

She started talking again, slowly. "I came here because every day I was turning on my computer and connecting to my email and not finding anything, and it was taking me back to a couple of times in my life that were pure blank pain. Blank like a computer screen after it flashes the message that it's checking for mail and then comes back with nothing. No cheery tune announcing that there's mail. But no Bronx cheer, either. No 'Nyah, nyah, you didn't get any.' Just an empty screen. Silence. That's the worst. I'd rather the computer jeered at me. I kept wishing I could reprogram it so that it would say something rude. The same way I wished that Alma Rose had written to say she didn't love me anymore and was having a wonderful life elsewhere. The same way I wished my mother could send back a message saying, 'It's unimaginably beautiful here, so don't feel sad for me.' Or 'There's nothing after death. I am now recycled carbon, so live your life and enjoy the flowers.' But there was just silence. And that's the worst.

"And I couldn't even complain, because I've been that silence myself. I've given off that blankness. Alma Rose used to rage at it. Probably it's why she left. Your mother puts up with me, luckily, and maybe I don't fall into that blankness as often now. But I know that silence really well, from the inside, and the one thing I know is that it doesn't go all the way through. It's like Styrofoam packing peanuts, absorbing the shocks. The more breakable the object, the thicker the cushion of Styrofoam.

"When I started meeting that silence on my computer screen, my first reaction was 'I can be more silent than you. There's no one alive who can be blanker than I can be.' It's always worked before. But I couldn't pull it off this time. I don't know why not. I've hardly ever gotten mad in my life, but this time I did. This was not going to happen to me again.

"When I started looking for you, I wasn't thinking about whether you needed help. The only thought in my mind was that you were one of the best things that has ever happened to me and I wasn't going to let you vanish. That's all. That's the only reason I'm here."

She had a very low-pitched, steady voice, even when she was talking about being mad. And even when she was talking, there was a part of her that stayed silent. I couldn't see her face in the darkness. There was just her voice, coming as close as she was ever likely to come to saying she loved me. It was like a gift, naked, no strings, and I didn't know how to answer.

She hadn't moved from her spot by the window. Her nightgown caught what light there was, a gray ghost. I stood up and crossed the room, put my arms around her. She hesitated, then tentatively returned the gesture. I leaned my head against her shoulder, with my face close to her hair.

Big mistake. My nerves weren't reliable right now. They were all wound up in a bruised tangle of confusion, and the moment I touched someone, felt the warmth of another person's body, they all let loose at once. I started crying, shaking with sobs, and words came pouring out, an incoherent jumble about Spider, and then about Bear, and then about June, and my knee was shooting knives up and down my bones, and my belly and chest felt the shape of her, a woman's shape, warm and soft, and I smelled her hair and skin, a woman's scent, warm and close against my face, and before I could stop them, my hands were traveling over her body, fumbling to reach past cloth and touch the warmth of skin.

Her voice was quiet. "Jordy, no."

Then a half-laugh. "I'm queer, remember?"

I wanted to yank myself away and flee, to the far side of the room where I could curl myself up into a ball. What hallucination had possessed me? It had passed, in a hurry, when she spoke.

She didn't let me pull away. She was stronger than I realized. She held me there, not right against her, but not letting me get away, either. Only her hands held me, but the grip was convulsive.

After a minute, I relaxed a little, and her grip relaxed a little, but she didn't let go.

"I'm sorry. That was crazy. I'm sorry . . . "

She shook her head. "There's no need."

Her hands dropped, and she looked away, toward the window. She seemed lost in some thought of her own.

"It would all be so easy, if feelings came along one at a time," she said slowly. "With a government label, so you knew what they were. If I'd known . . . "

She paused and then went on. "I spent two decades not knowing. People don't realize that not loving hurts as much as loving. It's like you've got a tourniquet on, closing off feeling. And when you finally release the tourniquet, the feeling can spurt out all over the place. Make you do crazy things. Carve a naked statue for the tourists to look at, two exits down from the Reptile Gardens."

She turned back and looked straight at me then. "Or start coming on to an old lady you absolutely would not want to find in bed with you in the morning."

"You're not old . . . " I said, because I thought I had to say something. I couldn't believe she had talked about it, straight out. Or maybe I could believe it. She couldn't make ordinary conversation, but this was exactly what she could do, talk about something most people wouldn't want to mention.

"I'm old enough," she said.

"Not to act like an idiot, you mean."

She laughed. "To have acted like one already."

Then she surprised me again. She took my hands in hers, lifted them to her lips for a quick kiss, then released them.

"Your mother is right," she said. "You're the best."

My mother. Shit.

"You're not going to tell her about this, are you?"

"What is there to tell? If people had to account for everything they ever thought about doing, we'd all be locked up."

The sky had lightened to gray behind the humped silhouettes of pine and hemlock. We agreed on breakfast, though it was not yet six. I made a pot of coffee and laid out my selection of cold cereal, apologizing because I only had canned milk.

"I haven't been going to the store very often."

"So I gathered," she said. "The man there was quite concerned. I've never met someone so eager to give directions."

"He was?"

"Sure."

"He never told me he was concerned."

"What you did wasn't any of his business. But he was very glad to meet someone whose business it was. He said you didn't like to leave your car."

As we ate, I began telling her a little about my time here. It was like looking back at a dream, now.

"I think I was going mental for a while there," I said. "It wasn't the car I couldn't leave. It was Bear. I thought something horrible was going to happen to him. I didn't dare leave him, even for a minute. Crazy, huh? But I'd been having nightmares, that he'd been stolen or shot or poisoned. It got so bad, I was afraid to go to sleep."

Pat's presence had been like daylight, dispelling wild imaginings, but now, describing the details of my nightmares, I felt the dread return. I told her about the images, Bear writhing in the snow, Bear peering through the mesh on the windows of the van, and as I talked, I began to sweat.

"There was one dream that kept coming back, over and over . . . " I said.

I told her about leaving Bear in the car, closed in, suffocating. I told her about being trapped in conversation, desperate to get back to him, but caught up in talk that went on and on. My throat seemed to close up, clamped in dread, as if I were the one suffocating.

"But this person wouldn't stop talking. And I knew something terrible would happen, but still I stayed there, talking and talking . . . I just fucking kept on talking . . . "

My body started shaking in spasms, and I couldn't stop them.

"Who were you talking to?" Pat asked.

"What?"

"Who were you talking to, when you kept talking and didn't leave?"

"I don't know. Nobody real. Just someone. It wasn't him that kept talking. That was what was so stupid. It was me. I could have left anytime, but I seemed to think I had to stay, that I had to go on chatting about nothing, to be nice . . . "

"What were you talking about?"

"Nothing. Nothing that makes any sense. Just chit-chat. Something about writing some graffiti, right at eye level, where people would see it . . . "

Graffiti. It all made perfect sense. I'd been having the dream for weeks, but it had been a masquerade and I couldn't see past the disguises. Now, describing it to Pat, the lights came up and the faces were so clear I couldn't understand how I had ever been mystified.

"It was Spider," I said. I could see his jacket, like the wall of a men's room, with pictures tacked up among the scribbles. "He wanted to leave, and I kept talking. You know, 'Hey, how's it going, man?' Like I'm cool, I'm hip. I can do this scene. And for some unfathomable reason, he decided to be polite and talk to me. He should have told me to buzz off. What did I know about him and his life? This nice little suburban computer nerd, trying to cross the culture gap, trying to show that we're all just human beings and if we would only talk to each other, the problems would all work out. And instead all I did was set him up to get slaughtered.

"If I hadn't been there, doing my bit for justice and harmony, he'd have been five blocks away when that gun started blasting. But he wasn't. He was there, talking to me about Shawn Kemp and what life was like in Kilgore. You know what the last thing he said was? 'How did you get out?' Like, 'How can I get out?' And about two seconds later he got his answer. 'This is your way out, sucker. This is the only way out you're ever going to see, so you better hope there is a god and that he has a guilty conscience about treating you like dirt while you were alive . . . '"

At that moment the sun found a gap in the trees and sent a shaft of golden light blazing through the window. As if god were saying, "Don't worry, son, I'm still looking out for *you*." The light hit the foil walls and fragmented, scattering patches of brightness around the room.

Pat was silent for a while.

"So what's the story with Cheryl Brisby?" she asked.

"Who?"

"You didn't read the newspapers afterwards?"

I shook my head.

"She was one of the witnesses. She saw you talking to Spider, and it made her nervous. You didn't look like you belonged there. She thought either he or you might be making trouble, somehow. So she crossed the street. She had just reached the other sidewalk when the shooting started. She said you could draw two lines, her path across the street and the path she would have taken to where you and Spider were standing, and the two lines would be the same length. So if you two hadn't been there, she would have been. She said she thought god must have been looking out for her that day."

"I suppose she meant the same god who looks out for the winning team in the Super Bowl," I said. "The one who wants to see the losing team suffer."

"I think she meant she was glad to be alive, that's all. Except for that one moment, she hadn't had a whole lot more luck than Spider."

Pat described a little of what the newspaper had said about Cheryl Brisby, the survivor who thanked god for her moment of good luck. Three kids with severe chronic asthma, their father in jail for possession. Almost a year out of work before she landed a temp job in the evenings, telemarketing, at minimum wage plus pocket change. No good aiming a lot higher. If she earned too much, Medicaid stopped paying for the kids. Her niche was carved out for her, precise as the crevice that makes some birds evolve a skinny beak.

"Is this supposed to make me feel better?" I said. "As if we were her one lucky break? As if we saved her life by standing there?"

"You didn't save her life. A million things could have happened differently. Spider could have gotten to that spot two minutes earlier, and you'd never have seen him."

"What is the point, then? That it doesn't matter what we do? Spider's jacket was right? Life sucks. Period."

"That's putting it in two words."

"You agree with me, then?"

"You're more concise than I could be."

"How would you put it?"

She didn't answer. She went to the stove and turned on the burner to heat up the coffee, then started carrying dishes to the sink. She didn't look like she planned on answering, so I prodded her.

"I want to know how you would put it. You can have three words. Four even."

"I'm not an oracle," she said. "I don't have an answer."

"You have your own point of view."

"My point of view has been changing, thanks to you."

"How?"

"You've made me recognize that life sucks," she said. Then she laughed. "Don't look so dismayed."

But I was dismayed. I felt as sick at heart as I would have if Bear had acquired the power of speech just long enough to tell me I was right and there was nothing more to be said. I must have been expecting her to argue with me, to tell me that life would be easier when I was older and wiser.

"I didn't really mean that," she said. "Not the way it sounded."

"What did you mean, then?"

"I meant that you are so . . . unguarded. It makes me feel like I've been sleepwalking. Like I've kept myself safe by staying with what I've always known. Like I suspected the world was painful, so I kept my distance. With you there is no distance. You let everything touch you. It's frightening sometimes to watch the world tear you apart and see you come back for more. The way you did with my dog Lucy, when I first met you. She had just ripped your leg to shreds, and all you could think about was how to save her, how to win her over with kindness."

"A lot of good it did. She still had to be put down."

"It did do good . . . I can't explain . . . " She stopped. She was over in the corner of the kitchen, fiddling with dishes, with her back to me. "Maybe it didn't change anything, but it did me good. To have someone else cry out against the pain. You're right. Life hurts like hell. And the way most of us handle it is with anesthesia. Don't care too much. Resign yourself. Turn cynical. Be cool and hip and streetwise, like you've seen it all before. Whatever it takes. Anything to stay alive and sane. Anything to get by. And I've been getting by all right. I could go on just the way I always have, living where I've always lived, saving money for a nice secure retirement. But then I look at my life and I think, that's what I've already had. A nice secure retirement. Now I want to do something."

"You made that sculpture. That's doing something, isn't it?"

She laughed. "My stepmother used to say I'd made the world's biggest tombstone. A monument to having loved somebody once in my life. That's what it might have been, too, if Donna hadn't come along."

"What will you do?"

"I'm not sure. All I know is, I've been safe and settled and middle-aged since I was about eighteen. Now that I really am middle-aged, maybe I'll try out nineteen. Or twenty-two."

Turned out she didn't have in mind anything simple, like buying roller blades or piercing her nostrils. She was thinking of something that, for her, was a lot more radical. She wanted to leave Kilgore. When she first said it, I couldn't believe it.

"You've always seemed so perfectly content," I said. "Like you belonged there."

"Do you know how many times I've closed out the cash register for the night?" she asked.

I shook my head.

"About nine thousand, give or take a few hundred. And you know what? I think I've finally got it down. So now I can move on to something else."

I stared at her and found myself breaking into a grin.

"That's awesome, Pat. What does Mom think about it?"

"She doesn't know yet."

"What? When did you decide this?"

"Today."

"She's going to freak."

"She knows I've been restless, ever since I hired an assistant manager."

"She's still going to freak."

"Maybe."

Panic thought. "You're not leaving her, are you?"

"Not a chance. I'm restless, not crazy."

"What if she won't leave Kilgore? You know she's not happy unless she can see twenty miles in every direction."

Silence, for a good long time.

"I hope she will. It doesn't have to be forever. I don't know if I'll be happy myself. I just feel the way you did, a few years ago. Get me out of this place."

Later in the morning, Pat and I drove into town, and she called Mom to tell her I was reasonably functional, no longer in immediate danger of cracking up. She left out quite a few details, although she did say it was good she had come, before I turned irretrievably peculiar.

Mom started making some noises about coming out to inspect me for herself, so I got on the phone and told her I was happy as a lark, that a six-month meditative retreat was exactly what I had needed, and I was now thoroughly in touch with myself. Like Pat, I left out a few details, like my going a month without changing my clothes and being afraid to leave my dog long enough to buy groceries. I also didn't mention how my stepmother had been obliged to fend off my juvenile gropings, or that my knee was feeling like it had broken glass where it should have had cartilage. I wasn't sure how Mom would react to the first piece of information, but I knew the second one would have her on the next plane east. I didn't want her there, telling me I would regret it every day until I was eighty if I didn't get the joint fixed.

The other little detail I couldn't face telling her was that I hadn't bothered to keep up the payments on my health insurance. It wasn't that I couldn't afford the surgery without insurance, but I knew she would be speechless at the stupidity of blowing $50K because I hadn't bothered to give the insurance company my new address. I didn't think I could explain to her where my head had been in the six months before Pat showed up on my doorstep.

Pat never asked me about my health. Maybe she didn't have to. She could see for herself that my leg didn't bend at all and that I had to turn my head to look at things on my right. Other people would have asked anyway so that I would know they cared. But it seemed that Pat had spent about a year's worth of speech since she'd arrived, and now she had reverted to her usual self, dropping a comment here and there but mostly quiet.

She never referred to what had happened that first night, but I didn't feel she was avoiding the subject. It hadn't bothered her, and she didn't need to talk about it, that's all. She probably would have called it her capacity for blankness. I thought it was another example of her not seeing the world the way other people did. It was as if she had her own definition of reality. She hadn't been shocked. She hadn't been morally outraged. I'm not sure she had even been physically repelled. She just didn't want to mess up a friendship that was important to her.

She might call herself an old lady, but she wasn't. She wasn't a parent, either. Parents generally had an air of knowing what's best, even my mother, who was a lot cooler than most parents. Pat never had that air. She was so totally in the habit of marching to her own drummer, she just assumed that everyone else did, too, and wouldn't want her advice about how to do it.

We weren't exactly friends, either, not the way Reba and I were friends. Pat was too old. Or I was too young. She might talk about going back to try out twenty-two, but she didn't totally mean it. She didn't mean she was going to zap a current through her brain to erase twenty-five years of experience. She just meant she wanted to take a chance on something unfamiliar. She and I would always be looking at the world from different points of reference. For me, Vietnam, the moon landings, Martin Luther King Jr. and Cold War bomb shelters were part of history. For her, they had been news. She still wore a watch with hands and a face. We would never be peers.

Still, in an odd way, we seemed closer in age now than we had ever seemed before. Here she was, itching to bust out and do something wild, and here I was, with both body and mind feeling bruised and cautious. Her silence was exactly what I needed. It was like her half-spoken offer of love. Just there, no strings. If I was silent, too, she didn't mind. She almost didn't seem to notice, and I was very grateful for that trait of hers, that not noticing.

I tried taking her around my long circuit of paths and logging roads through the woods, but after half an hour I had to turn back. I was pouring sweat, not from exertion, but from pain. It seemed like a faraway dream, that I had been able to walk for hours at a time and feel nothing I couldn't shrug off.

Pat accepted the change in plan without comment. We returned to my cabin, and she immediately went into the kitchen and put on a saucepan of water, saying she wanted some tea. She made a cup for me, also, and remembered how I liked it, sugar but no milk. We sat out on the front steps in the early May sunshine.

Bear was the one who had acted puzzled at the abbreviation of our usual walk. When I sat down with my mug of tea, he lay down facing me and stared, and I thought, that's all I need, a guilt trip from my dog. To cut off his reproach, I found the Frisbee and flipped it for him to catch. Unlike Skipper, he would chase and retrieve indefinitely, so I could always give him exercise without moving myself.

I knew what Mom would have said right then, that I should have the surgery now before my muscles started to atrophy again. I was enough like her that I could hear my rational mind saying the same thing. Probably Pat was thinking it, too. But Pat kept the thought to herself, and Mom wasn't there, and I had a gag tied around rationality, because for some reason I didn't want to hear what it had to say. At this moment, the idea of surgery was worse than the glass shards in my knee.

As far as I could tell, Pat had neither a particular purpose nor a particular deadline in mind for her visit. She had brought books with her and seemed content to sit for hours reading. At other times we sat together drinking tea and looking out at the pond, hardly talking. Whole days went by with only a few words of conversation.

I was surprised at her lack of concern for the time passing. In the past, she had treated the Mercantile like a rare orchid that might shrivel up and die if she left it too long in someone else's care. Now she didn't seem to mind if it shriveled. One evening, when she returned from her check-in phone call to Mom, I asked if the Mercantile was getting along okay without her. She shrugged and said she hadn't thought to ask.

Another evening she brought back some news that interested me. Mom had gotten an email from Mips, saying he was bored with computers and was going back to philosophy. He was entering a Ph.D. program and planned to teach and write books someday.

"He says, if there aren't any job openings when he graduates, he can always endow his own chair," Pat said.

"That sounds like him," I said. I didn't mention the other half of my thought, that his plan meant he wouldn't be starting any new companies anytime soon. Not unless he got bored again.

"He also wondered what you'd been up to lately," Pat said. "Should she tell him anything?"

I smiled a little. "Maybe she should say I've been doing more or less the same thing myself. Occupying a chair in philosophy."

In my state of mind, Pat was the only person whose company I could tolerate. She was the one person I knew who found solace in silence rather than talk.

As much as I could, I left it to her to communicate with Mom. If I went with her and spoke on the phone, Mom invariably came around to asking about my plans. I had no plans and was tired of saying so. I was simply not in the mood for conversation, about plans or anything else.

It almost seemed that Pat had settled in to wait until my mood changed. I suppose she knew that reticence was not my true nature, the way it was hers, so I was not going to stay silent forever. If there was anyone who could outlast a desert with silence, it was Pat, and after a while I did find myself starting to talk. I couldn't help it in the end. Her presence became a pull. The space needed filling.

It was raining, and we were still sitting at the table long after breakfast, because there was no particular reason to move. Outside the window, the evergreen trees looked almost black in the mist, but the grass and bushes were such an intense, translucent green they seemed lit from inside.

I remembered how this view had looked the previous November, like a root-bound plant, matted, faded and dried out, the water and sky as dull as pewter.

"When I first came, I thought this was the most desolate place I had ever seen," I said. "It wasn't even big, like the land around Kilgore. I thought it looked like a sickly version of the Northwest. But now I've grown a little attached to it. Not that it's grand or awesome or anything like that. You have to like details. Like hearing the ice crack and groan when the weather warms up. It's wet enough for me, at least. The sun used to drive me nuts out west. Day after day after day of it. Even in Seattle, in the summer. And then in the winter, day after day after day of gray. It isn't like that here. It's always changing. One day it's snowing, the next day it's ten below and crystal clear, and the next it's forty degrees and raining, then the day after that, you can't see the pond, the fog's so thick. It's more mixed up than I am. Makes you feel you can't count on anything to stay around. But you won't get stuck with anything for too long either. So it's good or bad, depending on your mood.

"In California, you hit May and you know it's going to be sunny for the next six months. What could be better, right? Everybody but me seems to love it. I loved it, too, for a while. But then it started to get to me, waking up every morning and knowing it was going to be a perfect sunny day. It stopped meaning anything, to have the sun shining. It got to be like eating when you aren't hungry, like I was bloated with too much sunshine. And at the same time, I thought, How can I not be happy, with all this money, and all this nice weather? What ails me?

"So now I'm in Maine, where people can't wait to talk about how rotten the weather is. If you're in a rotten mood, you can blame it on that, instead of feeling like you must be pathological. And whenever the sun is out, you really feel it. You just drink it in, because you know it's going to cloud up again before too long. And when it's cloudy, you can really wallow in the gloom, because you know it isn't going to last for weeks and weeks. You know the sun will be out again to rescue you before you sink into despair."

It surprised me, how much I remembered. I didn't think I had even noticed the weather, the sky, the vegetation or anything else during the last six months, but now that I had someone to talk to, I found it all reeling back out, as if I'd had a jetliner black box automatically recording my surroundings even when I thought my mind was blank. I started telling Pat about the pond and the marsh and how their colors would change every week, and about the different kinds of snow, some as fine and dry as talcum powder, some like a frozen margarita, some glazed with a mirror of ice. I told her how the light changed as the sun's arc climbed higher in the sky: milky, diffused and subtle in January; sharp blue shadows and yellow highlights in February; then March, bright and flat, not much character except on one rare day when the sun shone through a thin veil of falling snow; and then April, softened, muted by the warmth and moisture in the air. I told her about water falling, in mosquito specks of crystal; drenching, wind-driven sheets; pellets of stinging ice; slow floating clusters of fluff.

For the last six months, I had walked through water and air and sun, as unaware of them as they were of me, and they had offered beauty and harshness with equal absence of calculation.

For four days now, Bear and I had not walked more than a hundred yards from my cabin. My knee was hurting to the point that it intruded on thought. The less I walked, the more it hurt, but walking had become unendurable.

Pat still ventured no advice, but she did, finally, venture a question.

"What is it you dread?" she asked.

"Why do you think I dread something?"

"Because even a lab rat shuns physical pain, unless the scientist has found something it dreads more."

I tried to visualize the surgery, which some blind instinct was resisting. Was it the scalpel slicing through my skin? I flinched at the thought, but only for a moment.

Was it the months of laborious rehabilitation, the pages of exercises, the hours with weights and stationary bicycles? There would be women in Lycra. Why would I dread that?

Was it the anesthesia? I could feel myself sliding pleasantly and drowsily into oblivion. No pain at all.

And then I felt my body start to shake, uncontrollably, with disconnected images of bodies in pieces, of blood and of people crying, "How do I get out?"

"Jordy, what's wrong? What's going on?"

"It's the waking up," I said. "That's what I dread. It's as if, even though you're anesthetized, your mind has felt the pain. You don't escape. Not really. The anesthesia just keeps you still, so the scalpel doesn't slip. Inside, you know what really happened. And when you finally wake up, it's all right there, and you have to live through it. You thought you were blissfully asleep, but then you wake up and you realize all the horrors you thought you had escaped.

"And right now, my knee is like an anesthetic. Sure it hurts, but that pain is simple and physical, and it helps blot out all the other worse things I could be feeling. If that pain goes away, then I'll wake up. And it will all be right there. People killing each other for no reason. People picking on anyone who looks weak. People trampling each other to get more money. People hating their own families. Out here, I can watch the snow falling, and it's clean and beautiful. I can feel sleet blowing against me, chilling me to the bone, and that's a clean, hard sensation. And most of the time, I can block out the knowledge that I belong to a really shitty species."

There was silence for a minute, and then Pat smiled a little.

"Thanks for the compliment," she said.

"I didn't mean you."

"Who did you mean, then?"

I couldn't answer. Everyone. No one. All of us, sometimes.

That evening, Pat came back from the village with a bottle of wine. Neither of us needed much wine to achieve an altered state. Two glasses each, and we were laughing at nothing.

"I plan to be a tyrant in an easy chair," I said, "ordering my servants about."

"A gouty British lord, with a crimson smoking jacket and a rug across your knees."

"Exactly. Drinking stout. Or claret. What do British lords drink?"

"Everything, I think."

"Then that's what I'll drink. And I'll get a giant-screen TV, with two hundred channels."

"And an ergonomically designed recliner."

"Yes. And I can eat whatever I want, since I don't plan to move ever again. I'll get too fat to stand up."

"You'll need a catheter then."

"Good point. Do you think I can buy a recliner with a built-in toilet seat?"

"For a price, you can buy anything."

"In that case, I want it to be equipped with a Jacuzzi, too. It must have a hydraulic lift, to lower me into the water and lift me out again. I will keep my house at eighty degrees and dispense with clothing forever, and when I wake up in the morning, a servant will appear and start feeding me spoonfuls of chocolate mousse."

In the morning I was sober. "Don't you have to get back to the Mercantile sometime?" I asked.

Pat had been here ten days. "Would you like me to go?" she asked.

"That's not what I meant. I thought you might be worrying."

"It's just a store."

"What about Mom? Don't you miss her?"

"Of course I do. But we talk. We have plenty of time ahead."

"Aren't you bored? There's nothing to do here."

"I don't get bored doing nothing. I get bored doing something boring," she said. "What are you really asking me, Jordy? Would you like your solitude back?"

I shook my head. "I've had my fill, I think."

She waited, not saying anything. She took a couple of sips of her tea, then sat with her hands curled around the mug, not looking at anything in particular. I knew she would wait all day if she had to.

"Do you think . . . ?" I stopped.

She waited some more.

"Do you think the docs in Seattle could refer me to a surgeon somewhere around here?"

"Yes." Totally noncommittal.

"Would you stick around if they did?"

"If you want."

"They might not take me for a while."

She shrugged.

"Do you think they'll take me at all, with no insurance? I mean, I can pay, but how do they know that?"

Now she looked away, like she was uneasy all of a sudden.

"You do have insurance," she said.

"How?"

"Don't jump the fence. You know Donna well enough by now. It shouldn't be a surprise."

"She paid my bill for me."

"She can't help it, you know. If you blame anyone, blame Charles Darwin. There is strong selective pressure toward maternal instinct in mammals."

My surgery date was in Boston, later in the month. After looking at my X-rays and scans, the surgeon said it was physically impossible that I had walked almost a thousand miles on the joint. He said the end of my femur reminded him of what's left after a Bush Hog chews up a sapling. Shredded.

I said it had been mind over matter.

He said perhaps my mind should be X-rayed, too. He was smiling, though.

When the day was fixed, Pat asked me to do her a favor. "Call Donna, and tell her you want her to be here."

"I'm getting the surgery. Isn't that enough?"

"Would it be that hard for you, having her here?"

"She'll want to know what I'm going to do afterwards. She'll want me to have a plan."

"Tell her you don't have one."

"I've told her that a thousand times."

"So you have, and she still hasn't disowned you. I doubt she will this time."

"That isn't the point. Obviously she won't disown me. She's my mother."

"Not everyone can say that, you know."

Her voice was quiet, no trace of a reproof in her tone. Even so, my face burned. I knew what was in her mind. I could see the red furnace glare in my grandmother's eye.

I was already four years older than my mother had been when she stepped off a bus in Oregon with no money and no family except the amorphous clump of cells in her belly. It was no wonder she wanted me to plan. From the moment I was born, she had needed a plan, every day, just to pay the rent.

I suppose it's normal, to see a parent as the udder that feeds us. Babies bite down and mothers grit their teeth.

But I wasn't a baby.

"Hello?"

This time I had called, instead of Pat.

"Hi, Mom."

"Hey, Jord. How are you? I hear a rumor you're going bionic."

"Yeah, well, it's almost the year 2000. Everybody who's anybody has some titanium in their body."

"Your doc's the one who does football players, right?"

"So I hear. I had to get a letter from Mr. Ross before he'd take me as a patient."

"How did you get scheduled so quick?"

"It seems I'm an interesting case. They don't often see a joint so totally destroyed with so little damage in the rest of the leg. The surgeon is practically salivating over me."

"Good. That means you'll get good care."

There was a silence.

"How's Granddad?" I asked after a bit.

"Thriving."

"Did he do a lot of rehab?"

"Months. Grandma took charge, and he didn't dare not do it."

Another silence.

"Have they talked to you about yours?" she asked.

"They said it would be months."

"Where will you live?"

I felt my muscles start to tense. "I've found a furnished apartment. In Arlington. A little outside the city, but it's on a bus line. Ground floor, reasonably cheap and I can have my dog."

"Do you know anyone there?"

"Not yet."

Another silence.

"Pat can't stay indefinitely," Mom said. "For the time being, she still has a business to run."

"I know."

"How will you cope? Won't you be on crutches for a while?"

That was my cue, but half of me still resisted.

"I was thinking . . . " I stopped.

"You'll want someone to walk the dog, won't you? And carry groceries?"

"That's what I was thinking."

"Do you have a plan?"

I gritted my teeth and looked at my watch. Five minutes she had held out, before she asked. Still, I stayed on the phone.

"My plans are contingent," I said.

"Contingent on what?"

"On whether you have plans."

There was a long pause. I began to wonder if she had fainted from surprise.

"None I can't change," she said finally.

"People tell me it rains a lot here, even in the summer," I said. "Do you have an umbrella?"

"I left it behind in Oregon."

"Doesn't matter. I'll buy you one. And you'll need some wheels, too, to get out to the ocean. Otherwise, the trees back here will drive you nuts. I was thinking a convertible Porsche, so you won't feel closed in . . . "

"The umbrella is plenty. You can skip the car."

"I owe you at least that much, for paying my insurance bill last winter."

"You don't owe me anything."

"There must be something you want."

"I've already gotten what I want. If you're determined to spend more money, ask Pat. Your Porsche would make a pretty good dent in her tuition."

"Tuition? Pat?"

I looked across the living room of my newly rented apartment. Pat was absorbed in a book, sitting in one of the garish flowered armchairs that came with the place. Bear was lying with his head resting on her feet. No loyalty at all in that dog.

"Is she definitely leaving Kilgore?" I asked.

"It seems we both are."

"Where are you going?"

"I don't know yet. Somewhere with a university."

I laughed. "Well, whaddya know. After all these years, you finally persuaded somebody to go to college."

"I had nothing to do with it. You're the one who persuaded her."

"I did?"

"So she says."

The moment I was off the phone, I hobbled over and waved my

hand between Pat's eyes and her book.

"Mom says you're going back to college."

"It's not 'back,'" she said. "I never went."

"Why would you want to now?"

"To find out if I missed something. I've always thought that I did."

"Won't it be weird, hanging out with a lot of nineteen-year-olds?"

She shrugged. "I'm highly qualified for a position of weirdness."

I still had one more item to attend to before I got knocked unconscious again. Not that I rushed out to make a will or anything. But the idea of that needle pouring sleep into my veins made me want to tidy up any loose ends I could.

I wasn't quite ready to face a full-force blast of optimism and remorse and helpfulness, so I said a little prayer of thanks to the patron saint of well-intentioned cowards, the person who invented email, and logged into my new server.

> hi, breeze, i just wanted to let you know first hand that i'm okay. last fall i acted like more or less of a jerk, and i'm really sorry. i owe you big time, for all those weeks of care and for a lot of other stuff besides, mostly not tangible. you changed my whole way of looking at life, in all sorts of good ways. jordy

> Hello Jordy, Your email has made my day. My week. Maybe my whole year. Donna told me you are in Boston, scheduled for a new knee, and that relieved the worst of my worries, but it's a thousand times better to hear from you in your own voice.

> I expect you have enough to think about without any ideas from me, but I have to slip in one, just one tiny little one. Or maybe I can call it news, instead. I know there is absolutely nothing good about what happened, but good things seldom

get into the newspaper, and that story did, and an incidental consequence is that one of the local nouveau philanthropists got interested in Cyberplace, and we now have brand-new computers and a big pot of money, and if you ever happen to want to come back, you could call it an actual job. Although we haven't gone as far as a dental plan. Love, Breeze

I wanted to laugh and cry both. She had simply been born without a reverse gear. She was concerned only with things that could change, and that didn't include the past.

chapter seventeen

I floundered toward the surface, my arms flailing through water that dragged like gear oil. The current was pulling me down, and my arms and legs labored to move through the dark, viscous fluid. I thrashed, frantically, and suddenly my head burst free, into air, and I opened my eyes.

Within my narrowed field of vision, I saw a pastel blue pajama top and pants with a drawstring. Scrubs. I lay still for a long time, groggy, watching the scrubs move around the room, watching a black leather belt and white shirt roll a gurney past me and out the door. After a while the scrubs came over and stood next to me.

"How do you feel?"

"Rotten."

"Good. That means you're back with us and not delirious."

A gurney came rolling into the room, and the scrubs turned away to attend to it. I lay still for another stretch of time and gradually my head began to clear. I still felt dazed and a little queasy, but my thoughts no longer floated about like flotsam.

When the scrubs came back to my side of the room, I turned my head to look for a face. The face was beautiful, black hair, wide cheek-bones, wide mouth. I kept my head turned, gazing at her. She wasn't looking at me. She was looking down at a clipboard, making a note. Her eyes were brown, like Bear's.

She finished her note and moved away. For a long time I lay there, my eye following her around the room as she worked, checking vital signs of someone on another gurney, making more notes, sending that gurney rolling out the door. My mind felt a little lighter than air, but very clear. Sooner or later, she would come back to check my signs, write her notes about me and send me rolling out the door.

When she came to check my blood pressure, I could finally see her up close. Her eyes were looking at the gauges, though, not at me. They were terrific eyes, even darker than Bear's and very warm. She must have felt my stare, because after she wrote down her numbers, she looked at me and smiled, not broadly, just a little curve at each corner.

"Are you a lesbian?" I asked.

Her mouth opened in surprise, and then she laughed.

"Is there a reason for that question?"

"I'm scouting for hazards before I set out."

"Set out where?"

"To invite you to share my hot turkey sandwich and yogurt cup this evening."

"Is this a come-on?"

"I suppose so, yes."

"I have a six-year-old daughter. I'm divorced. How old are you?"

"Twenty-four. You still haven't answered my question."

"I just told you I have a six-year-old daughter."

"My mother has a twenty-four-year-old son, and she's a lesbian. So, are you?"

"Not as far as I know."

"*Argh.* Don't say that. Couldn't you be a little more definite, like, 'No, absolutely not?' Submerged rocks are the worst. They're the ones that cause shipwrecks."

"What makes you think I might be?"

"Painful experience. You're so beautiful. Every beautiful woman I meet discovers she's queer and becomes my best friend."

The nurse was laughing. "I'm revising your chart. You are delirious. Men have told me lots of things, like I'm funny or I have nice legs. They've even said they loved me. But not even in the hottest of hot pursuit has anyone ever said I was beautiful."

"I think you are."

"You are still under the influence of drugs."

"I'm wide awake."

"Not hardly. Anyway, I'm much too old for you. You'd start to feel like a Corvette going out with a Buick station wagon."

"A Corvette with a flat tire. How old are you?"

"I don't know why I'm letting you ask me these questions."

"And?"

"I'm almost thirty-one."

"Geriatric. You're not a station wagon. You're a senior citizens' shuttle bus."

Another gurney was wheeled into the recovery room, and she ducked away from me to tend to a patient who couldn't talk.

"Will you come see me after your shift?" I called after her.

"I pick up my daughter after my shift."

She signaled to the orderly.

"That one is ready to go up to the ward," she said, pointing at me.

"At least tell me your name. Your ID badge is microscopic."

"Meg."

"Short for Meghan?"

"Short for Margaret. I told you I was too old."

"What's your last name? I can't look up Meg in the phone book."

"You'd better try your luck on the ward," she said.

The orderly had swung my gurney around and was wheeling me toward the door. I pushed myself up on my elbows so that I could see her.

"You're my luck. What's your last name?"

She just laughed.

"Don't let him climb off that cart," she said to the orderly.

For the whole afternoon, Mom asked no questions about my plans. She had come to find me the moment I was in a bed on the ward. She had brought books and notepaper and some fruit, the usual stuff for people in hospitals, but for perhaps the first time since seventh grade, she didn't seem worried about my future.

I didn't see why she should be so confident all of a sudden. I was looking at six months to a year of physical therapy if I didn't want to end up back where I started, and apart from the PT, I had no idea what I was going to be doing. But she just flipped through the pages of exercises I had been given for pre-op entertainment and said, "Looks like you'll be ready for a triathlon when you're done."

"I'll be happy with a walk around the block, if it doesn't hurt," I said.

That was the last we talked about rehab. I guess we both assumed I would do it.

Instead, we talked about cities. What did I think about Boston, compared to Seattle?

"I've hardly seen Boston," I said. "All I know is that the drivers are maniacs. And the lane markings are like expressionist art, open to personal interpretation. Seattle . . . "

I talked a long time about Seattle. Not about the city. That could be summed up in a sentence. It's beautiful and pleasant, and way too many people have discovered that it's beautiful and pleasant. Instead,

I talked about Breeze, and Spider, and how it was that even in a place so beautiful and pleasant, life could be harsh for a lot of people, and how all the good intentions in the world couldn't change that reality.

"I had a go at changing reality, once," Mom said. "I personally was going to remake the world. I was eighteen. Then, when I was nineteen, reality got its claws into me good and deep, and I had to beg for negotiations."

"Did the world agree?"

"We're both still here, so I guess it did. I backed off and said I would aim for something in reach, and the world backed off and said maybe it would let me succeed at some of what I tried. And some of what was in reach has turned out to be really, really fine."

"Like what?"

"What do you think? You, of course. I got you through childhood all in one piece, and speaking entirely without prejudice, you are a positive addition to the world."

"What gives you such a high opinion of me all of a sudden?"

"What do you mean, all of a sudden?" she said. "I've had a high opinion of you from the word go. I knew you were going to do plenty when you sat up in your booster chair and talked your way out of eating peas. You said you were swallowing them whole to avoid the icky taste and I was wasting our money putting them on your plate."

"You didn't have such a high opinion when I was in high school. You were forever hounding me about college."

"Hounding you? If pointing out an application deadline is hounding, then I suppose I did. But you managed to resist my hounding quite successfully."

"You didn't let me go to L.A. with Reba."

"Let you? How did I stop you? I offered you an alternative, that's all."

"With the implication that I would be an idiot not to take your advice."

"Do you wish you were waiting tables in L.A.?"

"I wouldn't be lying here if I were."

"*Ah.*" She was quiet for a minute, gazing at my leg propped up on pillows. "So this is my doing."

"No, obviously it's not. This is bullshit anyway. I'm alive and rich and can buy spare parts. It's nothing to cry about."

"But your friend is dead and can't make use of spare parts . . . "

"He wasn't my friend. We hardly knew each other."

"If he wasn't your friend, why does it still bother you so much?"

"I don't know. It's not like it's a rational decision."

Why had I picked Spider? The city was full of kids like him, all shunted onto a track going straight into a ditch.

"I hoped we might . . . become friends. If I made the effort. I guess he was my negotiation with reality. I mean, I was racing around among a dozen different projects that Breeze thought would help save the world. And then there was Spider. And my gut was telling me that all the other stuff was a nice idea, but probably wouldn't really do anything, but Spider might be something that was in reach. Just one kid that I might connect with, and maybe I could open up a different track, if he wanted to take it. And instead . . . "

"He got killed before he had the chance to choose."

"Yeah."

Mom was quiet for a while, and when she did say something, it was gingerly. "You could always retire to a Club Med. Where it's safe and clean and amusing, and there's nothing to worry about except old age."

"Is that what you advise?"

"I wouldn't dare give advice, not after that last reaction. Anyway, even a Club Med isn't safe. Not really. Someone you love can have a stroke. Your spouse can cheat. Your daughter can fall in love with a televangelist. Your steak can be overcooked. There is no safe place, not unless you're brain-dead."

I looked at her, startled. It was like hearing my own thoughts spoken out loud.

"What's the deal here?" I said. "My whole life you've been telling me to do the prudent thing, and now all of a sudden you're telling me not to bother. I don't get it."

I said this half-jokingly, but she thought about it seriously for quite a while before she answered.

"These past six months . . . It's been . . . " She stopped, thought some more.

"I felt completely helpless. It was so clear you were miserable. And it was equally clear that I couldn't do anything about it. That I only made things worse. And it sent me into paralysis. Not just about you. About everything. If I couldn't do anything to help you, then why bother with anything else? At my job, I'd just as well have been sorting paper clips.

"I couldn't even let myself think about the possibility that you might . . . that it was something worse than wanting time alone . . . If I'd let myself think for one minute that I might not see you again, I'd have crashed completely. And I would have, anyway, without Pat. She just kept at it, searching for you, like it was another sculpture and however long it took, she was going to finish. Whenever she found me staring into space, she'd put a list of phone numbers in my hand.

"And then we finally found that animal shelter and it was . . . I don't know. Like I could breathe again. Like I'd been holding my breath all that time. And I wanted to jump on a plane and come, but I knew you wouldn't want that. Pat and I talked about it, and we both thought it was better for her to go. But it was the hardest thing I've ever done in my life. Waiting."

She was quiet a minute. Then she gave a little shrug and turned back to me, smiling, back to joking. "So we're both still here, and anything more than that looks like gravy."

That shrug and smile were completely familiar. That offhand look, like "Pain, who me?" A little current went through me, and I almost shivered.

Maybe I had joked about resemblances, said "It's genetic," but until this moment, I had never felt such an absolute, overwhelming awareness that her blood and nerves and skin and brain chemistry were elements in my own being. We were the same and not the same, simultaneously. If I had spent the winter going mental, then so had she, and if I had woken up screaming at the memory of Spider, the terror of what could happen to my dog, then how many nights had she been wrenched from sleep by nightmare visions of her own, rushing to fill the vacuum I had created when I fled?

I was finally outside her, looking at her, and the strange thing was, she looked more like me than she ever had when I was inside fighting to get out.

"I'm really glad you're here," I said.

She looked so surprised, I said it again. "I am. I mean it."

"So am I," she said.

We both smiled, but this was not the kind of moment where either of us was inclined to linger. The silence lasted maybe eight seconds, and then both of our inner timers went off, simultaneously.

"Are you really not—?" I said.

"What are you—?" she said.

We stopped, looked at each other.

"You first," she said.

"Are you really not worried any more?" I asked.

She paused, shrugged. "Not today."

"But how am I supposed to function without your worrying?" I said. "It's like losing one of the fundamental principles of physics."

She laughed. "Enjoy it quick," she said. "By tomorrow morning, I'll be demanding to know if you plan to stay in the east your whole life."

"Yeah, like I have a clue."

After Mom had gone back to my apartment to pick up groceries and walk the dog, I pulled out the notepaper she'd brought. She hadn't thought to bring my computer, but I didn't mind. I had a couple of things to say that maybe I wouldn't want to have blown away with one mouse-click.

> Dear Pat,
>
> Do you remember a conversation we had, years and years ago, when you said you thought the laws of physics applied to the spirit, too? I've been thinking about it this afternoon, and I think you're right, at least about one, Newton's Third Law, the one about equal and opposite reactions. Meaning that there are two sides to everything a person does, that we don't exist apart from our connection to people and things around us. I can't even decide to be alone by myself, because what means solitude for me also means my absence for everyone who knows me. (Not that they might not be glad of my absence . . .)
>
> So, in the opposite reaction category, I wanted to thank you for coming to find me, even though you refuse to admit that there was a speck of generosity or kindness in your action. I was in sore need of another random particle collision, to knock me back in reach of earth's gravity.
>
> Love,
> Jordy

That evening, I found a Post-it note stuck to the yogurt cup on my dinner tray: "My last name is Erving. No relation to Dr. J." And a telephone number.

It had to be an omen, that she mentioned basketball. But was it bad, or good?

about the author

Edith Forbes grew up on a ranch in Wyoming and has worked as a computer programmer, carpenter and farmer. The author of three previous novels, *Nowle's Passing, Exit to Reality* and *Alma Rose,* Forbes lives and writes in Vermont.

selected seal press titles

Alma Rose by Edith Forbes. $12.95, 1-58005-011-5. The engaging story of Pat Lloyd and her encounter with Alma Rose, a charming and vivacious trucker who rumbles off the highway and changes Pat's life forever.

Nowle's Passing by Edith Forbes. $12.00, 1-878067-99-0. A beautifully crafted novel about a woman who faces her exacting family legacy to discover her own life.

Exit to Reality by Edith Forbes. $12.00, 1-58005-003-4. It is the 29th century and all social problems have been eliminated. Lydian and Merle meet online and ignite an unlikely love affair of the minds—and bodies—leading to a confrontation between civilization and technology.

The Case of the Orphaned Bassoonists by Barbara Wilson. $12.95, 1-58005-046-8. A comic romp and an enlightening guide to the musical heritage of Venice that will delight Wilson's fans and charm new readers.

Gaudí Afternoon by Barbara Wilson. $10.95, 0-931188-89-X. Winner of the Lambda Literary Award for Best Lesbian Mystery and the British Crime Writers Association Award. Soon to be a major motion picture starring Judy Davis and Lili Taylor.

Seal Press publishes many books of fiction and nonfiction by women writers. If you are unable to obtain a Seal Press title from a bookstore, please order from us directly by calling 800-754-0271. Visit our website and check out our online catalog at www.sealpress.com.